Travelers

by

Edward Cox, Jr.

ISBN: 9781980967620

DEDICATION

To my wife, Christina and my children, Megan, Emily, and
Jeremy for making me the man I am today.

CHAPTER 1

Thunder rolled through the hot August night. Heat lightning lit up the sky, and the rain was a welcome relief from the humidity. Yet, there was no relief for Abigail Lane. She rolled around on the air mattress trying to get comfortable, but the more she moved her body, the more she heard the snores of her best friend, Courtney. Abby and Courtney were more like sisters than friends, but if the snoring didn't stop, they were going to quickly become enemies. As Abby tightened her grip on the pillow that would deliver a snore-stopping blow to Courtney's blonde head, the text alert from her cell phone snapped her from her focus.

Dad: Goodnight Ab. Be home around 10 tomorrow... Love you!

Of course her Dad would stop her from smashing Courtney with the pillow. Sometimes, it was like he knew her thoughts, which would be scary to some people, but Abby loved the connection she had with her father. Yet, his distraction made her smile and would calm her enough for her to go to sleep.

Abby: Goodnight Dad... Love you too!

Little did she know this might be the last thing she ever told him.

A few blocks away, Richard Lane smiled as he placed his cell phone on the night table. Lightning lit up his room as he yanked the sheet up over his body. Thunder roared through the night sky as the rain began pounding on his bedroom window. The rhythmic tapping of the rain helped Richard begin to drift off to sleep, but another flash of lightning lit up the room revealing the dark figures standing over his bed. Startled, Richard scrambled to get out of bed, instinctively knocking over the bedside table lamp. Yet, they were on him quickly, throwing a cloth sack over his head.

"Don't fight, and we won't hurt you, Traveler."

Richard immediately stopped moving, more from the shock of being called "Traveler" than from following directions.

"That's better," the voice said, raspy and commanding, "Now we're going to take a little trip to see some old friends. So, you keep your mouth shut and do as you're told and things won't get messy."

Richard knew there was no use fighting; he had seen at least three figures in the room before the sack was put over his head. If they were calling him "Traveler", then they were highly trained soldiers who probably had orders to kill if necessary. He quickly decided to wait for a better opportunity for escape.

"Ok," was all Richard could say.

"That's good, Traveler. Now where's the key?" commanded the voice.

"Key? I don't…"

The smack across Richard's hooded face not only cut his reply, but his lip as well. Richard's head was woozy, and he could taste blood in his mouth as his body was rammed against the wall.

"I said, where's the key?" came the voice, only centimeters from Richard's face, while strong hands braced him against the wall.

"Gone," Richard whispered as tried to pull in a breath through the vice grip pushing on his chest.

"What do you mean…Gone?"

"I destroyed it…melted it in a fire about ten years ago."

"Liar! I want the key!" The voice was now incensed. Richard felt like the pressure on his chest was going to thrust him through the wall, or at the very least crush a few ribs.

"Not…a…lie," Richard gasped, "I was…never…going back."

"Oh, you're going back all right...for good!"

CHAPTER 2

The sack on Richard's head did not stop him from knowing where they were headed. He could tell from the direction they went when they left his house exactly where they were in his neighborhood, and he was thankful they were going in the opposite direction of Courtney's house and Abby. What he didn't know was how they got through the door in the first place, or how they were going to get through it now?

Although he didn't look at a clock before they left, he figured it must be around four in the morning, which meant they had plenty of time to get to the door before sunrise. Questions ripped through Richard's head: How did they get a key? How would they get back? Could he escape? Did another group take Abby? But, most of all, how did they ever find him?

The quick rainstorm had stopped, but as they weaved their way through the neighborhood, Richard paid close attention to the turns they made. He quickly realized that they were headed to the woods east of the door. At four in the morning, there weren't many cars driving around, but anyone would notice a man with a sack over his head being drug down the street by a couple of other guys dressed in dark brown. Richard was hoping for a chance to get someone's attention, but these guys obviously knew what they were doing; the chance never came. In a matter of minutes, they were under the cover of trees that ran along the Poquessing Creek that borders Philadelphia and Bensalem in Pennsylvania. They made no hesitation in dragging Richard into the rain-swollen creek. Following the creek was not the most direct route to get to the door, but it was concealed, and the easiest way if you weren't familiar with the area.

Sloshing through the cool rough water made Richard uncomfortable. The rain from earlier disturbed the usually calm little creek and walking through it was a little difficult. If he was going to try an escape, time was running out. He had to get his bearings and come up with a plan. His best shot would be when they got close to the Route 13 Bridge because there may be people around, but to get away there would mean a tough run up a steep embankment. Suddenly, they veered left and Richard knew exactly where they were. He quickly stumbled to the right hoping they wouldn't notice his intent. Richard knew there was a small sandy area to the right that led through some underbrush to a parking lot. The sand would be wet from the rain and easier to run across. If he could make it through that lot, there was a machine shop and a small strip of houses where he could try to arouse attention. He also knew that the machine shop worked twenty-four hours a day and someone would be there; all he wanted was attention.

"Keep moving!" came the command.

"Ok, ok", Richard replied.

Yet, two steps later, Richard intentionally fell, again to the right. As he dropped to his knees, Richard reached up and unloosed the sack on his head in one quick motion. It wasn't that noticeable, but he could now look down and see some of the ground. As he stood, he stumbled again to the right and felt his sneakers sink into the wet sand. If he was going to escape, now was the time.

Richard now leaned to his left regaining his balance. As the man on his right reached to grab him, Richard quickly yanked him to the left, pulling him into the other man. As they collided, Richard ripped the sack off and ran across the packed down sand, up the small bank and into the parking lot. The machine shop was only a hundred yards ahead, and Richard began yelling.

"HELP! HELP!"

As the third help started to escape his mouth, he was thrown forward and tackled to the blacktop scraping his left arm, leg and side of his face; it was over.

"Nice try, Traveler," said the raspy voice, "but if you're not going to play nice, then neither are we." With that, he smacked Richard across the side of his head making his ear ring and sting at the same time. He then tugged the now soaked sack back onto Richard's head. Another man yanked his arms behind his back and tied them with a thick piece of rope.

The journey continued with the sack back in place and his hands bound behind his back. As the sun began to rise, the door was opened and Richard was shoved through.

CHAPTER 3

Abby rolled over on the air mattress to move the early August sun from her face. She pulled her shoulder length brown hair from under her, and reluctantly opened her eyes. She glanced up at the window where the sun was streaming through. "Another hot August day...another day closer to school," she thought.

Abby did well in school, but like most thirteen year olds, she wasn't looking forward to the work school would provide or the pressure. Abby always felt pressure to do well because it seemed to be expected, not only by her father and herself, but by her teachers too. Everyone knew that her dad was a Historian, which seemed to make everyone think she would be as smart as him. He just knew things that no one else did and could talk about almost any subject. Sometimes it was annoying to Abby, because people expected her to know, as much as him, which she clearly didn't. Plus, she would miss the summer hanging out with her friends at a local swim club, swimming, playing volleyball and just not being in school.

She stretched and prepared to get up when her cell phone buzzed. She continued the stretch, but now with the purpose of checking the message.

Bry: Yo, U goin 2 the pool 2day??

Bryan Johnson was one of Abby's closest friends, so close that most people thought they were more than friends. They weren't boyfriend and girlfriend, but many girls were jealous of Abby because of Bryan. To most girls, Bryan was "hot"; he had piercing blue eyes, dirty blonde hair and a well toned swimmer's body. Abby saw him as Bryan, her friend who lived two houses away, that she started playing with when she was two, and he was three. He was more like a brother than a friend; she couldn't remember her life without Bryan in it because he had always been there. She also knew that this year would be different for both of them because Bryan would be heading to high school. She wasn't worried about him because he was smart, fun, and would be the best swimmer on the team as a freshman. It would just be weird at school without him there. He seemed to feel the same way, as they spent more and more time together as school got closer.

Abby: Yeah, but not til later. Slept at Courts, gotta go home first. Txt you later.

Bry: Sounds good

Abby flung her pillow up at Courtney who was still sleeping, hitting her square in the face.

"Uh, what the…"

"Hahaha, wake up Court," Abby laughed.

"How can I sleep when you're beating the crap out of me with a pillow?!" Courtney replied sleepily.

"Girls! Breakfast!" yelled Mrs. Creely.

"Ok!" yelled Courtney throwing the pillow back at Abby, who caught it and dropped it on the floor. "I will get you back," snorted Courtney.

"Yeah, right," replied Abby confidently. Most people didn't mess with Courtney, she was quick witted and usually ready for an argument, which made people back down from her, but not Abby. They've had this relationship for years and Abby had no problem giving her a hard time.

The girls quickly got dressed and ready for breakfast. Mrs. Creely's chocolate chip pancakes were legendary to Courtney's friends who stayed over, so Abby threw on shorts and a t-shirt, pulled her brown hair into a ponytail, and brushed her teeth quickly. As they headed downstairs, the smell of bacon overtook the smell of pancakes, and they raced to the kitchen.

Mrs. Creely placed plates of pancakes and bacon on the table as the girls sat down.

"Look at you two sleeping until nine-thirty," she said.

"Nine-thirty? Wow, that is late," commented Abby. The girls were swimmers and were used to having practice at six every morning in the summer, but the summer season was now over and sleeping late before school started was a priority. "I have to hurry," she added, "my dad wants me home by ten."

"After you eat, I'll drive you home," said Mrs. Creely.

"That's ok, I'll walk. My dad will already be at work. He wants me to clean my room before we go to the pool," she replied.

"That could take all day," Courtney said.

"Yeah, I know", replied Abby, "I'll text you when I'm done."

"See you in a week," Courtney said slyly.

Abby finished her breakfast, thanked Mrs. Creely, grabbed her backpack, and headed home. She only lived around the corner from

Courtney, less than a quarter mile by distance, so walking was home was normal. They lived in a very nice neighborhood in Northeast Philadelphia that was not typical of city life. Of course, Abby's dad chose this area for it's historical significance, even though it meant a longer ride to work for him. Abby was grateful; she had met her two best friends here and wouldn't change that for anything.

Walking home from Courtney's house was a normal thing for Abby; she would walk down Courtney's street, and then cut through the Grossman's yard to her street. As she headed down her street, she slowed to see if Bryan was outside of his house. He wasn't, so she gave another glance and continued two houses down to her house. Her dad's car was in the driveway.

"That's weird," she almost said out loud. "He must have a late meeting."

Abby turned her key in the lock and pushed open the door. "Dad! I'm home!" she hollered. There was no answer. "Is he still sleeping?" she thought. Richard Lane never overslept. He was fanatical about being on time; to the point that he was always early and so was Abby. Since it was just the two of them, Abby learned everything from her father and shared a lot of his tendencies. She never met her mother, which used to bother her, but after thirteen years, it wasn't a big deal anymore. Plus, her Dad was so good at being both Mom and Dad that not having a Mom really didn't matter any more.

When she was younger, Abby used to ask questions about her Mom all the time. As a young girl, she used to pretend that her Mom was a great adventurer, who was exploring the world, or a movie star walking the red carpet. A young girl's dream of a Mom, who was special and better than all the other Moms she knew. Yet, as Abby grew older, she knew it was just a dream.

Her most vivid memory was sitting on the beach with her Dad at the Jersey shore when she was ten years old. The lifeguards had left for the day and most of the beach was empty, her Grandparents and Aunt had gone back to the house they had rented for the week, so it was just the two of them. He started by apologizing and telling Abby that when she was a baby, he felt like he had to save her from her Mom. He told her that she was an evil woman who was controlling, and he feared for their lives.

"Then why are you apologizing?" she asked.

"Because every girl should have a Mom…and I took that away from you. Not a day goes by that I don't wonder, if I did the right thing," he said.

She remembered her reply word for word, "Dad, I have a great life. I love you, and I'm sure you did the right thing."

He hugged her for a long time, and together they cried.

She knew that her Mom had problems and her dad took her away to be safe. Abby imagined that her Mom was involved with drugs, like many other kids she knew. Abby was lucky enough to have a great Dad, who took her from that situation and kept her safe. The only thing that bothered her was that there was no contact with her mother's side of the family at all. She was told that they lived far away and were embarrassed by her Mom. Over the years, Abby grew to hate those people that she never met for abandoning her and not caring enough to even try to contact her.

As she walked in the house, Abby noticed her Dad's wallet and keys on the small table by the door where he always put them. "He must still be sleeping," she thought. She dropped her backpack and hurried up the stairs to wake him.

"Dad!" she called, "Wake up!"

Again, there was no answer and Abby suddenly felt something

was wrong. As she hopped up the steps, two at a time, she noticed her Dad's bedroom door was open and a blanket lied on the floor. This was not right; her Dad always made his bed.

"Dad?" she questioned as she entered his room. She gasped as she saw the bedside lamp overturned and the sheet on the floor.

"Oh my God!" she yelled when she noticed a few blood drops on the floor, and a small hole in the drywall about six feet off the floor. Tears welled up in Abby's eyes as she heard the buzz of a cell phone. Her dad's phone lit up on the bedside table next to the overturned lamp. Abby lunged across the room to grab the phone, frantically wiping away tears to see the text.

`Adam: Hey, you coming in today or not?`

Adam was her dad's coworker at the Philadelphia Historical Society. Abby had met him a few times, but didn't know if she should answer or not. As she sat on the edge of the bed, she reached to pick up the lamp, but something caught her eye. There was a yellow paper attached to the bottom of the lamp base. Abby picked up the lamp and flipped it over to look at the bottom. She immediately recognized her dad's handwriting as she read the simple message: CALL MIKE PITMAN.

"Call Mike Pitman?" she said out loud, "Why would that be written there?" She knew that her dad was a planner. He was not a spontaneous person at all. As she looked closely at the note, she felt that it had been written a long time ago. She had heard the name Mike Pitman before, but had never met him. All she knew was that he was one of her dad's fraternity brothers from college, but why would her dad have written this under the lamp? So many questions raced through her head, but the two most important were: Where was her Dad, and should she call the police? She needed help.

It seemed like she barely hung up the phone and Bryan was knocking on the door. Abby whipped open the door and practically jumped on him, hugging him tightly while sobbing, "Oh my God, Bry! Oh my God!"

"Ab, what's going on? What happened?"

Abby brought him in the house and told him the whole story. She showed him the bedroom and the lamp. She ended with, "I don't know what to do."

"I say you call this Pitman guy and see if he knows anything, and then call the police. It's weird that that lamp is the only thing in the house that's messed up. It's like it got knocked over on purpose for you to see the note." Bryan said.

"It's not the only thing messed up!"

Abby led him to the back kitchen door and showed Bryan how the lock was pried open.

"It looks like something was shoved between the frame and the door that just popped it open," Bryan said.

"Yeah, but why would anyone want to take my Dad?" she asked with the tears coming back into her eyes.

"I don't know, but knowing your Dad, you have to call this Pitman guy."

Abby reached for her Dad's phone and searched through the contacts. Mike Pitman's number was not a local area code, but Abby didn't hesitate when hitting the send button. Each ring made her more nervous, and finally, on the third ring there was an answer.

"Lane! What's up, dude? Haven't talked to you in forever!" said the voice.

"Ah, this…is his daughter, Abby." Abby replied nervously.

"Abby? Oh sorry, I saw the caller ID and thought it was…wait, why are you calling from his phone?"

"Is this Mike Pitman?" she continued.

"Yeah, what happened?" Mike said concerned.

"How do you know something happened?" Abby asked beginning to get a little angry.

"Is your father missing?" he sighed.

"How would you know that?!" She was yelling into the phone now through tears.

"Listen," he said, "I can't tell you over the phone, just hang on and I'll be there in a few hours."

"A few hours?" she was growing more of an anger, now.

"Yeah, I live a few hours from Philly and I need to take care of a couple things, but I'll be there soon. Did you call the cops?" he asked.

"Not yet, but I'm going…"

"No," he cut her off, "don't call them yet."

"Why not? I think someone kidnapped him!" she pleaded.

"Someone did. Plus, I am a cop."

CHAPTER 4

The sensation of going through the door was always a strange one, but being shoved through the door made it even more intense. As Richard crawled through the tunnel, he could see the brightness of the other side through the sack. He was back. What that meant, he wasn't sure, but it couldn't be good. He crawled to the end of the tunnel and got to his feet. The hood was ripped from his head.

"You'll need to see to get up the embankment," the man said. Richard finally got a good look at him and didn't like what he saw. This man was battle worn, with a large scar that ran from the tip of his chin up to the corner of his right eye. He was a good six inches taller than Richard and muscles on top of muscles. Richard wasn't intimidated by his looks; he was scared. Obviously, this man had been through some ordeals and Richard didn't want to be the next one.

"Ok" was all Richard could muster.

"Move," was the reply.

Richard didn't hesitate, he moved. The man pointed toward the base of a bridge that Richard recognized as the clone of the bridge that ran over the Poquessing Creek at home. Yet, this bridge was graffiti free and not as weather worn as the one Richard knew. Richard was pushed up the embankment next to the bridge, it would have been much easier if he could use his hands, but he knew better than to mention that. He started to slip, but powerful hands grabbed him and flung him up the embankment. At the top, he steadied himself and started to turn around to the man when the sack was ripped back over his head making him blind again.

"Get him on the cart," came the command and Richard was picked up and tossed into a hay cart. He was then covered with a heavy blanket that would totally conceal him. He could hear muffled voices.

"Do you want him totally covered?"

"Yes, he cannot be seen by anyone."

"But the journey to the castle is long, he could die from the heat."

"Then, he dies from the heat."

Richard knew that from the door to the castle took about two days walking. As the sweat beaded on his face, he hoped the cart would move much quicker than that.

CHAPTER 5

Abby hated waiting, as did most teenagers, but knowing that her father was missing made time seem to stand still. Her phone had been buzzing all day with texts from friends asking why she wasn't at the pool. Apparently, Bryan and Courtney were getting the same texts since they were as glued to their phones as Abby. Everyone wanted to know where they were and none of them had a good answer. Shortly after her conversation with Mike Pitman, Abby texted Courtney and told her to "get her butt over here right now"; of course, she complied. Abby and Bryan told her about her Dad, the note, and the call to Mike Pitman. Courtney didn't react the same way they did.

"You're insane!" she said.

"What? Why?" Abby asked.

"You call some guy you don't know, tell him your Dad is missing? You don't call the police, because he says so, and you don't know why you're insane?"

"But…"

"But, nothing!" she yelled, "this nut might have taken your Dad!

29

Did you ever think of that? He's probably coming here to kill us all right now! And he knows...yes knows your Dad is gone!"

"But..."

"Oh my God, stop saying but!"

"Wait, Court, just wait", Bryan said breaking into the conversation. "Maybe you're right."

"Maybe? Who the heck would call some guy they didn't know and tell him..."

"OK!" Abby yelled. "I get it. I messed up! But I did know the name, and he is one of my Dad's friends."

"So, now what?" Bryan asked.

"Are you sure that he's one of your Dad's friends?" Courtney asked.

"Yes. I got his number from my Dad's phone. There are pictures of them together from college, and I know I've met him. I'm sure."

"Then I guess we wait for him," Bryan said.

"Yeah, but we don't let him know that we are here," chimed in Courtney pointing to herself and Bryan.

"That's a good idea," Abby said, "he doesn't know about you two, so when he gets here, you can hide in case there's trouble."

That conversation was hours ago. The three of them had plenty of time to calm down, especially Courtney. She was the planner of the group, so she might have been angrier at the fact that Abby and Bryan did something without her. Most people underestimated Courtney, maybe because of her blonde hair and all the stereotypes about blondes being dumb. She was far from dumb. She was analytical, figured out the smallest details and could be in your face in a second. It also made her the least adventurous of the trio, but on more than one occasion, she reeled in Abby and Bryan from doing something stupid. All in all, she was a good person to have around as long as her temper was kept in check.

Three hours passed, but it felt like twenty to Abby. The only good thing that came from the time was Courtney got a chance to plan how they would handle Mike Pitman. Abby would meet with him in the kitchen, while Bryan and Courtney would hide. Courtney would be upstairs hiding and waiting for a signal from Abby or Bryan to call the police. Bryan would be closer to protect Abby if needed. His job was to hide in the small walk-in pantry and listen to the conversation. If there were a problem, he would come out and attack Pitman. He really didn't like the idea of attacking a grown man, but for Abby, he would do anything. Plus, she could probably beat him up herself. Abby was the most athletic girl he'd ever met. There wasn't anything that she wasn't good at when it came to sports. Probably the only thing that Bryan could beat her at was swimming, and she would give him a good race. Abby wasn't like the other girls that were always trying to get his attention. She was smart, athletic and pretty, but she didn't seem to try at any of those things. She did well in school because, like her Dad, she just knew stuff and at sports, she was a natural. Everything was easy for her, and she was always competitive, yet the pretty thing was new to Bryan.

Abby was like a sister to him because she was always there from the time he was little, but as they got older, he was starting to notice her looks changing from cute to pretty. Abby wasn't one of those princess types that worried about their hair and makeup all the time. She was much more comfortable in shorts and a t-shirt with her hair in a ponytail than getting all dressed up. Yet, Bryan started noticing her getting prettier. It didn't help that TJ Callison asked Bryan if he thought Abby would go out with him. Bryan's jealousy surprised even himself, so he told TJ that Abby hated him, which was a lie. Bottom line was sister-like or not Abby was his, and he would protect her at all costs.

Just after three in the afternoon, an old model pickup truck slowly made its way up Abby's street seemingly looking for an address. Taking his turn peeking out of the window, Bryan alerted the girls that Pitman had arrived. They took their places.

Abby flung open the door before Mike Pitman got halfway up the walk; she waited over three hours and couldn't wait a second longer. The worst part was that she angrily opened the door, and then didn't know what to say. She took one look at Pitman, dropped to her knees and started crying. Pitman ran to her and dropped next to her, unsure whether to hug her or not. He simply put his hand on her shoulder and said, "You'll find him."

Abby, through tears, looked up at him skeptically.

Pitman gasped and actually leaned back, away from Abby.

"What's wrong?" she asked actually getting scared.

"Your...your eyes," he said then paused and said, "I'm sorry, I've just never seen that color before."

"It's ok, I hear that all the time," she said. She did hear about her eyes a lot and Pitman wasn't the first person to be taken aback by them. Her eyes were a very unique silver color. Her dad called them "storm clouds", but when she was little, kids teased that she was a "demon". Those same kids were now jealous of her eye color. "Now what about my Dad?"

"I can help," he said "let's go inside." He seemed so calm and sure that for some reason, she believed him.

Abby slowly got to her feet, wiping her eyes as she did. She hadn't noticed the package under Pitman's arm until he adjusted it as they stood up. Abby led Pitman into the house and went directly to the kitchen where she sat at the table with the walk in pantry to her left. She felt comfortable with this stranger knowing Bryan was literally only a few feet away.

Pitman approached the table. He was average height and very thin for a man who said he was a cop. Abby thought he looked more like a stereotypical farmer. He wore a dirty baseball cap with a tractor company logo on the front, a t-shirt, faded jeans and work boots. Abby found her thoughts move away from her Dad move to trying to figure this guy out. Did he really just drive over three hours in August wearing jeans and boots?

"Hi Abby, I'm Mike Pitman," he said with an accent that sounded a little Southern, but Abby knew to be from around Western Pennsylvania because some of her Dad's other friends spoke the same way. "We have a lot to talk about."

"Do you know where my Dad is?"

"No, but..."

"Then why do you think we'll find him?"

"Well..."

"Shouldn't we call the cops now that you're here? I read that time..."

Now it was his turn to interrupt. "No, and I'm not a cop."

"What!" she yelled as she jumped up knocking her chair to the floor. When her chair hit the floor, Bryan flew out of the pantry and tackled Pitman off his chair. Pitman had no time to react as Bryan straddled him with a fist cocked and ready to ram Pitman's face.

"No!" yelled Abby, "don't hit him!"

"Get off of me!" yelled Pitman.

Bryan, fist still cocked and ready to strike, looked confused.

"Let him up," Abby said more calmly.

"You sure?"

"Yeah, she's sure, you idiot! Let me up!" Pitman answered.

Bryan kept his fist at the ready position as he started to get up. Pitman pushed him off and scrambled to his feet.

"I come here trying to help you people and…"

"Ahhhhhhhhhh!" Courtney came flying into the kitchen with Abby's old softball bat aimed at Pitman's head.

"What the…!"

"Stop!" Abby yelled.

Courtney stopped, but her chest heaved sucking in air from her run down the steps and the adrenaline rush. She kept the bat ready to strike, her blue eyes locked on her target, which happened to be Pitman's head.

"You kids are crazy!" Pitman yelled.

"You're a liar!" Abby yelled back. "You said you were a cop!"

"Get your guard dogs off of me, and I'll explain!"

"Guard dogs?" Courtney questioned, cocking the bat. "Come on Ab, let me hit him," she said, her eyes never leaving the target.

"This is ridiculous! I came here to help you!"

"Then where is my Dad?"

"I don't know, but I think he left a clue with me. Let's all calm down, and I'll explain why I'm here."

Bryan and Courtney both looked at Abby for approval. She gave a small nod of her head and simply said, "Sit".

Pitman gave a small sigh and moved to a chair. Courtney pulled the bat down but continued to hold it as she sat down. Bryan and Abby took their seats as Pitman placed a small package on the table.

"These are my friends, Bryan and Courtney," Abby said.

"This story might take a while, but I should start at the beginning," Pitman said, not even acknowledging the introduction.

"Your Dad and I met in college. We were fraternity brothers, but quickly became best friends. Basically, we did everything together and were roommates in the fraternity house for two years. After college, your Dad moved back to Philly, and I moved back around Pittsburgh and then to a farm out near Lancaster. We stayed in contact, but it was hard to keep in touch. We did get together a couple of times, but the distance was a little too much. Plus, your Dad got a job that he loved for the Philly Historical Society cataloging artifacts; it was all he talked about. Then, it got weird."

"Weird?" Abby asked.

"Yeah, weird. Suddenly, there was no contact at all. It was like your Dad fell off the face of the earth. He didn't call or return calls; it was weird. For about a year or so, I heard nothing. Then one day he shows up at my farm; with you."

"Me?"

"Yeah, you. You were just a baby, only a couple of months old. I was shocked. He only ever talked about his job and then he turns up with a baby after he was sort of missing for a year. I didn't get it. So naturally, I wanted to know what the heck was going on, and where did he get a baby? I should have never asked."

"Why?" Bryan asked.

"He told me the most fantastic story that I never truly believed; until today. He told me about this book he found at work. He said it's William Penn's field journal or something that he started reading and found what he called clues to some hidden place that only the Indians knew about."

"Native Americans," Abby corrected.

"Yeah, whatever. So, then he tells me that he followed these clues, and they led to some 'other world' as he called it. Some parallel universe or something."

"Yeah right!" Courtney said.

"That's what I said."

"You can't be serious," Bryan said.

"Listen, I thought he was nuts. Then he tells me that he got this baby from this 'other world'.

"What?"

"Yeah, Abby, apparently you weren't born here."

"But…"

"I know. Just let me finish. So he says that he escaped with his daughter because of some danger and stuff. Then he tells me that he can't go back there, and no one can know about the place."

"Wait a minute. Escape from danger?"

"Yeah, that's what he said"

"That's the same thing he told me about my Mom," Abby replied with tears welling up again. "Could this mean my Mom is in this 'other world'?"

"Truthfully, I don't know what any of this means."

"Finish the story," Courtney said getting up and putting her hand on Abby's shoulder for comfort.

"Ok, so then he gives me this book that is vacuum-sealed. He tells me to never open it unless there is some kind of problem, and he makes me bury it somewhere on my farm. I was never supposed to tell him where it was unless something happened to you."

"To me?" said Abby.

"Yeah, he seemed to think that these 'other world' people might come and get you or him."

"Why would they come get us?"

"I don't know, but he was very paranoid about it at first. He told me that if he went missing, I was to dig up the book and try to find him, but after you got older, he said you should try to find him, because you are the only person who could really help."

"Me? How am I supposed to help?"

"He said that there were clues in the book, but I would have to figure them out. I guess it would be the same for you."

"Let's see the book," Bryan said.

Pitman slid the package across the table to Abby. She stared at it for a second before picking it up. The book looked like a rectangular piece of meat in a vacuum-sealed freezer bag. It almost surprised Abby that it wasn't cold when she touched it. Courtney was already looking through a drawer for scissors.

As they cut the plastic and air broke through the seal, the leather bound book began to take shape. Abby peeled the plastic off of the cover with the simple inscription of W.P. The book was small, about six inches by four inches with a leather bound cover and worn parchment type paper. Sticking out around the edges was a neatly folded piece of white composition paper that clear didn't belong in this book. Instinctively, Bryan grabbed at the edge of the unusual paper, but before he could pull it out of the book, Abby grabbed his hand.

"Wait, it might be marking an important page," she said.

"Good point," he replied as he let go of the paper, which was now about half way out of the book.

Abby slid the white paper back into place and wiped her hand across the front cover of the book which teetered on the table. Abby flipped the book over and noticed a bulge in the back cover. She opened the back cover first and found a long thin key, taped to the inside of the back cover. It reminded Abby of an old jail cell key from movies her Dad made her watch. She gently rubbed the key with her hand, but didn't remove it.

"What's the key for?" Bryan asked.

"Hopefully, to open up your brain!" Courtney said glaring at Bryan. "How the heck would we know what the key is for when we haven't even opened the book yet?"

"I just..."

"You're not helping," Abby said without looking away from the book or key.

She turned the book back to the front cover. "William Penn," she said out loud to no one in particular. She stared at the cover for a few seconds before shifting in her chair and opening the front cover. The first page simply had the year "1682". Abby knew that this was around the year that William Penn founded Philadelphia. Having a father that was a historian was both a blessing and a curse. Abby did well in school and knew many things that the other kids had no clue about, but it also made it difficult because some people thought she was the geeky kid, who knew everything.

She started paging through the book slowly. It was filled with rough sketches of animals and maps and even buildings. There was mention of a manor house and Native Americans. From Penn's writing, Abby felt that he must have been very interested in the Native American tribes of the area. He wrote a lot about Tammany or Tamanend and the Lenape Tribe that he ruled. Penn was enamored with the structure of the tribe and how they were ruled. He even mapped out the east coast of what is now Pennsylvania, New Jersey, and Delaware to show the area of tribe rule. The Wolf were to the north, with Tammany and the Turtle in the middle, where Penn was located and the Turkey to the south. Abby concluded that Penn and Tammany must have become friends and had regular meetings based on the writings. The book had pages about Tammany, then pages about other things, then Tammany again. Most of the Tammany writings were about the Lenape tribe and the land. The land writings and the maps freaked Abby out a little because they were about places she knew. Thinking about those tribes wandering around the area where she now lives was kind of weird. The maps showed rivers and streams all over the place, but the names were weird. Penn must have tried to spell them phonetically in the way the Lenape said them.

"Hey Court, Google this," Abby said without looking up.

Courtney looked startled for a second because Abby had been so focused on that book, that it was eerily quiet for almost a half hour.

"Oh," was all she could say. Courtney quickly searched the area to find the laptop sitting neatly on the couch in the living room. She flipped it open and quickly typed "google". "Ready," she said.

"Pemmapecka," Abby said then she spelled out each letter as it was written in the book.

"It has something about Hazard's Register of Pennsylvania, then a couple of Pa Archives sites and pages."

"Click on the PA Archives sites."

"Ok, the first one is about land being granted between the Pemmapecka and Neshaminch Creeks by Tamanen."

"It must be Pennypack and Neshaminy Creeks that they're talking about," Abby said. "It makes sense. That's exactly where we are, between those creeks."

Abby knew the area well, especially around Pennypack Creek. There was a bike trail that she rode a lot with her dad. Of course, he would constantly stop and give her history lessons about, "This Bridge was built in Sixteen-whatever for the King's highway, and it had to be redone in…" He was like a walking textbook, but Abby knew it made him happy to share the things he knew. She would listen and even ask questions at times, which would send him into a ten-minute talk about something else. Suddenly, she wished she had listened more intently at everything he told her.

"What does all this mean?" Bryan asked.

"Well the book tells about meetings with the Lenape Chief

Tammany, who was also known and Tamanen or Tamanend. He was the leader of the Turtle, who lived in this area. He controlled all this land, and then William Penn showed up with a bunch of settlers. Apparently, Tammany and Penn became friends and met many times, and they all lived happily in the same area. Yet, it turns weird in this part of the book. Penn writes about a secret that has something to do with the area between Pennypack Creek and Neshaminy Creek. It talks about another creek, but doesn't give a name."

"Well, the creek around here, that's between them is the Poquessing Creek," Bryan said.

"Yeah, that's what I was thinking," Abby said, "but there are a lot of small streams and stuff drawn on these maps. I hope the secret thing wasn't covered over by the city."

Abby then realized that when she turned the page, it would be to the folded piece of notebook paper; she turned. It took a lot, but she was determined to look at the book before the notebook paper. The page was a map that showed a creek between two others that were all unlabeled. The other small streams were eliminated from this map. The middle creek had a door drawn on it in the shape of a turtle. From the turtle came squiggly lines, which led to some trees and clouds. Abby had no idea what this meant. She reached for the notebook paper and slowly

opened it. There was nothing on it.

"Really?" Bryan said clearly annoyed. "Who uses a full piece of

paper as a bookmark?"

Abby just smiled. She lifted the paper to her nose and sniffed it.

Her smile grew as she inhaled deeply. Everyone was looking at Abby

perplexed except for Mike Pitman who also smiled. He was thinking

how much Abby was like her father.

"What was that?" Bryan asked.

Abby looked at him, smiled and said, "Turn on the stove."

"What?"

"The stove...turn it on."

"Oh good, I'm starving," Courtney said.

Abby just looked at her and laughed. "I need the stove to

activate the invisible ink my Dad used on this paper."

"What are you talking about?" Bryan asked.

"My Dad used to write me notes in invisible ink. He would use milk or lemon juice. They become invisible on the paper, but then you heat it and the message appears. It has something to do with organic stuff and how it burns."

"Your Dad's a weird dude," Bryan said.

"Richard always loved stuff like that," Pitman said breaking his long silence. "He liked talking about some Revolutionary War guy."

"Abraham Woodhull," Abby said, "he was from the Culper Gang during the Revolutionary War. They were spies for George Washington and delivered secrets by using invisible ink right under the British noses."

Bryan and Courtney looked at her like she was someone they had never met before.

"What?" Abby asked, "he told me all about it."

"So, we're not having food?" Courtney asked jokingly.

"Just watch the paper."

Abby carefully lowered the paper over the gas flame of the stove starting at the top left corner. As the paper got close to the flame, brown letters began to appear. The letters were crude, but decipherable. Abby made it a slow process, but she did not want to ignite the paper and lose

the message.

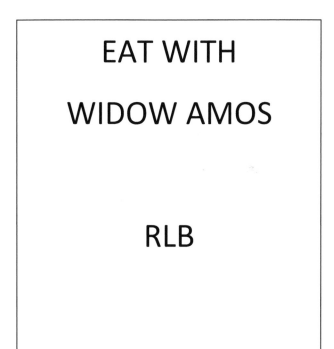

"Like I said, your Dad is a weird dude," Bryan said. "What the

heck does that mean?"

"I have no idea, but if my Dad really left this message for me, then he thought I could figure it out," Abby said. "But it doesn't look like his writing."

"What do you mean?" said Bryan.

"He writes all in capital letters a lot, but it just doesn't look like his writing."

"Yeah, but he's writing with like a toothpick or something and he can't see what he's writing, it's bound to look different."

"You're probably right", she agreed, "now we have to look this stuff up."

"I'm on it," Courtney said as she picked up the laptop again and began typing. "Eat with Widow Amos," she said out loud, "why did it have to be about food? I'm still hungry!"

"What does it say?" Abby asked moving to see the screen.

"It's all stuff about the Bible."

"Then try something else, it'll be about early U.S. history."

"Widow Amos is about Tori Amos, the singer," Courtney said.

"Let me try," Abby said.

She began typing different combinations of the words. Nothing was working.

"We're looking for a place, right?" Pitman asked.

"Yeah."

"So how about a map?" he asked.

"Worth a try," Abby said.

She typed 'Widow Amos map' into Google. The first result was about Rebecca Amos, an African American. It looked historical, so Abby clicked on the link. She started reading through the site info, but noticed that it wasn't tied to Philadelphia or the area, so she hit the back button. She scrolled down, looking through the links, none of them had anything to do with history, and then she saw it. 'Red Lion Inn'.

"This might be it," she said as she clicked the link. The site was from the Historical Society of Pennsylvania. Abby read, "It's a story about the Red Lion Inn, which was located next to the Poquessing Creek along the King's Highway. A license was given to Philip Amos to run a public house called the Red Lion Inn. When he died, it was given to Ann Amos, his widow."

"The Widow Amos ran the place," Courtney said.

"Yeah, but the Red Lion Inn isn't there anymore. My Dad told me about it. All the big names stayed there like George Washington and John Adams, but a few years ago it burned down."

"Great, back to knowing nothing," Bryan said.

"Not yet, we still have RLB. Plus, The Red Lion Inn was way after William Penn and Tammany," Abby said.

"Then, what's RLB? Shouldn't it be RLI for Red Lion Inn?" Bryan asked.

"Maybe", Abby said as she typed 'Red Lion Inn'. She read the first result, "The Red Lion Inn was a historic inn located near the Red Lion Bridge. There's the RLB. Now we just need the numbers."

"You think it's some kind of code?" Courtney asked.

"Not sure," Abby said as she typed in the numbers. First, she typed '400355 and 745852'. Abby laughed as Google gave her a calculator and added them up. "Guess, I can't use the word 'and'," she said.

She tried a couple different combinations, until she typed "40

74" and got the 40°74° Magazine.

"Could these be coordinates?" she asked looking at Pitman.

"With all those numbers, they would be very precise," he answered.

She brought up Google maps on the computer, but noticed that the coordinates were not posted. She then clicked on the Google Earth Application. When the app loaded, she clicked on the pin icon to mark the screen. She typed in the coordinates from the paper. She computer placed the pin at the fork of the Byberry and Poquessing Creeks, right next to the Red Lion Bridge.

"I got it!" Abby said.

"Really?" Bryan said.

"Yeah. We have to go to the creek right where it splits into the Byberry Creek and Poquessing Creek. That's right next to the Red Lion Bridge, which is next to where the Red Lion Inn used to be."

"Why the creek?" Courtney asked.

"I know my Dad pretty well," Abby replied, "and I think 'Eat with Widow Amos' has two meanings. The first is the Red Lion Inn, that's pretty obvious. It gets us to the area and leads us to the RLB part. The second meaning is the 'Eat' part. I think 'eat' refers to the 'fork' in the creek. So all together the invisible ink means: 'The fork in the creek, by the Red Lion Bridge, which is next to where the Red Lion Inn used to be located'.

"So that's where the turtle door is?" Bryan asked.

"Sounds good to me," Pitman said, "at least it sounds like something Richard would put together."

"Ok, so what about this door? It leads to another world?" Courtney asked. "Come on, you really believe all this?"

"According to the story Richard told me, it does," Pitman said.

"But this looks strange," Abby said now looking back through Penn's book. "On the next page is this drawing of a man dressed in Native American clothing with some kind of staff by what I think is the turtle door."

Abby thought that the man was doing something to the door. Then there was a sequence of pictures of a sun rising, then an arrow up and the turtle door.

"What do you think this means?" Abby asked Pitman while

showing him the book.

"It looks like an Indian putting a spell on the door. Maybe it only opens at sunrise?" he guessed.

"Maybe we have a key?" Courtney said.

"There's no key in the picture," Pitman said coming right back at Courtney, who was starting to annoy him.

"Then why would there be a key in the book?"

"It's in the back of the book, maybe it's to get back through the door from the other side!"

"Oh, that makes sense, let's make a door that you can't get into with a key, but you can get out? Great, just great. This whole thing gets dumber by the second."

"Maybe the dumb one here is..."

"Ok! That's enough! You two arguing about this does nothing to get my Dad back!" Abby yelled.

"You're right," Pitman said, "I just think that the picture shows a door going up at what looks like sunrise. You're Dad may have said the key was to get back. I don't know, it was a long time ago."

"Then we would have to wait until morning to find this door thing," Bryan said.

"Not necessarily," Pitman said, "we could go see if it's there, but we might not be able to open it until morning. We could at least find the right spot while it's daytime."

"Good idea," Abby said. "It's right near the swim club, so it's only a couple blocks from here."

"I'll drive us," Pitman said.

"You really think we want to get in a car with you?' Courtney questioned obviously still agitated with Pitman.

"Seriously?" Pitman said. "Fine, then we can walk. Happy?"

"No, you can drive us," Abby said giving Courtney a look.

"Ok," Courtney said, "but I don't like it."

CHAPTER 6

Time is a strange thing. Sometimes it feels like it is flying by and other times it stands still and the clock has trouble moving. For Richard Lane, this was one of those times. He didn't know where he was or how long they had been traveling. His body was completely covered in the back of the cart and the sweat was pouring off of him. When the journey began, he tried counting slowly to keep the time and also pass the time, but eventually, he scrapped that idea when his mind wandered and the noises of the cart and muffled voices attracted his attention. He spent some time trying to understand what was being said, but couldn't make out the mumbles. He couldn't even distinguish how many different voices there were. There were at least four men that came through the door with him. Originally, he thought there were three in his bedroom, but during his feeble attempt to make a run for it, he noticed there were four. There were at least two more when they put him in the cart. Richard doubted there would be more than six men traveling with him. If they had him this covered up, then they didn't want to attract attention, and too many of the Queen's men in one place was bound to attract attention.

Suddenly, the cart slowed and Richard could hear the low groan of voices in the distance. The cart veered to the right and stopped. This was the third stop they had made since they put Richard in the cart. The first two times they uncovered Richard and pulled the hood back just enough to thrust a cup to his mouth and command him to drink. It was encouraging to know they didn't want him to die. Yet, the background voices made Richard feel that he wouldn't be getting a drink this time.

The cover was slowly pulled back, and the sweat soaked hood lifted. The sunlight was blinding, but it was quickly blotted out by a face only inches from Richard's.

"You make a sound or move a muscle, and this cart will be carrying you to your funeral," he said. Richard recognized the voice from his bedroom. He was afraid to speak, so he just nodded.

That quickly, he was covered, and they were moving again. Richard still didn't know where they were, but he figured if they were on their way to the castle, the first major town they would come to would be Rivertown. It made sense, and meant they were about a third of the way to the castle.

"Not even half way there," thought Richard, "I'll need more water, or I won't make it." For all he had been through in his life, he never dreamed that he could die from sweating in the back of a hay cart.

His thoughts turned to Abby. "Would she find his clues? Would Pitman remember everything? Should she find the clues? Did he really want her here? And, what good would it do if he were already dead?" For so long, everything he had done was right, but now, it seemed all wrong. His past was coming back to haunt him, and his clues were going to drag his daughter right into the mix. He had to survive, not for himself, but for Abby.

His thoughts were disrupted by more voices as the cart slowed to a stop. After a few minutes, they began moving again. Suddenly, Richard noticed that the sound and lighting changed. He was moved indoors.

"Don't make a sound," was whispered to him.

Richard listened intently. He heard what he thought was the closing of a large door. "Did they leave him?" he thought. He quickly nixed that idea, feeling that they would have to have a guard watching over him. He continued listening, but heard nothing. Richard made the decision to move. He would turn his body and see what happened. His mind raced with how to move, slowly or quickly. He decided on one quick turn to his right.

He counted down in his head, 3…2…1…turn!

BANG!

His right arm was whacked with what was probably a stick.

"We said, don't move!"

Obviously, Richard knew there was someone there watching him, and his throbbing arm was all the evidence he needed to not move again.

There was not another sound for what seemed like a long time, but Richard was reluctant to try moving again. Then he heard the long sharp creak of a door opening and some muffled voices. We waited intently listening for any information he could get. The door creaked again, then a muffled bang of wood.

Richard felt and heard movement around him. He braced himself for another whack with the stick, but it didn't come. The cover was yanked off of his body and the rope binding his hands was loosened.

"Sit up," was the command.

As Richard sat up, the sweat soaked sack was pulled from his head. Richard squinted in the dull light trying to focus, but he was more interested in stretching his arms and flexing his wrists than seeing.

"Eat," said the man sitting on the edge of the cart. He still was out of focus to Richard, but the word 'eat' sounded good.

Coming into focus on his left was a bowl of some type of stew, and a pewter mug filled with water. Richard didn't care what it was. He devoured the stew that had some chunks of meat and vegetables; it tasted good and helped to satisfy his hunger and thirst. He looked at the man who was also eating stew, but with much less vigor than Richard. He was muscular and ate slowly and meticulously, savoring each bite. He wore all brown clothing that made him look like a peasant and not one of the King's Guard, but Richard knew better. This man may look normal, but he was probably a highly skilled soldier. Richard could see that this man's body looked sculpted out of stone. He had barely visible dark hair because of his soldier's haircut, a pointy nose and rock solid chin. The thought of attacking him almost made Richard laugh.

"It would be over in seconds," Richard thought, and he knew who would be the winner. So he tried another tactic.

"How did you find me?" Richard asked.

The man never looked up and continued to eat.

"I said, how did you find me?" he asked again.

Again there was no response.

"Oh my God, are you stupid or…"

The knife was against his throat before he could finish the sentence. Richard couldn't believe how fast the man moved, and he had no idea from where the knife came, but it was pressing hard enough that Richard held his breath.

"Shut up." The man said. Which made Richard nod his head to show he understood. He removed the knife and moved back to his food.

Richard was afraid to move or even breathe. He just stared straight ahead wondering if he should continue to eat or not. He definitely wasn't going to say anything. After a few moments, he slowly moved back to his food hoping he was allowed to finish eating. Then, the man spoke, startling Richard, who was waiting for the knife to slice the food out of his throat.

"I don't know anything, except that we were ordered to go to the other realm, find you, bring you back quietly, and present you to the Queen. Everyone else is eating and drinking at the inn, and I'm the one stuck here with you. So, if you had any brains, you would know that I know nothing."

"Sorry," Richard said while still looking for the knife.

"Why would you think that I know anything?" the man said.

Richard could sense the man's frustration of being left out and stuck here with him, so he tried again to get him to talk.

"I was just wondering how I was found after so many years, and since you were one of the people that found me, I thought you might know," Richard replied feeling a little more comfortable.

"I'm the newest guy here, so I get the worst job, which is watching you! Zareth doesn't tell me anything. I do my job and that's it."

"Zareth?"

Richard asked the question, but figured it must be the raspy voiced man's name.

"He's the leader of our squad, and you'd be wise not to ask him questions."

"Thanks for the warning," Richard said hoping to keep the conversation going, but still fearing the knife and the speed of the man.

The man just grunted while he continued to eat his stew.

"Sorry, I just thought you might know how I was found." Richard said. "I guess you know, but I'm Richard. And you are?"

The man looked away from his meal and glared at Richard like he wasn't sure if he should answer him or not. Finally, he spoke.

"I am Kason, soldier of the Queen's Guard, and now the Keeper of Richard, who needs to leave me alone so I can eat!"

"Hahaha, you're funny, Kason," Richard said, "But, can you tell me why I am here?"

"Why you are here?" Kason laughed, "Because you killed the Princess of Alden, of course."

CHAPTER 7

Pitman's car pulled into the lot of the apartment buildings where the Red Lion Inn used to stand. As they parked, Abby felt like her father. She began looking around thinking about all of the historical people who had been in this very place, from William Penn to George Washington. She looked over to Route 13, the road they just drove here on and wondered what it was like when it was "The King's Highway". She could imagine Washington on his horse leading his officers toward the inn, while the troops made camp in the surrounding woods. Today, there were no horses, no army camps, and no King's Highway, just the hustle of cars and people trying to get somewhere as fast as they could. Abby guessed that none of them knew the historical places they drove past every single day. As cars zipped by, she noticed the sign on Route 13, which she knew told about the Red Lion Inn. She had driven by it hundreds of times and like everyone else, never would have noticed it except that her Dad made her read it and explained what it was about. Now the significance of it made sense to her. They had passed other historical signs and places, which he would always point out, but here, at this place, he made certain that she read the sign and knew about it. He was always a planner and planned for this day, when Abby would need to know some things to follow the clues. She smiled and shook her head as she walked toward the bridge. Growing up without a Mom was difficult, but her Dad was always there for her, now she would be there for him.

"Let's go," she said leading the way.

The other three followed Abby to the bridge that crossed over the Poquessing Creek. She leaned over the side and looked down at the shallow water. Below her, the creek came from under the bridge and flowed to the left, while in front of her the small Byberry Creek ran into the Poquessing and formed one creek. She looked at the bank of the creek where they joined. Closest to her, there were some bushes and a small dirt area, the whole bank was covered with overhanging trees and vines. A little further away; there was a large concrete block that looked like it was dumped there. It definitely wasn't natural and could not have been there when Penn had this bridge built.

"I'm sure William Penn didn't put that concrete block there," Courtney said.

"Yeah, but that's where we want to look," Abby replied, "it's right where the two creeks join."

They moved to the end of the bridge, where it joined the road and peered down the embankment. Bryan led the way trying to establish the best footing for the rest of them to follow. It was only about an eight-foot drop to the creek below, but it was steep and muddy from the overnight rain. Carefully placing his feet at the top of the drop, Bryan peered over the embankment looking for footholds. He stepped down about a foot and then jumped to the bottom. The muddy sand mixture was soft and his knees bent to cushion the blow.

"Really? You expect me to jump down there?" Courtney asked.

"Sorry, it was just easier that way."

"Look out!" Abby said as she jumped off the ledge landing inches from Bryan and grabbing on to him for support.

"What was that?" Bryan said still holding on to Abby as she regained her balance. She just gave him a look, which he knew meant, "Shut up, we have work to do". It was the same look he had seen thousands of times, and he knew better than to question her again.

Abby turned and looked up at Courtney. Again, she said nothing, but Courtney knew it was time to jump. She did as Bryan and Abby both broke her fall and stopped her from tumbling into the creek.

Pitman quickly followed and the four of them stood on the muddy bank.

"This is disgusting," Abby uttered as she shook her head, "morons have no respect." Bryan also noticed the graffiti covered bridge and trash-strewn creek. This was an old stone bridge with three archways to let the creek through. It was a classic architectural design, but that didn't stop local kids from spray painting all along the underside of each arch and all along the side of the bridge. Again, Abby shook her head, but there were more pressing issues. They moved into the foot-deep creek and looked toward the concrete block. The water was cool, but refreshing due to the hot August day. Abby moved first, sloshing through the water making careful foot placements so as not to slip. The others followed like puppies. Abby reached the center where the two creeks merged and turned to stare at the bushes and weeds hanging over the creek. Here it was Pitman that moved first. He walked straight at the bushes and pushed them aside exposing the bank of the creek. Nothing seemed out of the ordinary, so the kids spread out to each side of the bank, with Abby going directly to the concrete block. It was smashed down into the muddy bottom of the creek, but about four feet still stuck out of the water like a fat javelin thrust into the ground. Abby moved around the block to the bank and like Pitman moved away some of the overhanging branches. Again there was nothing, so she started to look down into the water checking for some sign or symbol.

The others did the same moving branches and sloshing around in the cool water looking for something, anything that would make the journal true. It was Pitman who broke the silence.

"Got it!" he hollered although it was muffled by the branches that enclosed him enough that he could barely be seen. The others quickly abandoned their search and followed Pitman's voice into the bank.

As they drew closer they could see Pitman hunched over looking like a guy who had just been kicked in the privates, but quickly realized that he was holding up countless branches on his back. His face was caked with sweat and some wiped mud, but they weren't looking at his face, they were looking at a door.

"Is there a key hole?" Courtney asked.

"No! There's no key hole! So just shut up about the stupid key!" Pitman yelled still trying to hold up the overhanging branches.

"Oh my God, would you both stop!" Abby yelled back. "And, I thought we were trying to be quiet about this!"

It wasn't a normal door, it didn't really look like a door at all, but it was a large circular carving of a turtle. It reminded Abby of either Winnie the Pooh's house or a Hobbit hole. She ran her hand along the surface of the door noticing that there indeed was no keyhole. The carving was very elaborate, and must have taken a long time to do. Yet, the top of the door was flat with three small engraved drawings. The first was a turtle that looked just like the door. The middle engraving was a half of a sun with arrows on each side pointing up, while the third was an arrow pointing up. Abby didn't think it was too hard to figure out; when the sun goes up, the door goes up.

"We have to come back at sunrise," she said.

"At least we know where it is now," Bryan quickly said.

"Yeah, it will help because we'll have to be here in the dark, and that won't be easy."

"Wait, look at this," Pitman said pointing at the bottom of the door.

"A keyhole?" Courtney asked but all three of them gave her such a glaring look that she simply said, "Sorry" and put her head down.

Marked in the mud, there were four small holes on each side of the door.

"What does that mean?" Bryan asked.

"It means someone put their fingers in the mud and lifted this door," Pitman said, "and it wasn't that long ago or this creek would have washed those marks away."

"Do you really think that it opens at sunrise?" Bryan asked.

"Yep, and I think this door was opened at sunrise today. Which means your Dad will be one whole day ahead of us, if we go through tomorrow morning," Pitman said looking at Abby and pointing toward the door.

"Then we need to be here at sunrise to find my Dad."

CHAPTER 8

Richard Lane was a guy who always knew what to say. He could pick the right words in any situation and was usually the go to guy for a eulogy, toast or a quick speech. Yet, the words of Kason had him at a loss, "…killed the Princess of Alden". Those words seemed to bounce off his brain and around his head rendering him speechless and essentially declaring his guilt. Plus, Kason said it so matter of fact like, that felt like it wasn't even up for question. He then went right back to eating his stew leaving Richard dumbfounded and confused. When he regained his composure, dozens of thoughts ran through his head, but one part of the conversation jumped out at him.

"Did you say, you're part of the 'Queen's guard'?" he asked Kason.

"Yes, of course," replied Kason.

"Then, King Tammany is dead, and you think I killed Princess Kitane?"

"Of course, King Tammany is dead and has been for a few years. Princess Kitane is now Queen Kitane. You killed your own daughter,

Princess Abigail, and now you will pay, you demented fool."

The door to the barn burst open giving Richard no chance to respond.

"I see our esteemed guest survived his heated journey. The Queen will be pleased," said the man who Richard figured must be Zareth. "Now, get some rest, we leave before first light."

They settled down for the short night's rest. Apparently, some of the men had been drinking, because Richard could hear their soft snores almost immediately. Zareth declared that he would take the first watch, and Richard knew there would be no conversation with him. Richard was just happy that no one thought to put the sack back on his head or tie his arms.

He wanted to sleep so badly, but he couldn't stop his mind from racing. These people actually believed that he killed Abby. He didn't get it, how could anyone believe that he killed anyone, let alone Abby. Then, Tammany was dead and Kitane was Queen. That thought made him cringe.

Richard remembered back to the first time he met King Tammany XII. Richard had followed the clues from Penn's journal, found and opened the door which led him to the land of Alden. He journeyed many days through towns and villages meeting people, who were so content and happy. They treated him like a celebrity and affectionately called him 'Traveler'. He remembered not understanding how these people were so accepting when all Richard knew were people from home who were so engrossed in their own lives that they wouldn't even say hello to their own neighbors. Then, he found out why.

Richard was standing the center of the town of Kingswood talking to the townspeople, when they suddenly turned, recognized and dropped to a knee. Slowly riding into the center of town was a man astride a brown and white Palomino horse. He wore a simple Native American headdress, leather type pants, and a beaded vest. On each side of him rode a man dressed all in brown clothing. Both men had spears that were decorated with feathers and beads along with bows strapped to the horses and quivers slung over their shoulders. They looked menacing, yet the man in the middle wore such a smile that Richard found himself smiling back as he knelt with the townspeople.

"Rise, citizens of Kingswood and introduce me to your friend the 'Traveler'," Tammany said.

At once, they rose and approached him as he dismounted from

his horse. Richard could feel the love they had for this man. He also felt it was a huge statement that he traveled with only two guards, who now just sat on their horses seemingly confident that their King was in no danger amongst this crowd of people.

The crowd peeled back as Richard approached and instinctively extended his hand in greeting.

"Your Highness, I am Richard", he said.

"Hello Richard, please call me Tammany," he replied wrapping his hand around Richard's forearm, which made Richard do the same in return. Tammany's grip was strong, but warm and loving at the same time.

Richard marveled at how much the people loved Tammany, and how humble he was for a King. Of course, being allowed to marry his daughter a couple of weeks later showed how Tammany felt about him too, but all that was a distant past, as Richard sighed thinking about the death of his friend and former father-in-law Tammany.

Again, he tried to clear his mind and fall asleep, but thinking about his former wife as Queen was probably worse than Tammany's death. Yes, she was beautiful and he fell in love with her and married her, but before Abby was even born, he started to realize that she loved "The Traveler" and his celebrity and not Richard Lane. She was also power hungry and used his status as a celebrity to gain favor with the people. Richard found that as much as the people loved Tammany, they hated Princess Kitane. She just didn't connect with the people, and when Abby was born, all attention turned to Richard and Abby; jealousy became dangerous and Richard left. Now, he was back, Kitane was Queen, and he was going to have to face her in less than a day.

Richard was standing before he was even awake. Zareth had lifted him from a sleeping position and was now nose to nose with him. Like a camera trying to autofocus on an object that is much too close, Richard's eyes couldn't seem to figure out Zareth's scarred face, but Richard's ears had no trouble hearing the message.

"You're going back in the cart, if you make a sound, you're a dead man. Got it?"

Richard continued to try blinking Zareth into focus, but was able to nod his head, showing he understood.

"Good, Traveler. You're almost home," Zareth said with a slight chuckle.

The thought of home was so far from Richard's mind that he almost didn't get the statement. This place could never be his home, and really never felt like home even for the year he spent here. Home was Abby, and although he longed to see her, he was torn over whether he wanted her to find the clues. If everyone here thought she was dead, that might actually be a good thing; it meant they wouldn't go looking for her and she would be safe.

The sack was placed back over Richard's head and his hands were again tied in front of him as he was led back into the cart. The early morning was cooler than the heat of the afternoon; so being covered in the cart wouldn't be too bad for a few hours. He heard the barn doors open and felt the cool rush of morning air blow over his covering. The sun hadn't risen yet, and all was quiet except for the clop of horse hooves and the grinding of stone under the wagon wheels.

As they headed out onto the road, Richard knew they were headed through Rivertown and down the dirt trading path that led to Kingswood, the same town where he had first met Tammany; the place, where essentially, all of this began. A few hours later, he would arrive at the city and have to face the Queen. If he was going to escape, it better be before he was led through the city walls. He needed a plan.

Yet, how do you come up with a plan for escape, when you can't see where you are or who's around you? Although totally covered, Richard closed his eyes and tried to visualize the town of Kingswood. He had escaped from this place once before, and Kingswood was a major stop on his journey.

Richard's visual began with the road into the town. He remembered the first time he walked along this road and was stunned when he was suddenly crossing the small bridge into town. Apparently, it was a called Kingswood because the area around the town was not cleared of trees. It was sort of like taking a town and dropping it right in the middle of the woods. As Richard crossed the small wooden bridge over the Alden River, he noticed the small houses and how they seemed to be randomly placed as opposed to the way he was used to having houses line streets. There were no clear-cut paths through the houses, which were all built around a central center of town area simply called "The Circle". Richard visualized this area and again his first meeting with Tammany. Around "The Circle" were shops, tradesmen, and the

Broken Arrow Inn, which Richard knew had a stable in the back. He also

knew that beyond the stable were not houses, but woods that led down

an embankment to the river. Richard remembered this area well; it was

the first stop he made on his escape with Abby. There was a small

hidden cave on this embankment where he tried so hard to keep baby

Abby from crying and giving them away. This is where he would have to

go. Since they stopped at the inn in Rivertown, he hoped they would do

the same in Kingswood. Richard felt more of a connection here,

especially because he knew a hiding place, now he would just need an

opportunity to slip away. It wouldn't be easy, but hope was all he had.

CHAPTER 9

Abby didn't think she was going to be able to sleep, but it had been such a long day that she went right out. After they returned from the door, they had pizza delivered and decided on a plan for Bryan and Courtney to get away from their parents for a few days. Courtney was pretty easy because her and Abby were always sleeping at each other's houses, so for her parents it would be a normal event to stay at Abby's. Bryan would be a little different. He was pretty sure that telling his parents that he was sleeping over Abby's house wouldn't go over too well. They knew that he and Abby were best friends and all, but a sleepover was pretty much out of the question. So, over a couple of slices of pizza, they decided to tell Bryan and Courtney's parents that Mr. Lane was taking them to the beach for a couple of days before school got started. Luckily for them, Richard's phone was there, and they could just text them the plan without having to actually talk to them. The texts worked like a charm, Courtney ran home and packed a bag to stay the night at Abby's, and Bryan would get up really early to be at Abby's so they could beat the traffic.

Before she knew it, Abby's phone alarm was going off at 4am. She knew it was too early, but she was not missing sunrise at the door. She rolled over and flicked on the light, Courtney was awake and looking at her.

"Is this even right?" Courtney whispered.

"What do you mean?" Abby asked stretching her arms over her head.

"I mean, is this for real? Are we really going to do this? You really think your Dad was taken through some door to another world?"

"I don't know…but I do know that I need to at least try and see if this door will open and if there is really some 'other world'."

"Ok," was all Courtney could say.

"Court, if you don't want to come, I understand."

"No, I want to come, I just hope we're doing the right thing. I mean, we're trusting some dude we don't know and an old book."

"I thought the same thing, except, so far, the book's been right, and there really isn't any explanation for what happened to my Dad."

"That's the main reason why I'm going; the clues in that stupid book."

Abby got up, walked over and hugged Courtney. She didn't need to say anything the hug was plenty. They got ready and went downstairs where Pitman was gently snoring on the couch. Abby started over to wake him when she heard the weak tapping on the door. Courtney walked over and whipped open the door making Bryan jump back a step.

"What the heck, Court? You scared the crap out of me!"

"I know," she replied laughing.

Pitman woke with a snort, wide eyed and confused as to where he was. All three kids laughed at that.

"Good morning, Sunshine." Abby said.

"There is no sunshine, it's 4:30 in the morning. Even the Sun's asleep." He replied.

"Get ready, I want to go."

"We can't get there too early. People will wonder what we're doing, and we can't have anyone interested in us," Pitman said.

"Well, we can get something to eat and wait in the car then, I'm not going to miss this."

"Ok, give me a couple minutes to wake up."

The kids anxiously awaited Pitman getting ready. The three of them sat with backpacks on not even talking just waiting for him to come out of the bathroom. When Pitman did emerge, he looked at them and chuckled.

"I guess you're ready," Pitman said.

"Let's go," Abby replied hopping up from the couch and heading to the door. Everyone followed without saying anything.

By the time they left the house, it was a little after 5am, well before sunrise, but Abby was still in a hurry. She had checked the computer for the exact time for sunrise in Philadelphia and found it to be at 6:19am, which meant they still had about an hour to get to the door. Being early was Abby's plan; she wasn't going to miss this for anything. So when Pitman turned the car into a local store, she freaked out a little.

"What are you doing?"

"We're early, and I need some coffee," Pitman replied.

"If we miss this, I swear to God…"

"We're not going to miss it, I promise," he said as he got out of the car.

"We better not!" she yelled as the door closed

"We should take the car and leave him here," Courtney said.

"Don't tempt me," Abby answered still annoyed.

"I wasn't kidding," said Courtney smiling.

"It's ok, he's coming back already," Bryan said.

Pitman returned with coffee and some bottles of water for the kids. Just a few minutes later, they were pulling into the apartment parking lot next to the Red Lion Bridge. Abby couldn't contain her excitement and jumped out of the car before Pitman could even turn the car off. She quickly trotted across the bridge to the embankment they went down the day before.

"Yo Ab, slow down, I can't even see where I'm going," Bryan said as he followed her across the bridge.

Abby was not waiting for anyone, she was getting to that door and trying to open it as soon as she could. She didn't even wait for Bryan to help her down the embankment, she got to it and jumped into the dark, landing on the soft sand and walking directly into the cool creek water.

"Abby!" Courtney yelled as she saw her jump.

"Shh!" Pitman said, "We don't want to draw attention to ourselves. Be quiet."

"But she jumped!" Courtney said lowering her voice just a little.

"I know, we'll catch up, relax."

Bryan was already down the embankment when Courtney and Pitman arrived. Like the others they jumped down quickly and made their way into the creek. When they arrived at the bushes overhanging the door they could see a faint light coming from inside them. Abby was using her cell phone to light up the door while Bryan was trying to lift it. The door wasn't moving.

"Can you all see that it's still dark?" Pitman questioned.

"Yeah, but I thought it was worth a shot," Abby said annoyed.

"According to the time you looked up, we still have about a half hour before official sunrise," Courtney said.

"It will start to get light before that. Maybe it'll open then," Pitman said hoping to make Abby feel a little better.

The wait was almost unbearable. First, their anxiousness to open the door was driving them crazy, but the bigger problem was the bugs.

They were getting eaten alive by mosquitoes while standing in the calf deep water. Then it happened.

"Abby, look," Bryan said pointing at the door.

Faint glowing lines seemed to be growing along the edges and ridges of the turtle shell. They watched in awe as the glow grew. It was Abby who finally pulled herself out of the stupor and rushed at the door. As she dug her fingers into the mud and began to lift, the door came up easily like a well-oiled garage door. Behind it was a semi dark tunnel that Abby crouched into without hesitation.

"Wait," Pitman said, "let me go first."

Abby who was still anxious to keep going found herself stopping and letting him before she could really think about it. As they all passed through and crab-walked down the dry dirt tunnel, Abby turned and watched the door slowly close. She slid back and tried to open it again, but it was again sealed. She shined her phone flashlight at the door, which looked like the underbelly of a turtle with a keyhole in the middle.

"Wait!" Abby called to the others flipping off her backpack and opening it to get the journal. She opened it and took out the key. She dug a small hole to the right of the door and dropped the key in it.

"What are you doing?" Pitman asked.

"I want to leave the key here so we know we can return, and it won't get lost."

"That's actually a good idea," Pitman said, "We can't lose that."

They continue down the dark tunnel in silence with Pitman leading the way. After about ten yards, they can see a faint light up ahead which grows as they crawl forward. Suddenly, Abby feels and strange sensation come over her like she popped through an unseen bubble. As fast as she felt it, the sensation was gone. By the looks on the other kids faces, she knew they felt the same thing.

"Did you feel that?" she asked.

"Yeah, it felt like I got sucked through a straw," Bryan said.

"That was so weird like when you walk into a spider web because you can't see it," Courtney said, "but then suddenly, it was gone."

"Yeah, it's kind of neat," Pitman said.

"Neat?"

"Yeah, I think it feels kind of neat," he said shrugging his shoulders.

"Whatever," Courtney said as they continued toward the light. As the tunnel opened up a little, Abby could see what looked like the same creek in front of her glowing in the morning sun.

They stared in awe at what was essentially the same place that they just left. The biggest difference was the cleanliness. There was no trash strewn creek, no dumped concrete block, and most noticeably, no graffiti on the bridge.

"This is insane!" Bryan blurted out.

"You can say that again," Courtney said.

"This is…"

"Oh God, Shut up!" Courtney said whacking him in the arm making Bryan laugh at her.

"Let's go," Pitman said heading to the embankment, but suddenly, he stopped with Abby almost running into him. "Look," he said.

There were footprints leading up the embankment, at least a couple of sets of them. Abby knelt to touch the nearest print. Could it really be her Dad's footprints? Could he really be here? This whole thing seemed nearly impossible, but the more things happened, the more she believed. She felt herself starting to get emotional, but she didn't want to break down and cry now. She felt she was getting closer, so there was no time to feel sorry for herself or for her Dad. It was time to move and move she did. Abby scrambled up the embankment using her hands and feet like a well skilled rock climber. Yet, it was more a quick adrenaline rush that pushed her up that hill. The others followed with Bryan close behind Abby. He then turned and helped Courtney and Pitman to the top. When they got up, Abby was already in the middle of the dusty dirt road squatting down to look at something.

"What's that?" Bryan asked.

"There are hoof prints and some wheel ruts. By their placement, it looks like the horse was pulling a cart over the bridge and onto the main road. It's so weird how this is like the same bridge as home."

They all took a minute to look around. The similarities were scary to the kids. The creek and the bridge were exactly the same and so was the placement of the roads. The modern buildings where the Red Lion Bridge met Route 13 just outside of Philadelphia were not there, but the slope of the land was exactly the same. Instead of a concrete and asphalt city, there were rolling grass hills and forest area, but Abby still felt like she knew where she was. As they moved out toward the intersection of the dirt roads, Pitman pointed to the right.

"Look," he said.

There on the other side of the main road was a crude wooden stake with arrows nailed to it. A left arrow read 'Neshaminy Creek 1', while there were three arrows pointing to the right, 'Rivertown 1', 'Kingswood 2', and 'Alden Castle 2'. Courtney walked over to the signs to get closer. She pointed at the bottom two on the right and looked confused.

"How can they both be two miles away?" she said.

"I'm pretty sure it's not miles," Pitman said.

They all looked at Pitman, "Huh?"

"It's not in miles, it's in days. It means it takes 2 days to get to Kingswood and on that second day, you'll get to Alden Castle. That's how they're both a 2."

"Well, that sucks!' Courtney said.

"They must be taking him to the castle," Abby said almost to herself and not really paying attention to the others. She was deep in thought about her Dad and so focused that nothing else really mattered.

"I think you're right," Pitman said.

"What are we waiting for? Let's go," Bryan said.

He didn't have to tell Abby twice; she was already starting down the road before Bryan finished his sentence. They all followed quickly. Immediately they crossed what they knew as the Route 13 Bridge which in their world put them in the City of Philadelphia, yet here, there was no welcoming sign and nothing that looked like a twenty-first century city. There was a dusty dirt road full of wagon wheel ruts and hoof prints. The sides of the road were lined with trees and bushes. Off to the right, they could see through a layer of trees to a weather worn wooden fence that separated the road and trees from a field of what looked like young corn stalks stretching as far into the distance as they could see. They kept to the road, while looking for a farmer or farmhouse that was linked to those crops, but they saw no one.

They hadn't walked very far when they saw the first house. It was a small wooden house that was weather worn and in need of some new roof shingles. On the side of the house was a small garden, but what really caught their eye was a woman squatted next to the garden pulling weeds. She wore a long light blue dress with her dark hair tied up in a white ribbon. Abby thought she was plucked right out of a movie about the pioneers moving across the prairie. As they moved down the road, they got a little closer to the woman, but she was still a good fifty yards from the road. As they passed her, she noticed the movement and looked up. She stared for a second, waved, and went right back to her gardening. All four of the travelers waved back, but the woman didn't see them because her garden was way more important then a few people traveling down the main road.

"A lot of people must come down this road," Abby said, "because she paid us no mind at all."

"Exactly what I was thinking," Pitman said.

"Maybe we shouldn't be on this road," Bryan said looking first at Abby and then Pitman.

"Another thing I was thinking," Pitman said, "maybe when we get through this village, we should get off the road."

"Village? What village?" Courtney asked.

"There", Pitman said pointing up the road.

Up ahead the trees seemed to open up around the road and there also seemed to be some buildings on either side of the road. They quickly forgot about the woman and focused on the road ahead. As they got closer, they knew that Pitman was correct; this road went right through the center of this village. There were a few people walking around with some of the women carrying baskets full of goods from the stores that lined the streets. They were all dressed in the same fashion as the woman they saw gardening. The first man they saw looked like he stepped right off a pirate ship. He had torn brown pants that were rolled almost to his knee and what was once a collared white shirt, which now desperately needed a washing machine and some bleach.

At first, the people didn't seem to notice them, but once they did, they all seemed to slow in what they were doing and stare. Abby felt uncomfortable with the whispers and looks they were getting. She almost started running down the road, but was more afraid to attract more attention. Then an old woman wearing a long ankle length gray dress and a white bonnet covering her head approached from their right. She did not hesitate in coming toward them, but her age made her move slowly. Instinctively, the four travelers slowed as she grew near.

"Can I help you fine young people?" the woman said with an accent that Abby couldn't place but could easily understand.

"We are looking for a man," Courtney said.

"Aren't we all, Missy," the woman replied making herself laugh, and Pitman shake his head.

"He's my Dad," Abby said stepping closer to the woman.

The woman looked at Abby and her laughter immediately stopped, her smile was gone, and her eyes widened. She looked as though she saw a ghost and started backing away as she spoke.

"I'm so sorry, my lady. We of Dalusia cannot help for we have seen no man. I must go now," the woman said as she backed away. When she finished, she turned and ran across the street and between two of the village shops.

Abby turned and looked at the others perplexed.

"What was that?" Abby said.

"I don't know, but that old chick was pretty fast," Courtney said laughing.

Bryan was looking around, but the road was desolate. The few people that had been around were gone as fast as the old woman. "She's not the only one," he said.

"We should go," Pitman chimed in as he looked around the area.

"Yeah, I feel like we're being watched," Bryan said turning in all directions but seeing no one.

"We are being watched, that's why we have to go…Now!"

CHAPTER 10

Richard figured that it was mid morning when the cart finally came to a stop. He heard some voices getting closer to him, but he couldn't make out what they were saying. Suddenly, the cover was pulled back and Zareth was in his face again giving him the same speech as before they pulled into Rivertown. Richard nodded his head acknowledging that he would keep quiet. As before, the hood and cover were pulled back over his head and the cart pulled away. Richard took the few seconds of sunlight to try and look around. By the time his eyes adjusted, all he could see were trees and the road. Obviously, they had stopped before they reached Kingswood, but Richard was looking for something definitive to know where he was, a landmark, or sign, anything. Yet, it didn't happen.

As they moved along the road, Richard listened for sound changes. He heard the river first, and then the change of the cart crossing the bridge into Kingswood. Now he started to feel the twists and turns of the paths between the Kingswood houses. Richard tried to visualize the cart moving through the houses like a snake sneaking up some prey. Finally, after a few minutes, the cart moved straight and Richard knew they were in the center of "The Circle" amongst the shops and stores. He could hear the muffled voices of people moving around the area, but there was no way he was going to make a move now. Richard had bigger plans; he just needed a moment alone.

The cart made a sharp turn to the left, and Richard smiled under the hood. He knew exactly where they were going. The Broken Arrow Inn was the main spot for anyone who came into Kingswood. It was the only place to eat, have a drink, or spend the night if you were traveling around these parts. There were ten small rooms that could be rented for the night with a restaurant/bar that usually had some form of entertainment for travelers. Behind the inn was a stable, where travelers could leave their horses to be fed and watered while they stayed at the inn. This is where Richard knew they were going. He knew this area well and felt a moment alone could let him escape.

Finally, the cart came to a stop, and Richard could hear the horse being unhooked. He didn't hear the door of the stable and felt they were parked on the side of it. This would be even better for him, he wouldn't have to get out of the stable, just slip into the woods. He waited impatiently for the cover and hood to come off, but it wasn't happening. Richard started to feel defeat and thoughts raced through his head. "How could he escape when he couldn't see? Could he slip away with a guard watching the cart? Could he jump up and out run the guard?" He had so many questions, but no answers. He needed information. He listens intently, as the voices around him grow closer and a little louder. He can distinguish Kason and Zareth's voices over the others. Richard closes his eyes and listens.

"I think I should get to come in this time, I watched him the last time. Feston is new too. He should have a turn!" said Kason.

"You did a good job last time, I trust you," Zareth replied.

"He's newer than me!" came another voice that Richard didn't know and figured it must be this Feston guy.

"You know what, Kason is right, he can come in for a few minutes and eat and drink, while you stand guard out here. Then, you can switch," commanded Zareth.

"That isn't right, but I'll do it. You better eat fast!" Feston said.

Richard heard the men leave as their voices faded.

"Do I go now?" he thought. Then he felt the man, who had to be Feston, sit on the cart. Richard thought he weighed a lot because the movement of the cart was very noticeable. He also knew that this man wasn't taking the hood or cover off of him. Richard waited, afraid to move a muscle, for this man was already angry, and Richard didn't want to feel the wrath of it. Then, there was a shift of weight, a mumble of curse words and a sigh. Richard could almost feel the man's impatience. He didn't want to be here, and Richard hoped it would give in and go to the inn. After what seemed like hours, the man broke.

"Arrrruggh!" Richard heard as the cart practically bounced with the man jumping up and mumbling to himself as he made his way to the inn. Richard got a chill and knew exactly how the man's impatience felt, because he was now feeling it himself.

He made himself count slowly to ten before quickly slipping out of the cart and dropping to the ground. He ripped off the hood and let his eyes adjust to the distant sunlight. Crouching behind the cart, Richard peered around the back wheel closest to the stable as he undid the ropes binding his feet. He saw the man turn the corner to the front of the building. Richard knew it was only about twenty feet to the entrance of the inn. Once the man went inside, it wouldn't take long for Zareth to come racing back to the cart. He didn't have much time and was sure these men could track him through the woods. His only hope was the cave that was a good hundred yards from here. He scooped up the hay that had fallen with him out of the cart, stuffed it in the sack that had been over his head and slid it back under the cover that still lay in the cart. He quickly made it appear that he was still under the cover hoping it would buy him some time. Then, he turned and ran his hands still bound in front of him as he twisted them to try loosening the rope to no avail. It was awkward running like that, but he had not choice. He bounded through the trees and underbrush before turning to see if he was being followed. Richard again crouched and hid in the weeds trying to focus on twisting his hands free. He froze. From around the corner, came not Zareth, but Kason. He was walking quickly, but not with the urgency of thinking Richard escaped. Richard knew that from where he was spying on them, he could make it to the cave in less than a minute. He decided to wait and see what happened.

Kason approached the cart. Richard hoped that from Kason's view it looked like the lump under the cover was Richard. Then Richard noticed the piece of rope lying on the ground and some hay where he had been crouched down behind the cart. There was no way Kason could see it from the front of the cart, he just needed Kason to stay on the front side.

As Kason approached, Richard held his breath. "Please stay in front, please stay in front," he thought. As Kason got to the front of the cart, Richard saw his head turn side to side. "He must be making sure there is no one watching. They don't want anyone to know what's in that cart," he thought.

Then, with no one around, Kason put his hand on the lump in the cart where Richard's head should be and the lump collapsed. Kason was lightning quick as he hopped up on to the cart and began pushing all around, pulling the cover away to find a sack full of hay. He hopped off the end of the cart and noticed the rope on the ground. Kason grabbed the piece of rope and took off at a full sprint to the Broken Arrow. When he disappeared around the corner, Richard turned and moved deeper into the woods. He wanted to run to the cave, but needed to see what was going to happen first. He turned and crouched in the bushes again, further away and closer to the cave, but he could still see the cart clearly.

Five men came racing around the corner, Zareth in the lead; muscles rippling with the most determined look on his face. Richard felt he had to get out of there, but like bystanders at a car crash; he couldn't stop watching. They ran to the cart and surrounded it as Zareth leaped from a run to the middle of the cart, landing in the soft hay with a growl. Richard was far enough away that he couldn't make out the words being said, but there was a lot of pointing and yelling at Feston, the man who had left Richard alone. Feston was pointing and yelling at Kason. During the yelling and accusations, Zareth dropped from the cart and approached Feston without a word and with amazing speed, whipped out a knife and sliced Feston's throat. Richard gasped out loud as blood spurted from the wound, and Feston dropped to the ground. Richard felt frozen, staring at the dead man as blood pooled around the body.

Zareth began pointing for his remaining men to search in different directions, but grabbed Kason and threw him toward the body of Feston. Kason began pulling the body toward the cart as the other men began their search. Zareth said something to Kason, turned and began jogging directly toward Richard.

"Oh no!" Richard whispered to himself as he turned and ran toward the cave. His mind raced hoping his throat wouldn't be next. He hopped over a fallen branch, trying to keep his balance with his hands still tied in front of him, stumbled, regained his balance and saw the familiar bushes that covered the entrance to the small cave. Zareth had to be into the woods by now, and Richard prayed he didn't leave behind any prints on his trek to the cave. One last glance behind him revealed exactly what he had hoped, no Zareth. Richard smiled as he turned toward the cave and was completely blindsided and slammed to the ground. With his hands tied, there was no way to cushion the blow as he hit like a box of rocks. Stunned, Richard almost blacked out when the drool hit his face. He focused his eyes on the bared fangs and green eyes of a snarling wolf that had him pinned to the ground.

CHAPTER 11

It only took a few minutes to be out of the village and back under the cover of trees. Quickly and silently they made their way down the dusty road filled with tracks from wagon wheels, which made walking fast a little tricky. A turned ankle was easy to come by and none of them wanted that problem to slow them down. About a quarter mile outside the village they paused and the three kids turned to Pitman.

Bryan broke the silence, "How do you know we were being watched?"

Pitman laughed a little, "Were being watched? It's not were, we *are* being watched, right now. Which is why we need to keep moving and then get off the road as soon as possible."

"How do you know?"

"Just keep walking, and I'll explain, but think about this, if you were them, would you be watching us?"

The looks Pitman got were enough to know the answer. They began moving again in silence, but more intent to sounds and trying to look inconspicuous in their search for people watching them. They saw no one and probably heard nothing, yet in their minds they could hear many threats.

Finally, after walking for another twenty minutes or so, Pitman broke the silence. "I think we're alright now, let's move off the road and see if we can find a parallel path."

"Are you sure?" Abby asked.

"No, but we walked a while, so…"

Courtney exploded at Pitman, "Wait a sec! You say people we can't see or hear are watching us for miles and miles. Now, you say, 'We're good', but you're not sure? What the heck does that mean?"

"Courtney, relax." Pitman said.

"Relax? Are you kidding me? We go through some tunnel and end up in like 1680 world with some old chick looking at Abby like she's the Zombie Queen from Hell, and now we're followed by ghosts for miles through the woods, and you tell me to 'Relax'! Are you serious?"

"Yeah, relax."

Abby grabbed Courtney and pulled her back before she could fully lunge at Pitman. Bryan, who was stunned that she would go after a grown man, quickly helped, but agreed with Courtney saying, "You need to explain why you think we're not being watched now."

"Ok, think about it, if they wanted to hurt us or do anything, it would have happened right away. When we left, they probably followed us to make sure we left their village and didn't do anything. After they followed us for a while, they probably figured that we were just leaving and went back home."

Abby loosened her grip on Courtney, "He's probably right, Court. It does make sense."

"Yeah, but he said 'probably' way too much for me," Courtney said calming down enough that Abby let her go.

"Now, do you want to stand here and yell at me or go find her Dad?" Pitman asked pointing at Abby, but directing his question to Courtney.

Courtney shook her head, smiled and was ready to start yelling, when Abby just grabbed her arm and said "Let's go," pointing at Pitman to lead the way.

Pitman led them off of the road and through the underbrush. It was an awful trek with branches whipping against their legs and arms, which they held in front of their faces for protection. About fifty yards in, they came to a small clearing and paused to regain themselves.

"Well, that sucked!" Courtney said. They all nodded in agreement while probing their legs and arms for small cuts.

"It sucked, but it might have worked," Abby said pointing to a small footpath leading from the clearing.

"That'll work," Pitman said leading the way down the path, which they figured ran pretty much parallel to the road.

It wasn't like the road, but traveling single file was fine and the war with the branches was much easier on the path. Another good thing was the path seemed to move straight and was not winding, making it easy to follow. After about a half hour, they came to another clearing, which was bigger than the last one and they were able to spread out and rest for a few minutes. They dropped their backpacks and plopped down on the grass, listening for any sound of followers, but they heard nothing.

Abby was the first to break the silence, "I have to go to the bathroom."

"Number one or number two," Courtney giggled.

"Funny," Abby replied while standing up and ripping open her backpack. She pulled out a few perfectly folded paper towels. Holding them in her hand, she stared and smiled. It was strange how something so simple like paper towels could take a person totally away from the situation at hand. Looking at those paper towels made her think of her Dad because he was like the Paper Towel King. It was a weird obsession of his that he always seemed to have some paper towels on him. It was an unwritten law that they had to have them in the house at all times. Of course the were used for the normal things that everyone else used them for, but Richard used them for so much more, like blowing his nose. Abby could never remember ever having to ask someone for a tissue, because in one little sniffle, Richard would whip out a paper towel. At least once a week, they were picking pieces of them off of clothes from the wash because one was left in his pocket. It drove Abby crazy, but right now, she wished he was there to hand her some so she could go to the bathroom.

Her smile faded and she snapped back to reality. "I'll be right back," she said.

"You want me to come with you?" Courtney asked.

"Nah, I'm good."

"How about me?" Bryan said laughing.

"Thanks for all the concern guys, but I'm pretty sure I can pee by myself."

"Seriously, don't go too far," Pitman said breaking up the laughter.

"I won't."

Abby scoped up her backpack and headed into the trees. She knew she couldn't go far from her friends, but she also didn't want to go to the bathroom right in front of them. She pushed through the bushes and small trees for a few yards looking for a secluded place. She figured that she moved about thirty yards away from her friends to an area that they couldn't see her, but she was still within ear-shot if there was a problem. When she was finished, Abby felt a sense of relief, grabbed her backpack and headed back to the clearing.

After a few yards, she heard some voices that she didn't recognize. They were deeper than her friends and didn't sound like Pitman. Abby froze. Thoughts raced through her head, "Were they still followed after all this time? Who could these people be? Are they the people that took her Dad? Should she hide? Could she just leave her friends?" She was torn. If she ran back and her friends were being taken, then she couldn't help them or her Dad. Yet, staying here meant she was alone. She decided to sneak closer and see what was going on in the clearing.

Abby crept slowly and quietly through the bushes, trying not to move any branches or step on anything that would make a noise. Finally, she could distinguish a few different voices and knew that her friends were not alone. She crouched in the bushes and listened as best she could. She couldn't really make out the words being said, but it was clear that these people were not happy.

Abby decided that she would be more important to her friends if she was free and could possibly help them. She rose from her crouch to move backward when a hand clamped over her mouth. She felt her body being pulled backward and pressed against the person holding her. She wanted to scream, but the grip was so tight, she could barely breathe. Then she felt it, a strange cold sensation extending from the hand, around her mouth and deep inside of her. It seemed to last for a few seconds and as quickly as it came upon her, it was gone. Later, Abby would compare the sensation to downloading something on a computer. The cold was like that line shooting across the screen to download a new program. Then she heard a voice, "Shhh, let's get out of here. Quietly walk backward with me and don't make a sound."

As they moved back toward Abby's recent bathroom, the grip over her mouth eased. She still wanted to scream, but wasn't sure if it would do any good. Her friends already seemed to be captured and now she was too. Yet, the man's words triggered in her head again, "Let's get out of here," seemed more like an escape plan than a capture. The voices of her friends and their captors faded away as Abby was pulled gently from the scene.

Finally, the man spoke again, "I'm going to let you go, if you scream, the Queen's men will get us both. Do you understand?"

Abby nodded and the man removed his hand from her mouth and let her go. Abby quickly turned to face the man. When they looked at each other, both took a step back. He was startled by Abby's eyes and the shock of them made him gasp. Abby had no reaction to his gasp because reaction to her eyes was normal. The reason Abby stepped back was the man who grabbed her was not a man at all, but a boy, a very handsome boy. He was not much older than her, maybe a year or two and he had black hair that was kind of long for a boy, but it was kept out of his face by a crimson cloth. His eyes were light brown and had a wild look about them. Abby thought he looked like he jumped out of a movie about Native Americans, with his tanned skin and rippling muscles. He wore no shirt and had only crude knee length pants, but on his belt was a tomahawk and a large knife. She found herself staring and at a loss for words.

"I am Lakota. Are you a Traveler?" he asked looking her up and down, which made Abby uncomfortable until she realized he was checking out her clothes.

She wasn't ready for the question and simply replied, "Huh?"

"Are you a Traveler?" he said again, "I mean, from another place?"

"Yes, I...I guess I am," she had found her voice and finally answered, "I'm Abby."

"Nice to meet you Abby. Why are you here?"

"I'm...Well, my friends and I are looking for someone," she replied being kind of vague on purpose. She wasn't sure if she should trust this guy, but he didn't do anything to harm her yet, so she didn't totally lie.

"Another Traveler?" Lakota asked.

She saw her opportunity and took it, "Yeah, he was with us, but we got separated. We were searching the woods for him. You didn't see anyone, did you?"

"No, just you and your friends."

"What about my friends, where are they? We have to go find them and help them!"

"Wait here," Lakota said leaving Abby by herself as he moved silently into the woods where they just came from.

Now, she was really confused. This boy, who had just practically kidnapped her from her friends, was leaving her alone. She could escape and run off to find them herself, but then she remembered her biggest problem; she had no chance alone in these woods. She decided that if the boy was going to harm her, he would have done it by now, or he at least wouldn't have left her alone. Abby plopped down in the grass and waited. It wasn't long before Lakota returned.

"They were taken by the Queen's guard and it looks like they're headed for the castle," he said as he returned.

"But why? We didn't do anything."

"Travelers are not always welcome, because some people fear them. We can follow at a distance and try to find them, before they get to the castle. Yet, it won't be easy."

"Well, why are we still here and not following them?"

"There are only so many routes to the castle, and they all take about the same amount of time to get there. If they are traveling with a group of people, it will take longer then it'll take us. They are also highly trained soldiers, so we can't be too close, or they most certainly will catch us. We need to keep our distance and maybe even wait until they get in the castle to meet up with them."

"Are you serious? We need to get them...now!" Abby said.

"Ok, let's go rushing in there to get them. The two of us against a whole group of, what, twenty soldiers. Sounds like a plan for disaster to me."

Abby knew he was right, but didn't want to say it. She felt like she was abandoning her friends and was lost without them. She put her head in her hands, closed her eyes, and took a few deep breaths to stop herself from crying. She was so torn. She really felt that it might be better to just run after her friends, so that they were all caught together. "At least we would be together," she thought.

Lakota looked down on her and looked torn. He really didn't

know what to do, but he knew he had to keep her away from her friends and get her to the castle as quickly as possible. After a minute, that felt like hours, he found his voice, "I have a plan, but you have to trust me."

"Trust you? I don't even know you!" Abby yelled.

"Shhhh! They will hear you and find us."

"I don't care…"

"Yes you do!" Lakota said as he grabbed Abby by the arm and yanked her to her feet. She was running before she realized what she was actually doing. The bushes smashed against her as Lakota drug her through the woods. The ground went by rapidly as Abby tried keeping her head down to avoid losing an eye from the whipping branches. Hey didn't run far or for long, but the speed burst had Abby gasping for air.

"What…was…that…about," she panted trying to catch her breath.

"We couldn't stay there with you yelling! They are trained soldiers and are probably checking out where we just were. You can't take chances like that, you don't know who you're dealing with here."

"Well…I…How are you not out of breath?" she asked looking perplexed.

"I'm used to running from people like that," he answered still looking around to make sure they weren't followed. "Come on, we need to keep moving."

They did. Abby followed Lakota like a lost puppy, not having any idea of where they were or where they were going. He convinced her that they were taking a parallel route to the road, which would lead them to the castle. It was a long journey that would take them over a day to finish, but Abby knew, she had no other choice.

CHAPTER 12

Sitting in the back of a cart with four men watching their every move was not how Bryan and Courtney envisioned this trip going. Less than an hour ago, they felt safe that whoever they thought was following them was gone. They sat and relaxed in the small clearing, even letting Abby leave alone to go to the bathroom, when they were ambushed by brown clothed men carrying primitive weapons like swords, bows and arrows, and clubs.

Bryan felt they came out of nowhere, silently surrounding them in a matter of seconds. He replayed the scene in his mind, seeing Courtney's eyes widen as she spotted the first man stepping into the clearing. He saw Pitman jumping up to confront them, and the vicious thud of a fist smashing into the right side of his face. Then, there were five of them all around, and he hadn't even had the chance to move. "A big help I am," he thought shaking his head to himself.

He glanced over at Pitman, who sat sullen with a darkening bruise on the side of his cheek and dried blood caked to the side of his mouth. Bryan didn't like the guy, but at least he tried to do something, unlike himself. Courtney sat close to Bryan, her tear streaked face, stoic

117

since they were placed in the cart. Bryan knew she was thinking about Abby. They were so stunned at the time that they didn't even realize that Abby wasn't captured. As they were led away by the men, Bryan and Courtney made eye contact, and it was like they could read each other's minds; both thinking should they give up Abby, or let her be free? They made their decision by saying nothing.

Now, riding in this cart, Bryan was scared for Abby, who was now alone and lost in these woods. Questions raced through his head: Did she see them get captured? Did she follow? Could she keep up with the cart? He had no answers. He glanced at Courtney and could almost see the same questions running through her mind. Courtney took a huge sigh, which drew the attention of the men in the cart, but it meant nothing.

Taking their attention away from Courtney, the men began looking around as if they were looking for something. Their demeanor stoked the interest of Bryan and Courtney, who also began scanning the landscape expecting to see Abby come running out of the bushes. Then, the cart slowed and Courtney perked up even more. One man stood and jumped out the back of the slow moving cart like he had done it thousands of times. Bryan still scanned the sides of the road behind the man, hoping Abby would pop out, but she didn't. Voices from the front of the cart drew his attention away from his thoughts of Abby.

"Griffin! You've returned," a man said approaching the cart, "And you've brought guests."

"Yes, go tell Vala to prepare for three guests," said Griffin, who was obviously the leader of the raiding party, and also the man that cracked Pitman in the face. Bryan stared at him with contempt and awe. Griffin was tall and muscular with the crew cut hair of a soldier and the menacing look to match. Yet, Bryan could tell that he was not a big, dumb soldier. There was a leadership look in Griffin's dark eyes that made Bryan want to know more about him.

"Let's go," said the man who had jumped from the cart. He held out his hand to help Courtney down, and then did the same for Bryan. As Pitman approached the edge of the cart, he removed his hand and simply said, "Jump."

They were led from the cart into a small village that had only a few people visible. There were small wooden houses that were strewn around the large clearing in the woods. They were led to a large wooden house and greeted by a woman, who they figured must be Vala. She was middle aged with long graying hair neatly braided down her back. She wore a long dark bluish colored dress, but the best part of her was her smile. It was genuine, friendly and welcoming. Bryan couldn't help but smile back at her as she welcomed them into the house.

"Come in and welcome to Sono," she said. As Bryan smiled back, Courtney gave her a strange look of confusion and Pitman simply kept his head down. They were led to a room with a table and chairs that looked like a meeting room. There was a basket of bread and fruit on the table along with a pitcher and some wooden cups. "Eat," she said as she closed the door. They heard the lock turn and they were alone.

"Are we prisoners?" Courtney asked immediately after the lock turned.

"My face thinks so," Pitman mumbled.

"I have no idea," Bryan said grabbing a small loaf of bread. "We're not tied up or anything, but I don't think we can just leave, so I guess we are. Might as well eat."

Courtney pulled out a chair and grabbed an apple from the basket. Pitman sat with his head down and didn't make eye contact with anyone. Bryan continued to eat like a starved dog, scanning the room, which was pretty bare except for the table and chairs. Courtney was finishing up her apple when the lock turned. They all looked up.

A group came through the door with Griffin leading them, which made Pitman lower him head.

"I am Griffin, and we are the Fighters For Alden, known as the FFA. Who are you, and where are you from?"

Bryan and Courtney looked at each other and Pitman kept his head down, but none of them spoke. The silence seemed to last forever. Bryan wasn't sure if he should answer or not. He looked around the room at each of the four men's faces. They all looked stone-faced and soldier like, except for Griffin, whose gaze reminded Bryan of a teacher waiting for a class to answer. His look almost made Bryan answer him, yet Bryan knew that they shouldn't really give up any information to these unknown men. Courtney looked over at Bryan and apparently she had the same feeling about Griffin's gaze. Her eyes were telling Bryan that she wanted to speak, but Bryan gave the slightest shake to his head telling her no. She understood and gently put her head down like a student who didn't complete her homework. Griffin watched stone-faced.

"Ok," he finally said, "You're dressed like Travelers and look like Travelers, but we haven't seen Travelers in a long time. How did you get here and where is Richard?"

That did it. Courtney's head shot up and the silent treatment was gone. "Oh My God! You know Mr. Lane?" she said.

"Oh my God, shut up!" Pitman yelled suddenly interested.

"Maybe they can help us!" she yelled back.

Bryan didn't know what to do or say. He agreed with both of them. Maybe they could help them, but maybe they couldn't trust them either. Torn between the two, he just sat there.

"Help us? They're the Queen's soldiers!" Pitman yelled back waiting to be punched again, but not really caring.

"What?" Courtney asked.

"What do you know about the Queen's soldiers?" Griffin asked standing and looking confused.

Bryan and Courtney were more confused than Griffin. They looked at each other and then at Pitman.

"Who is Mr. Lane?" Griffin asked Courtney directly leaning over her as she sat still confused about who the Queen's soldiers were.

"Richard Lane." She finally said staring up into Griffin's teacher gaze.

"We don't know…we're looking for him," said Bryan finally finding his voice.

"Would you two please SHUT UP!" Pitman yelled as he stood.

Griffin turned to the man next to him and nodded. Pitman was sure he was getting hit again and quickly sat down glaring at Courtney and Bryan. The man turned and left the room without a word.

Griffin relaxed and sat down. "So it's true," he said, "Richard is back."

Pitman put his head in his hands knowing Richard was in trouble if the Queen's soldiers knew he was here. He didn't even look up when a new man walked in the room. He was smaller than Griffin, but had the same commanding presence about him. He had short blonde hair and blue eyes and the same brown clothing as the others, yet he had a sly smile on his face. He nodded at Bryan and Courtney then looked directly at Pitman.

"Hello Pitman…Remember me?" he said.

Pitman paused with his hands running through his hair and slowly lifted his head. "Oswyn." Pitman replied. It was a statement and not a question to which Courtney reacted.

"You know him? How could you possible know him?" Courtney asked.

Pitman gave a loud sigh, and Oswyn's smile grew. "I've been here before," Pitman said looking dejected and putting his head down again.

"Did you bring Richard back?" Oswyn asked.

"Are you serious?" Courtney yelled as she jumped to her feet, "What's going on Pitman?"

"Hahaha, they don't know?" Oswyn laughed, "You better start talking!"

CHAPTER 13

Richard lie pinned to the ground with the fangs of a snarling

wolf only inches from his face. His brilliant mind searching like Google

through lists of historical people he had studied, and he couldn't recall

anyone who was killed be a wolf. He almost smiled that his death would

be that unique, then the reality of how much pain this was going to be

brought the fear back. He stared into the green eyes of a stone cold killer

and hoped that death would come quickly.

Suddenly, over the snarl, he heard the quick pounding of running

feet. Thoughts raced through his head, would Zareth save him or let him

be killed? Would the wolf go after Zareth and let him go? The scariest

question of all was, where are the other wolves? Richard knew that

wolves lived in packs and if there was one, there was usually a half

dozen more. They hadn't shown themselves yet, but Richard was sure

Zareth was now in a lot of danger.

The footsteps slowed to a stop like the wail of a fire truck that

has arrived on the scene. Richard scrunched his eyes shut and waited.

"Ok, Shifter, he's mine, let him go!" Zareth yelled to the wolf.

Richard was confused, but felt the weight of the wolf easing off of him. He opened his eyes to see a gray haired, green eyed man standing over him in a dark heavy cloak and ragged clothes, but to Richard's shock, the wolf was gone. Richard's eyes darted around looking for the beast, who was so close to ending him, but there was no sign of him. Could this man be the wolf?

"How can he be yours, if I have him here with me?" came the reply from a deep gruff voice. "You must not be doing a very good job of keeping the prisoner, Zareth."

"I'm doing just fine, Mika," Zareth said, "one of my men let him get this far, and I've taken care of him."

"Soldiers are a direct reflection of their leader," Mika responded.

"That's why he's no longer a soldier," Zareth stated becoming impatient. "Now, I have somewhere to be with this prisoner, so we will be going. Thank you for your help."

"I was sent to keep an eye on you, and it's a good thing I was here. If you or your men mess up again, it might be your blood staining the road."

Zareth reached down and grabbed Richard by the shoulders

yanking him to his feet. "Let's go" was all he said, but Richard couldn't take his eyes off this man, Mika. He was so confused about who he was and if he could have been the wolf. Zareth didn't seem to care as he walked quickly almost dragging Richard back toward the cart. Richard could feel the anger pulsating through Zareth's hands as he stumbled back toward the cart.

Richard was scared of Zareth, but through all of this, he found out two things. First, he knew that Zareth wasn't allowed to harm him and second, Zareth couldn't get any angrier then he was right now. So, Richard took a chance and spoke.

"Did that wolf turn into a man?"

Zareth turned so quickly, Richard thought he made a huge mistake. He waited for the knife to slice his throat, but it didn't come. Instead, Zareth yanked him by the throat and pulled him so close that Richard could have kissed him.

"You never saw that man or that wolf. If you ever speak of it again, there'll be an unfortunate accident during our trek to the castle. You understand?"

Richard nodded slightly since he couldn't speak over the death grip on his throat.

"Now walk!" Zareth commanded.

Richard took a deep breath as he strode forward toward the edge of the woods. He sighed when he saw the cart and Kason in the distance and cringed seeing the blood of Feston staining the dirt road. As they moved out onto the road, Zareth gave a loud, high-pitched whistle that Richard knew was to call his men back to the cart. Quickly they started to appear from all directions. Richard dropped his head knowing his only hope of escape was lost.

Kason rushed toward them with a rope in his hand. Zareth pushed Richard toward him and walked away clearly disgusted with both of them. Kason pulled Richards arms behind his back this time and wrapped the rope around each wrist. He pulled it so tight that Richard knew it was going to leave a mark. He wanted to talk to Kason, even tell him that he was sorry, but he didn't. He kept his head down as he was led back to the cart, Kason keeping a firm grip on him. He really didn't want to look at the pool of blood lying on the road, but his eyes were drawn to it. Richard felt responsible for the man's death and the image of his limp blood spurting body dropping to the ground was going to haunt him for a long time. He also noticed the trail of blood leading to the cart where the hay was now blood stained like the road. Without a word, Kason lifted the tarp to expose the limp body of Feston, his blank eyes still open staring at Richard.

Richard bent and threw up as Kason pushed him into the cart next to the body. He landed in the blood soaked hay continuing to try and spit out the rest of his stomach contents as the tarp was pulled over him again.

It was over and Richard knew it. Once he passed through the city walls and into the castle, he would have no chance of escape. The cart pulled away and Richard tried to keep his mind occupied, so as not to think about the lifeless body snuggled against him. For once in this ordeal, he was happy to have the hood over his head and the subsequent darkness. He did not want to see the body of Feston lying next to him. The smell of blood and the taste of his own vomit were enough reminder of what happened and the responsibility he felt.

The journey continued and Richard's thoughts fell into the gentle movements of the cart. The rocking of his body due to the cart trudging along the dirt road made him doze off to sleep. He dreamt of Abby and her despair at losing her dad, her searching for Mike Pitman, looking through the book for answers and finding the door. Even in his dream,

Richard was so proud of her for figuring everything out. Then, he was walking across the castle bridge alone in a fog. In the distance he could see the figure hanging from a rope off the side of the bridge. Dangling helplessly and lifelessly over the water surrounding the castle entrance. As Richard approached, he knew the figure was himself, hung by the Queen as a final revenge for taking Abby. He approached slowly trying not to look at himself, but being drawn to the figure as the body swayed in the breeze. The rope turned, Richard looked up at the face; it was Abby.

CHAPTER 14

"You've been here before!" Courtney yelled about to completely lose herself. Both her and Bryan were standing with Courtney's chair sideways on the floor behind her. Only the table separated her from attacking Pitman.

"What do you mean, that you've been here before?" asked Bryan slightly calmer than Courtney, but with noticeable anger in his voice.

"Yeah, Pitman. They say that every man has a story, and I can't wait for this girl to hear yours," Oswyn chimed in making Courtney all the more volatile. Oswyn could feel her glare, but he never took his eyes off Pitman.

Slowly, Pitman raised his head and stared at Courtney. "This is exactly why I told you two to keep your mouths shut! This here man is the leader of the Queen's Guard not some FFA crap! There was probably a rumor that Richard Lane had returned to the Land of Alden and these men were sent to check on that rumor. They probably weren't sure if it was true, but you two and your big stupid mouths have removed all doubt and told them that he is here!" Pitman's voice rose as he got angry.

Bryan plopped down in his chair realizing what they had done.

Courtney was unwavering. "That doesn't tell us, how you've been here before! Ya big, stupid jerk!"

"I love this kid!" Oswyn said looking at the other men in the room.

"Just because he's an ass," she said pointing at Pitman, "doesn't mean I like you!"

"Like you said, I love this kid!" Griffin chimed in getting a glare from Courtney. "But enough of this. Everyone have a seat, and let's discuss saving Richard from the Queen."

"How are we saving her from the Queen, when you work for the Queen?" Bryan asked looking confused.

"Well, that's where Pitman here is wrong," Griffin said gesturing to a man to pick up Courtney's chair.

Courtney reluctantly sat down, still angry and confused about what was going on but wanting to hear what these people had to say.

"Thank you," Griffin said as Courtney sat. "Oswyn, would you please explain."

"Sure. He is correct that I was once one of the leaders of the Queen's Guard and that's where we met. Yet, I am no longer in that position. I resigned from the Queen's Guard claiming that I could no longer complete my duties due to age. The Queen let me retire gracefully with a full 'changing of the guard' ceremony, but I knew deep down that she was happy to get rid of me because I was really her father's man and not hers. She longed to get her own people in all the high power positions and replace those, like me, that worked for King Tammany. What she did not know is that for about a year, I had been working with Griffin to develop a group to go against the Queen. We have been friends for a very long time and do not like the direction that Alden is taking under the direction of the Queen. She is all about herself and doesn't care about the people at all. Our goal is to organize enough people to go against her and eventually try to overthrow her."

"Then, why would you leave?" asked Bryan, "I mean, most groups try to get someone on the inside to help them. You were already there. It doesn't make sense that you would leave."

"You actually believe this load of crap he's giving us?" Pitman said, although he kept his head down probably waiting to get smacked again.

"Haha, you're right, kid," Oswyn said ignoring Pitman's comment. "The original plan was for me to try and continue working for the Queen and staying on the inside as long as she trusted me. Then, things changed when he arrived," he said looking at Pitman.

"Him?" Courtney asked.

"Yes, he changed everything."

"How?"

"Well, here's the short version. Richard came here, married Princess Kitane, they had Princess Abigail and everyone seemed happy."

"Oh my God," Courtney said shaking her head.

"What?"

"Princess Abigail? That's just crazy."

"Anyway, then, Richard and the Princess went missing. There was a search, that I led and it was determined that he must have traveled back to his realm with Princess Abigail. There was no key to open the door, and every blacksmith in Alden sent to make one. They all failed. The Princess was distraught and became almost unbearable to live with.

The King set her straight, but there was always underlying tension. Alden moved on and things were normal for a long time, then the King mysteriously died about two years ago. Princess Kitane became Queen Kitane and all hell broke loose. She has been a tyrant from day one, just demanding and ruthless to everyone. The people despise her, but are in such fear that they do whatever she says. I tried to help in my position, but it was tough."

"So where does, he come in?" Courtney asked pointing at Pitman.

"About six months ago, there was news about a 'Traveler' in Alden. The Queen freaked out. Everyone in the castle thought that it was Richard returning, or even an adolescent Princess Abigail. Word spread throughout Alden and the people were rejoicing. They thought that Richard had returned and could dethrone the Queen. Every soldier was sent to find the Traveler."

"And you found him."

"Yes, we found him. Pitman was taken to the Queen, who welcomed him with open arms and got all the information she needed from him..."

"Wait a minute," Pitman finally spoke, "if you're going to talk about my part in this crappy story, I want to tell it!"

"Finally!" Courtney said.

"Go ahead, Pitman, tell your story," Oswyn said.

"Richard gave me that stupid book a long time ago, and I did what he said and buried it on my farm. I forgot all about it for years, and then one day after a storm the tree where the book was buried next to was uprooted. I started cutting the tree up for firewood and remembered the book. I dug around a little and found it. Being bored and curious I opened it up. I followed all the clues, just like you kids did. I even remembered about the invisible ink thing that Richard used to do in college. I drove to Philly, found the door and figured out when to open it. I came here and started walking around. The people got freaked out. They were awesome and treated me like a king, calling me Traveler and giving me whatever I wanted. Then, the soldiers arrived and took me to the city with the castle. Suddenly, I'm meeting a queen, and she's beautiful and treating me like a king. It was awesome. Then the questions started and unfortunately, I mentioned Richard. I was beaten and thrown in a cell. I didn't know what the hell was going on. She turned on me so quickly, I was sure that I was going to be killed. Then, there was a deal. They would let me go home, but I had to do certain things. First was to give them the key. I hid the key and book when I came through the door, but I wanted to go home, so I told them where to find it. They came back with the book and key. I overheard people talking about making a copy.

"Yes, that was the Queen's main goal, a copy of that key," Oswyn confirmed.

"Then, they wanted me to get Richard to come here. They would let me go home and bring him back. I explained about the book and the key, and that he would never come without them. They gave them to me and took me back to the door. I figured if I could get back, they would never see me again and I would stay away from Richard to keep him safe."

"Apparently, that didn't work!" Courtney said.

"No, they were smarter than me."

"Like we didn't know that!"

Pitman just glared at her.

"You backstabbing..."

"I know, I know! I was scared. I thought I could just go through the door and never come back here, but they sent a man with me, and I had to show him where Richard lived and how to return. He made me take him to Richard's house. I tried going to a fake place, but he knew Richard and waited to see him. I tried different places, but finally had to really show him. He was going to kill me. After he saw Richard, the man left and I thought I was free. I was supposed to try and get Richard to come back, and I wanted to tell him so badly, but I was so scared. I was afraid for my friend, but more afraid for myself." Pitman now had tears in his eyes, but that did not curtail the wrath of Courtney.

"So, you let them come get him, and then sat there all innocent with us trying to find the stinking door, when you knew exactly how to find it and where it was!"

"Yes, but I was also shocked! It had been six months and I heard nothing. I made no contact with Richard, but texted him every week or so, just to make sure he was ok. I hoped something happened and their key didn't work. They were able to copy it, but I hoped it got messed up. Then, you called and my worst nightmare came true. That's why I came with you, to try and right this wrong that I caused."

"That is what happened," Oswyn said. "I was the guy that made the deal, not that I wanted to, but those were my orders. It's also what made me retire. I knew that if Richard came here, I would be the one guarding him and delivering him to the Queen. I couldn't do it and figured I could help Richard more from the outside if we could get him before the Queen did. That's also why we dress like the Queen's soldiers. People stay away from us and leave us alone to do what we want.

"So, now what?" Bryan asked.

"Well, we know that Richard is here and was brought here by the Queen's soldiers. We do not have his location, but based on where we found you, he is closer to the castle than we thought."

"Great!" Courtney said throwing her hands up in disgust.

"Relax," Griffin said, "All is not lost, yet."

"But..."

"Yes there is a but," Oswyn said cutting off Courtney.

She looked at him strangely, trying to figure out what he meant by the statement and a little annoyed at being cut off. "What?" she finally said.

"Where is Princess Abigail?"

There was a dead silence. Courtney looked at Bryan, Bryan looked at Courtney, and then they both turned and looked at Pitman. He had put his head down again and they were both sure he wasn't going to put it up. Slowly they both put their heads down waiting for either Oswyn or Griffin to speak, but they didn't. The question just lingered in the air waiting for someone to take control of it. Bryan finally had enough and raised his head to speak when Courtney beat him to it.

"I'm the Princess," she said so calmly and easily.

The room froze for a second. Bryan couldn't believe his ears. Why would she say that? If these men, who they didn't really know, were lying and were really the Queen's soldiers, then she was as good as dead. He couldn't say anything. He just stared in disbelief.

Pitman raised his head from his lap and continued all the way to the ceiling, letting out a deep sigh in the process.

Oswyn and Griffin looked at each other and then at Courtney before both of them bust out laughing. Courtney, of course, took offense to the laughter.

"What's so funny?" she yelled, "You are speaking to a Princess and should have respect!"

That made them laugh even louder.

"I will not stand for this disrespect!" Courtney hollered getting up as if to leave

"Relax, and sit down 'Your Highness'," Griffin said mockingly. "Let me tell you another story."

Reluctantly, Courtney sat, but she obviously wasn't happy.

Griffin continued, "I am happy to see that you care that much for your friend to try and help her, but you are *not* the Princess Abigail. Please do not say so again, because no one would ever believe it."

"Why not?" she exclaimed clearly frustrated with their laughter.

"If you must know, it's your eyes. Princess Abigail was only here a few months in Alden, but she has the unmistakable eyes of her mother, which you obviously, do not."

Courtney didn't know what to say. There's nothing quite like the feeling of getting caught red handed in a lie. Now she was embarrassed. Bryan put his head back down and Pitman broke from the ceiling at looked at Abby. A slight smile broke across his face. He knew this girl hated him, but she sure had some guts.

"Eyes?" she questioned, not quite giving up yet.

"Yes, Princess Abigail has the mysterious eyes of the queen. They are her signature trademark and all of Alden knows it."

"That's why the people were scared and backed away from Abby when they saw her," Bryan said.

"She is here?" Oswyn asked.

"Yes, she came with..."

"Here we go again, telling them everything," Pitman interrupted.

"They have to know, Pitman. She might be in trouble," Bryan fired back.

"Was she taken with Richard?" Oswyn asked.

"No, she came here with us," Courtney said finally giving up on her lie. "But she went off into the woods to go to the bathroom just before you captured us."

"We don't know where she is now," Bryan said.

"This is not good," Oswyn said.

Griffin motioned to one of the soldiers in the room to him. He whispered something inaudible to the man. He rose at attention, saluted and left the room quickly. Griffin then joined the conversation.

"You should have told us that she was with you sooner," Griffin said.

"Oh yeah, that would have been real smart as you were capturing us! 'Hey, don't forget our friend over there peeing in the woods'. Just great! Courtney said throwing up her hands in disgust.

A small smile came to Griffin's face. "I understand that," he said, "I meant after we told you who we were."

"Yeah, like we really know who you are," she said looking bewildered at the statement. "We don't know squat about you! For all we know, you might have Mr. Lane, tied up in the basement of this dump!" Courtney was ready to cry. She held back as much as she could, but it didn't stop the tears welling up in her eyes at the thought of Abby out there alone and in danger.

"I totally agree," Griffin said, "you don't know who we are and you don't have to believe our story. I do assure you that it's true, and we have your best interests at hand. I have sent a group to search for Richard and another to find Princess Abigail. You are free to go search for them yourself, or to let us help you. You could also return to your home, where you would be totally safe."

"You really think we would leave without Abby?" Bryan asked.

"I don't know," Griffin said, "I don't know anything about you." He looked at Courtney, trying to show her that he was sincere about their story, but understanding her skepticism.

"We will not leave here without her and Mr. Lane," Bryan said.

"I understand your frustration, but this will not be easy. We have highly trained people looking for them both. As I said, you are free to do whatever you want, but let me suggest the following. It's getting late and nightfall is coming. You do not want to be alone in this land that you do not know at night. There are wolves and other animals that wander the forests looking for prey. I suggest that you stay the night, and if you're serious about finding your friend, then we will set out in the morning to search for her."

Pitman lifted his head and finally spoke, "We don't really have a choice."

"There, you are mistaken, Pitman, you most certainly do have a choice, but staying the night is by far your best option," Griffin said.

"Then we will stay," Pitman said.

"Oh, so now you're in charge of making decisions for us?" Courtney said mockingly.

"So, you want to leave?" Griffin asked.

"No, we'll stay," she said.

Griffin just shook his head and smiled.

CHAPTER 15

Richard woke with sweat beading on his face and a gasp of air ripping into his lungs. It took him a second to realize that the vision of Abby was just a dream. A sick joke his mind was playing on him to punish him for leading Abby here. Yet, the darkness under the hood did not help to remove the vision of Abby hanging helplessly from the castle bridge. Richard could feel the cart rattling along toward the castle. More and more voices on the road let him know that they were getting close. Richard knew that the traffic around the castle would be the busiest part of the trip and they would soon be approaching nightfall. This meant that peddlers and farmers would be heading away from the castle city back to their villages and farms for the night. It also meant that his time was running out. Richard's spirit was waning. He was so excited about the chance to escape in Kingswood, but now the reality of facing his wife, the Queen, was weighing on him. Then, the cart stopped.

Richard could here voices going back and forth. He knew that every cart into the city was searched, but would they search a cart led by soldiers, he was sure the answer was no. He listened as intently as possible, but to Richard's dismay, the banter sounded jovial like old friend reminiscing. After a short time, the cart lurched forward through the city's gates and rattled toward the castle, closer and closer to Richard's doom.

The cart sauntered along for a few hundred yards before stopping again at the castle gate. Richard could visualize were they were, and what the scene around him looked like. The city gate they had passed first was a stereotypical twenty-five-foot-high wall with huge thick wooden doors, while this inside gate was made of huge iron doors connected to a fifteen-foot high wall. Richard pictured the view, through the magnificently designed iron doors, of the castle set in the middle of a huge lake that served as a moat and protection for the castle. Just beyond the gate lies the castle bridge extending a good hundred yards across the lake to the entrance area of the castle. Yet, Richard's mind was stuck on the middle of the bridge and the thought of the gallows that protruded out over the lake and the dream image of Abby hanging there. He shook the image out of his head and refocused his mind on the journey across the bridge to the castle and the final door that would lead to his doom. The large wooden doors were usually opened due to the fact that any enemy would have to get through the previous two gates to even get to the castle. Those gates would give the Castle Guard plenty of time to seal the castle doors and prepare for a fight. There would be no fight when Richard arrived, just a defeated man worried about his daughter.

Richard heard the muffled talking again of the guards with the soldiers guarding him. This time the pleasantries were shorter and the cart moved on through the gate. After a short rumble on gravel, the cart bounced onto the wooden bridge and Richard knew that his time was up. In a few hundred yards, he would be trapped inside the castle and probably in the dank rat's nest of a dungeon with his evil wife in charge. He sighed at the thought.

The cart jerked to a halt, quite unexpectedly as Richard's head raced trying to think of an explanation. Suddenly, the tarp was pulled off of him and he could feel Feston's body being pulled from the cart. Voices followed commanding the other in just above a whisper.

"Tie the larger one around his chest," the voice commanded.

"Should this one go around his feet or knees?"

"Feet," came the reply, "We have a third for his waist."

"Right."

"That looks good. Now bring him over here."

"Oh hell, he's really heavy now."

"Alright, on three, 1, 2, 3, up!"

Before Richard heard the splash, he figured that they were tying rocks to the body and throwing it in the lake. He hoped his splash wouldn't be next.

Again the cart started forward without even recovering Richard. Although he still had the hood over his head, Richard could tell that nighttime was setting in from the dim light he could see.

"This is it," he thought as he rolled helplessly toward his demise.

Suddenly the sound of the wheels changed and the dim light Richard could see was gone. He knew they were inside the castle. The cart stopped, and Richard was yanked from the cart by his legs. His feet firmly hit the stone ground, with strong arms grasping him from each side. They led him away to the right confusing Richard. Although he had not been in the castle for many years, he knew the layout like the back of his hand. The Throne Room was straight ahead through the entrance. He was sure he would be meeting the Queen as soon as he arrived and couldn't figure out why they took him to the right into a smaller room.

After a short walk, the hood was pulled off Richard's head. The room he was in was only about the size of his modest living room at home. The walls were stone with brilliant tapestries hanging from the high ceiling; the lighting was dim with a few torches on the walls and some candles on a large wooden table. Sitting at the end of the table with the remnants of a meal in front of him was Raftis, the Queen's right hand man a loyal advisor. Richard was surprised that after thirteen years, he basically looked the same. During his time in Alden, Richard became fairly close with Raftis. He did everything for Princess Kitane as her advisor, and now did the same with her as Queen. As always, Raftis wore a long elegant robe that Richard always felt made him look like a priest. He had shoulder length black hair and a neatly trimmed goatee, which Richard knew he was meticulous about. He stood and slowly walked around the table to Richard looking him up and down.

Richard thought that he must be quite a sight to a man as well groomed and orderly as Raftis. Richard was a complete mess with dirt and blood from the corpse he shared a ride with covering most of him. Luckily, he had gone to bed in black gym shorts and a black t-shirt, so the blood was only really seen on his arms, legs and face.

Raftis came within a few feet and shook his head slowly simply saying, "Richard".

Richard stared into Raftis's black eyes and said, "Raftis". The soldiers on each side gripped him tighter and seemed ready to strike him for speaking, but Raftis put up his hand stopping them.

"Take him away," he said, "I will inform the Queen of your mission's success."

With that, Richard was led out of the room and toward the steps to the dungeon. He had been to the dungeon before, but never as a prisoner. He dreaded knowing the horrors that would be awaiting him, especially since there would be no mercy from the Queen.

to follow Lakota silently as they moved along the small path. It reminded her of following the horse paths through Pennypack Park, which was not far from her house. Abby and her Dad would ride their bikes along the bike path, but her Dad liked to take their mountain bikes onto the dirt horse path to get what he called "a more fun ride". This path was just like that one as it was only about two feet wide and had some underbrush sticking out ready to poke an unsuspecting traveler in the leg. Unlike the trails Abby traveled at home, this path journeyed out of the woods and across some rolling hills and open fields. Abby moved a little quicker through the fields hoping the men that took her friends would not spot them.

The journey was not that difficult since they moved at a normal pace stopping every once in a while to drink from a small stream, which was a new adventure to Abby, who lived in a large city where the creeks and streams had long been polluted. She wouldn't even think of drinking from the trash-strewn creek where she opened the turtle door to get to Alden. So watching Lakota cup his hands and suck down some cool water was so against the norm for her that it took a moment for her to muster up the courage to do it herself. She was glad she did, amazed at the clear crispness of the best water she had ever tasted.

Finally, after what seemed like hours they stopped. The sun was getting lower in the sky and it was starting to get late. With no sign of her friends or the men, Abby was very concerned.

She wondered how long it would take to get to the castle. She wasn't even sure that she wanted to go to the castle, but since they stopped and Lakota sat and leaned against a tree, she figured she would try to get some answers.

"How long until we get there?" she asked.

"We have a long way to go and won't get there until tomorrow," Lakota replied.

"Tomorrow?"

"Yes, I told you that it takes over a day to get to the castle."

"But where do we go for the night?" Abby asked.

"We will stay here, of course."

"Here? I can't stay here. I..."

But Abby was cut off by the sudden movement of Lakota quickly jumping to his feet and turning to the path that turned around some trees. Through the trees, the light was fading and Abby couldn't see much into the forest. Suddenly, she saw some movement from around a tree a few feet away. She froze in place thinking that the men had finally found them and her questions had given their location away. Lakota never moved from his original jump to his feet, but he stood in a ready position looking to Abby like a ninja ready to pounce.

The movement Abby saw slowly began to take shape. It was an old woman dressed in what could only be described as rags with a long staff to support her. Her feet were so dirty that Abby first thought she was wearing shoes, but then realized her feet were bare and filthy. Although it was an old woman, Lakota stayed in the ready position as she slowly approached.

"It's nice to see young people in love," she said as she approached.

The comment was not what Abby was expecting, but she could feel herself turning red with embarrassment. She hadn't thought about Lakota much because of all the turmoil of losing her friends and trying to follow them. She was so focused on their journey and the task of saving her friends that she didn't think much about how good-looking Lakota was, and how nice he had been to help her. She wished she could walk into school with him just to watch her friends swoon. She could hear them now: 'He's so hot!', 'Are you going out?', 'What's his name?', 'Where did you find him?'. It would be awesome, but that would never happen.

She shook her head out of her daydream and noticed Lakota still ready to pounce on this old woman.

"We're not in lo..." Abby started to say when Lakota cut her off sharply.

"Be on your way woman, we have nothing for you here."

"Just a few scraps for an old lady?" she asked looking more at Abby than Lakota.

"I said, be on your way," he said again sharply.

Abby was surprised that for someone who had seemed so nice to her that Lakota was being so mean to this old woman.

"Sorry, we don't have any food," Abby finally said.

"Thank you, Miss," she said in her old crackling voice. "I have something for you though."

A quick as a cat, Lakota pounced and the old woman was dropped to the ground like a box of rocks. He pinned her arm behind her and drove one knee into her back.

Abby screamed.

"Quiet!" Lakota commanded. "Gather our things," he said with a snarl.

Although still pinned to the ground, the old woman managed a smile at Abby and said, "See darling, never trust a Shifter."

Lakota hopped up with the woman and drug her away. She let out a high-pitched eerie laugh that made Abby's blood run cold. Lakota drug her down the path away from where they were going. Abby stood almost stuck in place. The old woman continued her laugh, then abruptly it stopped and she yelled at Lakota.

"Don't even think about it, Shifter!"

Abby couldn't hear Lakota's response, but the old woman got a stunned look and pulled away from Lakota ambling down the path as quickly as she could go. Abby was confused with the whole situation and questioned Lakota when he returned.

"What was that about?"

"What do you mean?" Lakota asked.

"I mean some sickly looking old woman comes looking for food and you tackle her like a linebacker on a goal line stand!"

"A linebacker?"

"Forget that! Why did you tackle her?"

"She was not a sickly old woman. There is ancient evil in this forest, which includes witches that will give unsuspecting little girls presents that will take over their lives or even kill them."

"She was a witch?" Abby asked.

"I'm not positive, but I think so. At least, she acted like one." Lakota said.

"Wow," was all Abby could say with a shocked look on her face as she remembered all the fairytales she had ever been told about witches and how they tricked girls.

"Yeah, we should go."

"Hey," she said stopping Lakota and making him look at her, "What's a Shifter?"

Lakota looked oddly confused, but replied, "I don't know, maybe she thought I was someone else, too."

For the first time, Abby didn't really believe him. She felt there was more to the woman calling him Shifter, but she simply shrugged her shoulders. Lakota quickly looked away, staring down the path where he had released the woman.

"Hey," she said again grabbing Lakota's arm and turning him toward her. "I'm not a 'little girl'."

He looked at her very seriously and said, "You are when you get tricked into talking to a witch." Then he turned and started walking down the path away from where he took the old woman.

Abby stood stunned for a second, then followed, feeling more like a little girl than ever.

CHAPTER 17

Courtney could not get comfortable in the small guest room where she was supposed to be sleeping. From the window, she watched the sun set and the world around her turn to darkness except for the candle that flickered a dull light throughout the room. She wanted to go to sleep, but was afraid for Abby, who she knew was still out there in this dangerous land with no one to help her. She shook her head and stared at the candle trying to get the nightmarish thoughts of what Abby was going through out of her head.

A dull thud hit her door. It sounded more like someone tapping a microphone to see if it was on then someone knocking. Then, it came again.

"Who is it?" she whispered.

"Me," came the reply, to which Courtney smiled

"Thank God for Bryan," she thought. Originally, when they first were led down the hall, she thought they were going to have to sleep in the same room together and was a little freaked out. Then the woman, Vala, pointed to rooms across the hall from each other and Courtney was relieved. Now, she wished they were sharing a room because she didn't really want to be alone. She smiled as she opened the door.

"What's up?" she asked.

"Nothing, just can't sleep."

"Thinking about Abby," they both said together, then laughed.

"You know, they weren't lying about us being free to go," Bryan said.

"What do mean?" Courtney asked.

"Well, I've been snooping around a little. There are no guards or anything. We could just walk out and go.

"Yeah, and where would we go?"

"That would be the problem. I also thought that they don't really need guards, because we have no where to go," he laughed. Then added, "You think Pitman would know where to go?"

"Even if he did, I don't want to go anywhere with him!" Courtney said raising her voice a little. "I hate that man! I'll never trust him again!"

"I can't believe he's been here before."

"I can. I told you and Abby that she shouldn't have called him."

"I knew I didn't trust him. The first thing that dude did was lie. Saying he was a cop on the phone and then, 'Oh, I'm not a cop'. We should have ditched him right there."

"Well, it's too late now."

"Maybe not. maybe we can get Griffin to leave him here when we look for Abby."

"Not a bad idea." Bryan said.

Pitman had already been placed in a room down the hall, when the kids were shown to their rooms. The door latched behind him and he sat on the lumpy bed putting his head in his hands. He couldn't believe his predicament. He never wanted to hurt anyone. It had been so long since Richard showed up at his farm with baby Abby and the book. He really had forgotten all about it being busy with his farm and wife, but then she left and he had gotten bored.

While bailing hay one day, he took a break in the shade under a tree. There, sitting in the shade, something triggered his memory of the book he had buried in a plastic bag under that very tree so many years ago. Later that day, he dug it up. He told himself it didn't mean anything since Richard never talked about it again. They had grown apart over the years, with Richard busy being a single parent and him caring for his farm that Richard would never know. Plus, it was something to do.

He never thought that he would be so drawn to the book and its stories and clues. For days, he couldn't put it down. Using the internet to figure out clues and pull up maps and names from the past. Just like the kids did, he figured them all out and had fun doing it, but then, he had to know. Was there really a door? Another world? In Pitman's head, there was no chance, but he gathered some supplies and headed to Philadelphia to check it all out. Little did he know that he would be in a fight for his life with a crazy Queen, who saw him as her ticket to Richard.

All he wanted to do was go home so he led them to Richard. The story he told the kids was totally true, he really thought he could lead them astray without giving Richard up, but it didn't go as planned.

Now, he was back, trying to right a wrong, but these kids didn't trust him, Abby was lost, and he saw no way to get to the castle to save

Richard.

Pitman slowly raised his head. There was clarity in his eyes with the realization that there was only one thing left to do.

"It's time to go home," he said to himself.

CHAPTER 18

The dungeon stayed the same at all times. There were no windows to tell whether it was day or night and only the flickering light from wall sconces lit the dark dreary halls. Richard knew that night was upon them, but only because of his journey. He was not looking forward to the dungeon with it's cold, damp conditions and creeping rodents searching for food scraps left in cells. As Richard was led down the tunnel of cells, he tried to peer through the darkness searching for other prisoners. He saw none, but he surely smelled them. The stench of the dungeon was probably the worst part. Prisoners were not bathed, stayed in the same clothes at all times, and relieved themselves in a two-foot-wide trough that ran across the front of the cells and the length of the cell tunnel. The floor of each cell had a slight angle to it, so everything flowed to the trough, including sleeping prisoners if the fell asleep at the wrong angle and rolled into the sloppy trough.

Richard crinkled his nose as they moved deeper into the cell tunnel. As the smell grew stronger, Richard could hear low moans coming from a cell ahead on his left. Richard hoped his cell would be far enough to not hear the moaning. He also knew they were running out of cells and those moans would become a part of his dungeon life. Finally, they stopped abruptly at a cell door on his right. The guard produced a large iron key that undid the lock and the door creaked open.

"Welcome home," the other guard said giving Richard a slight push toward the blackness of his new cell.

A third guard carrying a torch chimed in waving the torch toward the cell, "I hope you find the accommodations to your pleasing. We wouldn't want the famed Traveler to feel slighted.

The light gave Richard a quick chance to take in his new home. The stone floor looked damp and hard, but there was fresh straw piled in the corner where he could sleep. He hoped that the furry residents of the dungeon didn't already call that straw home. As he entered the cell, a dull thudding bang came from the door of the final cell at the end of the tunnel. Richard paused and looked toward the banging, but could see nothing.

"Quiet down there!" the guard yelled and the banging stopped. Richard's hesitation made the torch-bearing guard give him a one-handed shove into the cell. Richard stumbled, but kept his balance enough to turn as the door closed and latched.

Darkness, total complete darkness encased Richard when the door closed and the flicker of the guard's torch left. Richard felt along the cool, damp wall slightly shuffling his feet and hoping not to fall. He reached the corner of the cell and slid to his right, never taking his hands off the guiding wall. Finally, his feet crunched on the straw and Richard slid down the wall and into his new bed.

High above Richard's new cell home, his fate was being decided.

"The prisoner is taken care of, Your Majesty."

"And the Traveler door?"

"The lock is in place, my Queen. You shall have the only key."

"Destroy it."

"Your Majesty?"

"I said, 'Destroy it'!

"Yes, I heard you, Your Majesty, but this lock took many months and many lives…"

"I know all about it! I know the price! I also know that destroying the only key, seals that door forever!

"I shall take care of it, My Queen."

"Good, Raftis. I want that taken care of tonight, right after you take me to see the prisoner," the Queen said in a much calmer tone.

"My Queen?" Raftis questioned.

"You heard me. Take me to see the prisoner."

"But, My Queen, he is in the dungeon. There are reasons that you don't go to the dungeon. I will bring him to you."

"No. He will not leave the dungeon. I will go to him."

"But…"

"Don't lecture me Raftis! I will go to the dungeon to see the prisoner!"

Richard Lane sat in the corner of his cell, the dampness of the stone walls chilled him, but the feeling of déjà vu overtook him to a time many years ago when he sat in Castle Erawaled. Then, he was preparing to marry the Princess, but now he was a fugitive who had been caught. He would most certainly be sentenced to death, but maybe, just maybe the Queen would not kill him and just leave him here in the dungeon to rot. That would give him the opportunity to try an escape.

The long journey to the castle had given Richard a chance to think about his situation. As he sat breaking pieces of straw between his fingers, he kept returning to one thought, "Why was he hidden so well on the ride to the castle?" If the Queen wanted to look like a hero for finally finding him, wouldn't she want him paraded around in front of everyone like a prized catch. Why the secrecy? He came to one conclusion. The Queen must be hated by the people and she was afraid that the people would help him. If that assumption was right, then he needed to have the people find out that he was here. The problem was time. If the Queen wanted him killed, it would probably be done quickly and there would be no chance to escape.

Jumping to his feet, Richard ran forward to the metal cell door and began pounding on it with his fists. "Guards! Guards!" he yelled. He continued pounding on the door hoping for some kind of response. After minutes which seemed much longer, his arms grew weary and his pounding slowed. He then heard a response, but it was not what he wanted. The moaner across the hall began wailing louder than before, and the thuds from the end cell down the hall began to answer Richard's banging with louder thudding of his own. Richard smiled, if he was going to be stuck in the dungeon, at least he wouldn't feel alone.

The answers to his pounding gave Richard some much need adrenaline, and he resumed his pounding with the wails and thuds of his unseen friends echoing through the dungeon. Richard forgot how tired he was and actually enjoyed the cacophony he created. Finally, Richard heard the sound he wanted; footsteps. The synchronized footsteps of guards approaching were music to his ears. Richard stopped his pounding to make sure they were coming to his cell and not one of the others. He stood straight up facing the door as the flickering light of the guard's torches slipped under the door. He heard the key enter the lock and prepared himself.

The door whipped open and the torch light blinded Richard. He squinted and shunned away from the light holding his arms up to cover his face. His eyes had betrayed him, but his ears didn't.

"Hello, Richard."

He froze not expecting a woman's voice. His eyes were still squeezed shut from the light, but he responded.

"Kitane"

"It's Queen Kitane to you," she replied.

"Queen? How did that happen?" Richard asked.

"When a King passes..."

"Yeah, yeah, I know how it works," he said starting to lower his arms from shielding his now adjusted eyes. He got his first look at the Queen in over ten years. Not much had changed, she was still stunningly beautiful wearing a dark colored flowing robe and a diamond studded gold crown on top of her dark cascading hair. Yet, it was her eyes that drew Richard's attention. As usual, they were uniquely gorgeous and almost exactly the same eyes as Abby. The biggest difference was these eyes were boring a hole right through him.

"Where is the Princess?" the Queen said through tight angry lips.

"She died," Richard said bluntly.

"Guards, you all heard that. He admits that his actions caused the death of the Princess."

The guards nodded in unison as the Queen moved very close to Richard. For a second he actually thought she was going to kiss him, but she put her mouth right to his ear so only he could hear her.

"You're a liar, Richard. She is alive. My men saw her bedroom, and it was the bedroom of a very alive girl. They searched your house for her, but she was not there.

Yet, I am happy, because your lie will secure your death sentence at your trial tomorrow."

She moved away from him, her eyes still locked in a death stare, but a small grin appeared on her lips. Richard knew he was in trouble, but the only thought on his mind was Abby. For the first time, he hoped she didn't follow him.

CHAPTER 19

Twilight was upon them quickly as Abby followed Lakota through the woods. Her mind was still racing, trying to make sense of their encounter with the witch. It seemed impossible to Abby. Witches were from children's stories to scare little kids, they weren't real, were they? Yet, she was in a world that couldn't be real, too. Yet, no matter how boggled her mind was, she kept returning to the one thing that dominated her thoughts; "never trust a Shifter". It was what the old witch said that she couldn't shake. What did it mean and what did it have to do with Lakota? There had to be a reason that the witch said that to her, but she wasn't getting any answers from Lakota.

They trudged along in silence as the sky grew darker. Finally, they reached a small clearing next to a stream when Lakota stopped.

"We can camp here," he said moving toward the stream for a drink.

Abby didn't need to be told twice, she flopped down on the ground next to a tree totally exhausted. She wanted some water, but would wait a few minutes just to sit and rest. She watched Lakota suck in handfuls of water then gather pieces of wood for a fire. She wanted to help, but sitting felt so good. Physically, she was tired, but mentally, she was totally drained. She didn't want to think anymore, so she just sat and watched as Lakota gathered wood, arranged it and started a small fire by using something from his bag and a rock to create sparks. She found just enough energy to speak.

"Won't a fire give away where we are?" she asked.

"Yes," he replied, "but, it will get chilly tonight and you will need it to stay comfortable and sleep. I will stand guard, and we will be fine."

"What about you sleeping?"

"I will be fine. I have trained myself to live on very little sleep," he said confidently. "Now, you should get a drink and go to sleep. We have a lot more traveling to do tomorrow to get to the Castle."

Abby slowly got on her aching feet and made her way to the small stream. The water was refreshing, and she could actually feel it rushing through her body. She drank her fill and moved back to the campfire. It didn't take long for her to be curled in a ball and sleeping by the small, warm fire. Lakota sat and watched as she drifted off.

Some time during the night Abby stirred and opened her eyes. There on the opposite side of the now smoldering fire was a huge gray wolf. Abby couldn't move, she lie frozen on the hard ground not daring to move. The wolf was wandering around, but seemed to be looking away from the camp. Suddenly, the wolf turned her way and for a split second they locked eyes. Abby wanted to close her eyes so bad and go back to sleep hoping this was just a bad dream, but she couldn't take her eyes off the wolf. She waited to be attacked, but the unthinkable happened. The wolf walked away into the woods. Abby laid for a few more minutes before moving. She sat up looking around for Lakota, who was nowhere to be found.

A noise behind her made her jump to her feet. She grabbed a long stick unburnt and protruding from the almost dead fire. The silhouette coming through the trees was familiar and Abby sighed in relief. Lakota was back.

"Oh my God! Where were you?"

"Ah, sorry," Lakota replied awkwardly, "I had to go to the bathroom."

"There was a huge wolf here!"

"A wolf?"

"Yeah, a wolf! And you were nowhere to be found! Do you know how scared I was? I was, like frozen!"

"It's ok," he said taking Abby by the shoulders to calm her down. She immediately stopped talking and stared into Lakota's eyes. For some strange reason, she believed him, that they were 'ok'.

Lakota stared back into Abby's amazing eyes. So many thoughts went through his head, but all he managed to say was, "Where did you come from?"

"What?"

"I mean, who are you? We've been walking for a day looking for your friends, but we haven't talked at all. Who are you? Where are you from?"

Abby was shocked. She forgot all about the wolf and tried to figure this guy out. Yes, they had been walking for almost a day and hadn't really talked, but he didn't try to strike up a conversation. He just walked, and Abby followed like a lost puppy. Now, he suddenly wanted to talk, when all she got since they met was 'trust me' and 'you're a little girl'.

"Oh, now you want to talk?" she said. "How come you didn't want to talk during the thousand miles we walked yesterday? All you said was 'trust me, we'll find your friends', and 'they must be going to the castle'. You didn't want to talk to me then, how come you want to talk to me now?"

"I couldn't talk to you then," he said apologetically, "you were loud and upset and would have gotten us caught. I wanted to talk to you when we stopped, but the witch came. Then, you were so exhausted, I thought you just needed sleep. So, here we are, dawn will be soon, and we will have to walk again. This is our best time to talk."

Abby knew he was right about everything he just said. It made her feel a little better and a lot more trusting, so she began to talk.

"My name is Abby. My friends and I came here through a secret door from I guess another world. This has to sound so weird," she started.

"You are Travelers," he said. "We know about the door, but they have been sealed for so long that it was weird to see a Traveler again."

"Anyway, we came here looking for my dad. He was kidnapped and brought here, but he left me some clues that led me through the door." Abby paused. She couldn't believe she was saying this much, but it just kept flowing out of her mouth. "I don't know why he was taken, but we came here to find him and then go home."

"Who is your dad?" Lakota asked.

"His name is Richard, and he does historical research."

"Wait," Lakota said putting up his hand, "Your dad is Richard? As in Prince Richard?"

"Prince Richard?"

"Oh my," he replied knowingly, "I knew it. Those eyes, you're Princess Abigail."

"What?" Abby said shaking her head. "What are you talking about?"

"It actually makes sense," Lakota said. "Who is your mother?"

"I don't have a mother," Abby said looking confused.

"Everyone has a mother," said Lakota, "and yours is the Queen."

Abby was stunned. She knew that her mom might be in this world, but she didn't think the Queen. She stared at Lakota almost waiting for a smile or laugh, like this was the punchline from some sick joke, but it never came. Lakota stared back just as stunned, but shaking his head up and down like he figured something out.

"It makes sense, Princess," he said knowingly.

"I don't care what you think or know or whatever, you will not call me Princess! My name is Abby!" she retorted.

"Ok, ok, just listen. Almost fifteen years ago a Traveler named Richard, your dad, came to our land. He was welcomed by King Tammany and his daughter, Princess Kitane. Princess Kitane and Richard fell in love and got married. They had a daughter, Princess Abigail, but soon after the princess was born, her and Prince Richard went missing. At first the people thought they were kidnapped, but clues were found and the King's guard figured out that Prince Richard took the princess and fled. The whole land was searched, but the only signs of them were found near the Traveler door, which was locked. Prince Richard must have had a key to get back to his world. There have been legends and rumors about a key to the Traveler world throughout our land, but no one is known to have one. Since then, many years have gone by and no one has seen the Prince or little Princess since. I was very young when all of this happened, but learned about it through the years. Many believe that Prince Richard feared for the safety of Princess Abigail, because Princess Kitane is beautiful, but not very nice. She has gotten worse over the past year or so, since she became the queen. There are rumors that she has been searching for a key to the Traveler world and even sent the two best blacksmiths in the land to try and make a key. They have never returned."

When he stopped speaking, a tear rolled down Abby's face. She put her head down knowing that this story blended perfectly with what Pitman had told them. She had no reply knowing it was all about her and her dad. It was too much to grasp in one moment. Her dad had kidnapped her to save her from her mom, who she never really met, but was a Queen; an evil Queen, but a Queen. She was a princess. It was every little girl's dream that suddenly felt like a nightmare.

"I'm sorry," Lakota said moving toward Abby and putting his arm around her. She didn't really know this guy, but she needed a hug so she nuzzled herself against Lakota and let him hug her.

Finally, she found her voice through the sobs. "I'm the one that's sorry. It does make sense, but I just don't get how I'm in the middle of this, and I didn't know any of it. Do you know what it's like to have someone tell you that you're a princess?"

"Ah, no," Lakota answered with a smile on his face. It was exactly what Abby needed. She moved away from his embrace and laughed through her sobs. "You know what I mean", she laughed.

"I know, and I am sorry, but you had to know. From the first time I saw your eyes, I was pretty sure that you were the Queen's daughter. She has the same eyes, and they are so unique, there was almost no doubt. Then, when you said that Richard was your dad, I was positive."

"Now what?" Abby asked.

"Well, I think we still need to go to the castle. I think your friends were taken by the Queen's soldiers and your Dad was kidnapped by them as well. They are all in danger. We need to get there quickly and find out what's going on."

Abby nodded as she wiped away the tears from her face. She didn't know what she would do when she got there, but she felt she needed to get to the castle. She moved toward Lakota and said, "Thank you," as she hugged him tightly. She felt safe as he hugged her back.

CHAPTER 20

Courtney jumped to her feet. The pounding on the door waking her from her sleep. It took her a second to figure out where she was as the pounding continued.

"Wake up, Traveler!" came the call through the door.

"I'm up, I'm up!" she answered back stumbling to the door. She unlocked it and opened it to see one of the guards, his arm still raised to knock again.

"Your friends are..." He paused looking past her to the room behind her. "Oh," he continued, "Griffin wants to see you immediately. Him too," the man said pointing behind her and turning to walk away.

Courtney turned to see Bryan stirring from sleep and then realized that she had been using him for a pillow.

"Oh my God," she said out loud. Then thought, 'my parents would kill me if they knew I slept in the same bed as a boy'. "Hey, wake up. Griffin wants to see us," she said acting like him being in her room was no big deal.

Bryan sat up and wiped the sleep from his eyes. He looked around still trying to figure out what was going on.

"Come on!" she said again grabbing his arm and yanking him from the bed.

Bryan was still a little disoriented as he walked down the hall following the guard. He led them to the same meeting room they had been in before, but Griffin was not there. The room was empty except for a bowl of fruit on the table. Bryan woke quickly at the sign of food and grabbed an apple from the bowl. Courtney glared at him like he was a child stealing from the cookie jar.

"Seriously?" she asked.

"What? I'm hungry," he said as she shook her head and sighed with a small smile.

The door opened slowly as Griffin began to come in, still talking to someone down the hall. "Get back to me in an hour, either way," he said as he turned to the kids.

"Good morning," he said. "Apparently, you didn't like your accommodations," he added looking at Bryan.

"Ah, no," he stammered, "I was lonely and went to talk to Courtney.

I fell asleep."

"How old are you?'

"Fifteen," Bryan answered.

"Yeah, when I was fifteen, Vala and I liked alone time together too. Then, we got married."

Bryan blushed and put his head down.

"Ewww," Courtney said, but she was blushing too.

"Enough of you two. Did Pitman talk to you last night?"

"No, why?" Bryan asked raising his head.

"He's gone."

Courtney jumped up slamming her hands on the table. "That son of a..."

"Court!" Bryan stopped her. "Why didn't you stop him?" Bryan asked Griffin.

"I told you that you were not being held here and were free to go if you wanted. You were not being guarded. Some of our guards did see him, but they were under orders to let you all go, so they did. He seemed to head North, which is away from the castle."

Bryan shook his head with a frustrated look on his face trying to take in the information he just received. While Courtney sat quiet, but angry looking like she was ready to explode. The silence was awkward and lasted a few minutes, Bryan and Courtney going through their meeting of Pitman and their journey to this world. Griffin finally broke the silence.

"I'm sorry about your friend," he said.

"He's not my friend!" Courtney retorted.

"It doesn't make sense," Bryan said still shaking his head, "it just doesn't make any sense at all. Pitman and Mr. Lane were best friends. I know they grew apart, but I can't see that guy just giving up and leaving his best friend. I couldn't see myself leaving you or Abby, Court. It just doesn't make any sense. I know the guys a jerk, but even jerks have feelings."

"I have other news that's more important."

"About Abby?"

"Yes, we have some news. One of our search teams ran into an old beggar woman, named Esma. Some think she is a witch, but that's not that important. Esma said she saw a Traveler girl walking through the woods with a Shifter."

"A what?"

"A Shifter."

"What the heck is a Shifter?" Courtney asked.

"There are four known Shifters in our land. They are Shapeshifters and can change into different animals and people that they have touched. So a Shifter can be a man, and then turn into a wolf or a bear or an ant or even a person."

"How is that possible?" Bryan asked.

"I don't know, but I do know that they can change in an instant. One second you see a man, and then there's a bear there ready to maul you to death. They can only turn into things that they've touched for a few seconds. It's like they hold on to the animal or person for a few seconds to generate the power to be them."

"Sounds like they download the animal into them."

"Download?"

"Yeah, it's something in our world that happens with computers."

"Computers?"

"Not important. Tell more about the Shifter thing and Abby," Courtney said.

"Well, Esma said she came upon the young Shifter and a Traveler girl. She tried to warn the Traveler about him, but was chased away. Since, she said the young one, it had to be Lakota, the wolf."

"The wolf? You mean this guy held onto a wolf long enough to become one?"

"Yes, there are four Shifters that we know of Lakota is the youngest, only a few years older than you. Lakota and Mika are known as the wolves, because that is their main animal. The other two are Kuruk and Gawain, they are known for changing into bears and hawks."

"Bears! These dudes are crazy!"

"The Shifters usually keep to themselves and wander the forests, but the scary part for Abby is that all four of them work for the Queen."

"So, Abby was taken by one of the Queen's men, who can change into a wolf?" Courtney asked.

"Unfortunately, yes," Griffin replied, "but if it makes you feel any better, Lakota is probably the least loyal to the crown. The others having been lurking in the kingdom for a long time and are very powerful."

"Oh, yeah, I'm sure Abby can just put a leash on the wolf and teach him tricks, so she doesn't get eaten!"

"Courtney, I understand your frustration, but he hasn't done anything to her yet, and he might not know who she is. Maybe we can stop them before they get to the castle and he finds out."

"We better before she becomes Kibbles and Bits!"

"What?"

"Wolf food!"

"We have a search team looking for her now. We need to see what they find before you leave here. As Travelers, you will become targets for the Queen's men and we do not want to draw their attention. It would only let them know that there are young Travelers here and that the Princess may be one of them. Remember, the last time anyone saw her, she was a baby. So, no one knows what she looks like, unless she looks just like the Queen," Griffin said with a laugh.

"Oh no," Bryan said, "What color are the Queen's eyes?"

"Lakota the Shifter will know her," Griffin said realizing that Abby must have distinctive silver colored eyes like her mother the Queen.

"The Queen has amazing silver eyes, doesn't she?" Courtney asked.

"We need to find the Princess."

CHAPTER 21

Abby walked along the small dirt path not behind Lakota like the day before, but next to him. Her purpose was renewed. She had to find her friends, but more importantly, her dad. She didn't feel relaxed, but she was optimistic. She now had an ally in Lakota and that gave her a chance to find her father and her friends.

Abby almost had a smile on her face when Lakota's pace slowed a bit. It happened quickly and made Abby turn to look at him. He kept walking, but looked around intently almost as if she wasn't there. Abby began to take notice of their surroundings. The path was the same, but the forest was getting a little darker and denser. Lakota was on alert like when the old witch came toward them.

Abby looked at him and was about to say something, when Lakota turned to her and placed his hand over his mouth to tell her not to speak. He then pointed to his ear telling her to listen. She felt a chill, but followed his silent directions and listened. Their pace went from a normal walk to almost stopped.

Then, she heard the growl. It was low and barely audible, but she definitely heard it. Lakota stopped and flung his arm out to stop Abby from walking like a parent stopping quickly in a car and throwing out their arm to protect their child. Suddenly, their path was blocked, by an angry, snarling dog. Abby took a step back until she heard the growl behind her. They were surrounded. The third dog came from the right. All three dogs had the same look about them. To Abby, they looked like small speckled German shepherds, but three of them descending upon her and Lakota was more than she could handle. Abby's emotions were already running high and the sight of three dogs ready to maul her and Lakota was more than she could handle.

Instinctively, she grabbed a three-foot length of branch that was lying on the ground next to her. Swinging it at the dog on the right and yelling "Get away!" Obviously, she was ready to fight. She turned to make sure Lakota was with her when to her astonishment, he was gone. Lakota, who was so strong and had been at her side was not there; he was replaced by a huge wolf. Abby took a step back and dropped the branch, thinking that her life was over being surrounded by three wild dogs and a huge wolf. Suddenly, the wolf bounded in front of Abby in a protective mode and the dogs backed up. Abby was frozen in place and didn't dare to move. She stayed still, but her eyes searched the area for Lakota, but he was no where to be found. Yet, the wolf protected her growling at the dogs, who were suddenly defensive and not ready to pounce anymore. The wolf attacked barking and striking the front dog across the snout with a sharp paw. He yelped and vanished down the path. The other dogs snarled, but did not advance. The wolf turned to the dog on the right, who was now closest to Abby and bared his teeth. Abby stood frozen putting her life in the hands or paws of a wolf, who was suddenly her protector. The dog on the right turned and ran without a fight.

While the wolf watched him run, the dog behind them attacked Abby. He ran at her and leapt toward her. Out of nowhere, the wolf slammed into the dog with a complete body block sending him to the ground and landing on top of the dog. The wolf pinned him down with his mouth on the dog's throat. The dog writhed in pain desperately trying to free itself from the wolf's grasp.

Abby screamed backing away from the scene holding the branch in front of her as protection from the wolf. He saw her backing away and let go of the injured dog who yelped in pain, but was just happy to be out of the wolf's grasp and retreated quickly. Abby backed away wary of a possible attack from one of the dogs, but more terrified of the huge wolf who was now walking toward her. The change was quick and immediately the wolf was gone and Lakota was in it's place. Abby shook her head and blinked her eyes trying to comprehend was had just happened.

Lakota spoke first, "Abby, it's ok," he said, "it's me."

"What?"

"I'm sorry. I should have told you. I am the wolf," he said looking dejected.

"What?

"I am the..."

"How is that possible?" she interrupted. She continued to back away from the guy she had come to trust and like. She still held the branch in front of her for protection.

"Are you ok?" he asked.

"Ok? I just got attacked by dogs. Then, they get attacked by a wolf, and the stinkin' wolf is you!" she said pointing at him. "No! I'm not ok!"

"I'm sorry," he said again, "I should have told you, but I thought you would think I was crazy and run away."

"You're right! I do think you're crazy, and I do want to run away!

What's going on?"

"Let's keep moving, and I'll explain."

Abby was reluctant to do anything with Lakota, but she was still wary of the dogs and was afraid they would come back. She stared at him for almost a full minute before starting down the path where they were originally going. Lakota moved with her, and they walked side by side again. Abby kept a close eye on him making sure that Lakota was next to her and not a ferocious beast ready to pounce on her. He noticed her skepticism and just walked for a bit before saying anything. Lakota also knew that taking some time could possibly calm Abby down so that he could explain himself to her.

"I am a Skinwalker or Shapeshifter, as some people say."

"You lied to me," she said.

"I didn't really lie; I was just afraid to tell you the truth."

"In my world, that's called lying!'

"Again, I'm sorry," he sighed, "but most people are afraid of me and stay away from me. I thought if I told you that the old witch was right about me, that you would be scared and run away.

"What's with the wolf thing?"

He sighed again, but this time it was more of relief because he thought she was going to let him explain himself. "I am a Shapeshifter, like the old witch said, a Shifter. That means that I can change myself into different thing that I've come in contact with, like a wolf."

Abby looked confused.

"If I touch a living being for a little bit of time, then I can change into that being. When I was a child, another Shifter named Mika changed into a wolf and let me touch him long enough that I could be a wolf. It's my main animal, but I can change into over fifty different beings. I don't like doing it because it drains my energy, except for the wolf. For some reason, I am connected with the wolf and it is very natural to me."

"So when I was sleeping..."

"Yes, I was the wolf you saw. While guarding you, my senses are much better as a wolf than as a man, so it was only natural for me to change and protect you. The same thing happened with the dogs. As a man, we could have fought them, but as a wolf, I knew they were no match."

Lakota was explaining, but Abby's mind was wandering back to when they first met and he had placed his hand over her mouth so she didn't yell. She felt a coldness come upon her and started to wonder. "Can you change into me?"

"What?"

"When you first saved me, and my friends were caught, you touched me. I remember a cold feeling coming upon me when you did. Were you stealing me?"

"Stealing you? What's that mean?"

Abby stopped walking and stared into Lakota's eyes. "Can you change into me?" she asked.

"I don't know."

"Oh my God, stop lying to me!" She was angry now and it showed on her face.

Lakota tried again to calm her down. "Seriously, I don't know. Changing into a human takes a lot of effort and a lot of strength. I have only done it once when I was young, and it was very hard to do. When I touched you, I did take something from you, but I don't know if it was enough or if I could do it. Besides, I have to want to change. I don't want to change into you. When I change into a wolf, it's so natural that I can do it without really thinking about it, but a person takes effort." When he finished, Lakota changed into the huge wolf and quickly sat to let Abby know that there was no danger.

Abby was startled for a second, but reached over to pet the wolf who immediately changed back to Lakota, who now had Abby's hand touching the side of his face. She pulled back awkwardly, almost wanting to slap him.

"I promise that I will not change unless I have to change and only for protection."

"Ok," she answered, but her mind was much deeper in thought as they began down the path again toward the castle. She trusted this guy, and he lied to her. Why would he lie? Was he hiding something else from her? Suddenly, she went from optimistic that they could help her Dad and friends to wondering if she was in danger. The scariest thing was that she didn't think she could survive on her own. She might have to stay with Lakota, even if she didn't trust him any more. If she found her friends, she had no idea of how to save them or her Dad, but she thought that having a wolf might help. Her options were limited and some crazy wolf boy was better than her alone. If she could get to the castle, then she could possibly get away from him if there were other people around. Alone in the woods with a wolf was not the place to try and escape.

CHAPTER 22

The torch light ripped through the darkness of the dungeon bringing voices and waking Richard. He pulled himself to a sitting position against the side wall of his dark cell. He could hear mice scurrying around the base of the walls avoiding Richard while searching for food scraps, but tried to focus on the flickering light bouncing off the walls. Richard wiped the sleep from his eyes and waited for the cell door to open. He was sure they were coming for him. 'Nothing like having a trial that's already decided,' he thought.

Yet, Richard was surprised when the soldiers passed his cell and continued down the hall.

Richard listened intently when he heard a guard say, "The first rule of this job is we always attend to the Unknown first."

"The Unknown?" came a reply.

"The second rule of this job is don't ever ask about the Unknown Prisoner."

"Ok," said the second guard, who Richard figured must be new to the job.

The first guard continued, "The Unknown has been here for over two years. The only one who knows his identity is the Queen. Any one else that found out his identity has gone missing. He is treated better than any other prisoner and give many amenities like light, books, comfortable furniture and good castle food. His cell is cleaned every three days. If you have to clean the cell, make sure he places a hood over his head before you go into the cell to clean it. You do not want to know his identity."

Richard was thankful for the small hallway and the echo of the dungeon to give him information, but now he was intrigued by this unknown prisoner thing. 'Why was he treated so well and who could he possibly be?' His mind was wandering when suddenly the lock clicked on his cell door, and it was flung open. Richard jumped back startled at the sudden intrusion and blinded by the torch light.

"Hands on the wall, Traveler," came the command from the experienced soldier.

"Isn't that..."

"Quiet! We do not speak to the prisoners or about them."

"Sorry."

Richard did as he was told. The new guy knelt down and placed iron shackles around Richard's legs with a short chain. The same was done with his arms in front of him. Then, Richard was led out of the cell and down the hallway away from the Unknown's cell.

Richard shuffled along getting used to the chains length on his legs and how far he could step. His biggest issue was the weight of the shackles. They were heavy and bulky, not only on his legs, but they drug his arms down as well. He was led up the stairs from the dungeon and into the halls of the castle.

Richard knew they were headed to the Throne Room, where his trial would take place. He almost laughed out loud, 'Yeah, some trial this will be,' he thought. They stopped in front of the huge doors that led to the Throne Room.

"Wait here," the main guard said as he slid through a small door on the right, which led to the same place, but was not as formal. Richard could hear grumbling from behind the doors. Then they started to slowly open.

Richard stared straight ahead as the gap in the doors widened enough for him to see the Queen sitting on the raised throne about fifty yards in front of him. Even from that distance, she looked beautiful in her gold crown and long beaded red and gold dress. She stared directly back at Richard unwavering in her contempt for him. He would not give in to her and continued to stare back even when the gasps started and conversations erupted around the room as the gap in the doors became wide enough for everyone to see him. Richard could tell there were a lot of people in the room even though he kept his eyes locked on Queen Kitane. He shuffled forward dragging the heavy shackles across the floor. The conversations grew louder though Richard could not make out what was being said. He was too busy staring down Kitane and remembering the first time he entered this hall.

He thought back to Tammany sitting on the same throne and how he stood and walked toward Richard to meet him halfway down the red carpet. It was such a show of friendship and humbleness from a King, Richard would never forget it. He also knew, the same would not happen today. There was no red carpet for him this time, and Kitane would never stoop to meet him. Staring at her and her love of power made him realize that taking Abby away from her was the greatest decision he ever made. She was not the same girl he saw that first time here when Tammany greeted him. That girl was beautiful with the most mesmerizing eyes he had ever seen. She was a Princess, but humble like her father which made it easy for him to fall in love with her. Then, she changed. Richard realized that she was in love with him being a Traveler and not in love with him. The longer Richard stayed in this world, the more common he became, and the more distant they grew. By then, there was a baby involved, who had those same mesmerizing eyes. He saw how loving, beautiful and compassionate they could be through Abby. Now those eyes were boring a hole right through him as Richard steadily made his way toward her.

Finally, the guard leading Richard along stopped. Raftis, standing on the steps that led to the Queen, banged a large wooden staff on the ground silencing the crowd. The guards moved away and Richard stood alone with all eyes on him.

Raftis spoke, "My Queen, I present to you Richard Lane, formerly known as Prince Richard. He is accused of the kidnapping and murder of Princess Abigail."

This brought gasps and murmurs from the crowd of people.

"Silence!" Raftis commanded.

Queen Kitane sat stoic when she said, "Do you have anything to say for yourself?"

Richard was not prepared for the question. He never thought he would be given a chance to say anything, so he stood silent and slowly bowed his head.

The Queen continued, "Do we have witnesses?"

"My Queen, may I present Zareth of the Queen's Guard."

Zareth emerged from the crowd and stood right next to Richard making him very uncomfortable. Richard kept his head down, not wanting to look at Zareth.

"My Queen, my team was sent to the Traveler's land to find him and the Princess and return them here. We found Prince...excuse me, we found Richard, but there was no sign of the Princess at his home or anywhere in the land. Upon our return, Richard tried to escape by killing one of my men, but he was unsuccessful in his escape."

Richard raised his head and looked at Zareth quizzically. Even Queen Kitane looked at Richard obviously surprised by the accusation. Richard noticed her look and shook his head in disgust as he lowered it again.

"There was no sign of the Princess?" she asked.

"No, my Queen, we searched the whole land."

Richard smirked and shook his bowed head some more, which gained a menacing look from Zareth that Richard never saw.

"Thank you, Zareth. Any other witnesses?"

"Yes, my Queen, may I present Multon of the Queen's Guard," Raftis said.

Multon moved next to Richard and nervously spoke, "My Queen, while standing at the prisoner's cell, I heard the prisoner tell you that the Princess was dead."

"Thank you, Multon. I'm glad that I wasn't the only one to hear those words come from his mouth," the Queen said. "You are dismissed."

Queen Kitane looked hard at Richard. "Before I decide your fate, do you have anything to say?"

Richard slowly raised his head. "You're going to believe want you want, but I will say this. Yes, I took Abigail, but I took her to give her a better life."

Some in the crowd laughed at the thought of a Princess having a better life away from being a princess.

Richard continued, "I did not kill anyone. I did not kill Abigail and I, by no means, killed a guard trying to escape. Now, do with me what you wish." He then lowered his head again and was a little surprised that there was no reaction from the people. They stood silently, mostly stunned, staring at Richard.

The Queen stood, which broke them from their stupor and made them all bow their heads like Richard. Then she spoke, "I will do with you as I wish," she said. "You have admitted to kidnapping the Princess Abigail, which holds a death sentence. As for her death, we are still unsure of that, but if she has died, then you are responsible. Finally, a leader of my guard has accused you of murder and I believe him. So, on the second sun from today, when the sun is highest, you will be taken to the bridge bound with chains and a large rock and thrown into the moat to drown."

Gasps came from the crowd, Richard raised his head and stared at the Queen, who had a sly smile on her face. He was quickly taken back many years when a murderer was given the same sentence. Richard remembered telling his then wife that drowning would be a terrible way to die. Apparently, she remembered that conversation too.

"Guards, remove the murderer," she said without taking her eyes off of him.

Richard was led away to think about dying in two days and wonder if the man who helped him escape last time would show up to help again.

CHAPTER 23

As they walked, Abby's thoughts jumped around her head. She wondered if she should wait until the castle to get away from Lakota or try and find a town or village and seek help to get away from him. To ease her mind, she started asking questions.

"How long until we get to the castle?"

"It's not that far now, we need to be there before they close the city gates at sundown. We definitely will be. We can even rest if you are tired."

"No, I'm good," she answered, "What is the plan when we get there?"

"I'm not sure yet. I think I will be able to find out information to see where they are holding your friends and your Dad. We can figure out our next step when we find that out."

Abby nodded her head, hoping Lakota could come through with information, when suddenly Lakota stopped walking and turned to look Abby in her eyes.

"I'm really sorry that I didn't tell you about me. Most people are afraid of Shifters and stay away from us. I liked having someone to talk to and travel with and thought you would run away from me if I told you. I...I... that's all, I'm sorry." He then turned to walk again, but Abby grabbed his arm to stop him.

"Ok," she said, "Thank you for apologizing." She was happy that he took the chance to say that to her, but thought he looked like he wanted to say something else, but he didn't. They just turned and began walking silently again.

They walked for a while before Abby finally broke the silence. "It's a shame that no one takes the time to get to know you," she said, "You're really very nice." Lakota looked shocked, but didn't know what to say, so she continued. "I'm glad that I met you, I mean, I'm not happy that my friends were taken and all, but I'm glad I'm not looking for them alone. I still think the wolf thing is a little weird though," she finished with a smirk. Lakota smiled "And not knowing that you're a Princess is a little weird, too. I mean, who doesn't know that they are a Princess? At least, I know I can be a wolf."

"It is weird," she said. They had stopped walking and just stood there talking. "The craziest thing of all is that I don't even know my mother, and you knew who I was based on the color of my eyes. Can you tell me what she's like?"

"Well, the Queen is...," Lakota stopped and quickly looked to his right.

"What...", she started to say, but Lakota put his hand up to silence her clearly listening as intently as possible.

Suddenly, three men came running out of the bushes toward them. They were dressed in brown and carrying spears, clubs, and bows and arrows. Abby knew immediately that they were the Queen's men.

Lakota yelled, "Run!" and immediately turned into a large bear shielding Abby from the men. She was scared, but she turned and ran as fast as she could away from the path and into the brush for more cover. She sloshed across a small stream and up an embankment turning quickly to see what was happening. Arrows and spears flew toward the bear, who suddenly disappeared. Abby knew the men would chase her, so she ran as fast as she could. She thought of the horror movies she had seen where the girl was running for her life, but was eventually going to get caught. She didn't want to be that girl. So, she ran through the bushes snapping back in her face trying to find a clear path. Then, she was hit with a thought. 'I escaped from Lakota! I am free from that lying wolf/boy'. Then, still running, she thought of Lakota, 'He let me go. He tried to save me. If he was truly bad, he would have never let me go. I need him! I have to go back to him!' In a split second, she decided to go back to Lakota.

Even though she had trust issues, she felt that he was her best chance to survive, so she ran for her life. Abby knew that being smaller than the soldiers would help her through the underbrush, and she was right. The distance between her and her chasers widened and Abby started to angle to her right trying to make a huge arc that would bring her back to the path they had been traveling and hopefully to Lakota. More questions raced through her head, 'What if I never find him again? Would that be so bad? I wouldn't have to worry about trusting him again,' she thought. She did realize that she would miss Lakota and not just because he was good looking. There was something about him that she really liked.

Abby continued to run, thankful for being a swimmer and the endurance it had brought her. She could no longer hear anyone behind her, so she cut her arc a little sharper hoping to get back to where Lakota had been. Finally, she popped through some trees and saw a small dirt path, she couldn't be sure, but she thought and hoped it was the same one that they had been following. Now her dilemma was whether to continue

on toward the castle or to go back to where she left Lakota. Lakota said

the city doors closed at sunset, she wasn't sure exactly what that meant,

but thought she needed to head to the castle. She hoped to find Lakota

along the way, but figured staying the night in the city would be better

than out in the woods alone.

The path was fairly straight through the trees, so Abby could see

ahead of her and a good distance behind her too. She walked at a decent

pace trying to make up the lost time from being chased by the men, but

was still scared that they would go back to the road, too. Then she heard

a rustling and voices ahead of her, but not on the path. Abby quickly got

off the path and ducked behind some bushes and trees. The voices got

closer and she tried to control her breathing so as not to be heard.

"I'm not telling him, you tell him," the first man said.

"Why do I have to tell him?" came another voice.

"I'll tell Oswyn," said a third voice, "he'll understand that the Shifter

was the problem. He went from a bear to probably an ant when we

attacked him. By then, the Princess was gone."

"Should we say that we chased her, and she got away?" said the first voice again, it was high pitched and easy for her to distinguish from the other two, but they were getting harder for her to hear as they moved down the path away from the castle.

"Bear, ant, Princess gone, that's all he needs to know. He doesn't need to know that the girl was faster and smarter than us. She will get caught though."

"Yeah, but by who?"

The voices faded away down the path, but the last question made Abby uneasy. 'By who? what did that mean,' she thought. Abby wondered who was after her besides the Queen's men. Yet, she had to shake that out of her head at this point and stay focused on escaping from these three men. Luckily for Abby, they were going away from the way she wanted to go. It was good for her, but it made her wonder, if they were going to give up and tell this Oswyn guy that they couldn't find her, then why were they going away from the castle? There were many things that she didn't understand, but the more pressing issue was to get to the castle and stay hidden.

Abby emerged from her hiding spot and moved back toward the path. The men were too far down the path to be seen or heard, so Abby continued her journey. She moved a little slower this time watching and listening as intently as she could a little more concerned that there were more people looking for her.

After, what Abby figured was a few miles, she began getting frustrated at how slowly she seemed to be moving. Then, she heard a rustling noise in the bushes behind her. She quickly dodged behind a tree in front of her and looked back to see the source of the sound. Bounding through the bushes and across the path was a young deer, eyes wide and legs bounding over the path. Abby sighed with relief, then the bushes where the deer came from moved again and a large gray shadow emerged; a wolf. He raced onto the path and skidded to a stop sniffing the ground all around, then sitting down in the middle of the path. Abby wanted to show herself, but if it wasn't Lakota, she was dead. She held her breath not making a sound, hoping the wolf would go back after the deer. The wolf stood and immediately changed into huge man with gray hair, bright green eyes and ragged clothes. Abby let out a little gasp and the man turned and looked in her direction.

"You can't hide from me," he said, "you might as well come out."

Abby didn't move. She wasn't sure what to do, Lakota was a Shifter and he had been nice to her, this guy might be too. If she told him that she knew Lakota, then maybe he might help her, too. She also knew that she could not outrun a wolf in the forest, and he could sniff out her hiding spot in a second.

"Ok, have it your way," he said in his gruff voice, and the man was gone again replaced by the wolf with the same green eyes.

Abby jumped out of her spot, "Here I am," she said before really thinking about what she was doing. In her head, it was better to try to talk to the man, than get pulled out of the bushes by a wolf.

The wolf did not change. He stared at her and slightly turned his head with that quizzical look dogs sometimes give like they are trying to understand. Abby stared back trying not to be scared, but not doing a very good job of it. She remembered reading that animals can sense fear and go after the weak and fearful. She stared down the green eyed wolf trying to look tough, but inside, she wanted to pee her pants.

Suddenly, the wolf bared his teeth, raised his head and began sniffing the air. Abby stepped back dropping the whole not being scared thing. The wolf saw the step back and slowly moved forward stalking his prey. Abby continued to take small steps backward, while the wolf kept inching closer to her ready to pounce.

She could feel the numbness of fear closing in on her body knowing there was no chance to get away. She thought of her dad and wondered quickly, what he would do.

The wolf shot forward leaping at her. Abby stumbled backward shutting her eyes tightly, falling, and hearing the thud of bodies colliding. There were growls and grunts, but she felt nothing. She lie on her back, but felt no pressure on top of her. She opened her eyes to a cloud of dust and two wolves rolling on the ground and snapping at each other. Abby sat up and backed away ready to run, when the wolves rolled away from each other. They stared each other down. The green eyed wolf on the path facing Abby and the other wolf standing between them. Abby blinked her eyes and the wolves changed into two men. The gray haired green eyed man and Lakota. His back was to Abby, but she had followed him for so long, she knew instantly that it was him.

Lakota ripped the tomahawk and knife from his belt and held them up ready to fight. The green eyed man laughed, "You are getting stronger, young Lakota," the man said. "But, you know our rules, we share prey, but do not take prey from each other."

"Exactly," Lakota said, "she is mine. I have traveled with her for two days, and I'm taking her to the castle."

"You do know who she is."

"Of course, I do," Lakota said, "you taught me well."

"Not well enough. You left her alone in the forest."

"We were attacked, and I told her to run away while I protected her."

"Attacked?"

"By brown shirts, looking for her, but I am taking her to the castle."

"Understood," the man said, "You may take her, but you should hurry and be wary of the night. You want to get there before the gates close."

"That is the goal," Lakota replied.

"It is good to see you, Lakota. I have missed you. We should travel together soon." The man walked toward Lakota and they hugged. The man whispered, "Be careful of her. Do not fall for her beauty or it will cause a lot of trouble." They pulled apart and the man looked at Abby and said, "Be safe, Princess. You are in good hands. Now, I have a meal to catch." He clapped Lakota on the back, morphed to a wolf and bounded through the bushes

Abby stood stone-like trying to understand the conversation and then wondering what was whispered. Lakota turned to her and smiled. "I thought you would return to the path," he said.

"Thank you," Abby said running toward Lakota a grasping him in a huge hug. "You keep saving my life," she added letting go of him, but keeping her arms on his shoulders. He looked at her with his light brown eyes and for the first time in her life, Abby wanted to kiss someone. She was frozen and didn't know what to do. Lakota broke the silent awkward moment.

"It's fine," he said, "we need to hurry to get there before the gates close." Totally breaking the moment that Abby was having and making her drop her hands from his shoulders.

"Yeah...Yeah, we should go," she said stammering. "By the way, who was that other Shifter?"

"His name is Mika. He's my father."

"Your father! Oh my God! He's your father?"

"Yes, he taught me everything I know, but the way our land works, we don't get to see each other too much. When I first attacked him, I wasn't sure it was him, but quickly realized who I was dealing with."

"He's your father?" she said again.

"Yes, why do you keep asking."

"I'm sorry, I just never thought about you having parents."

"It is part of life. I wasn't dropped from the sky," he said laughing at her.

"Hahaha," she laughed back, "but what did he whisper to you?"

Lakota lowered his head and got a shy smile on his face. He raised his head, stared into Abby's eyes and replied, "He thinks I like you."

She blushed. She could feel the blood rush to her cheeks, and there was nothing she could do about it. She wanted to say something, but was at a loss for words.

"He's right," Lakota said and walked away from her up the path toward the castle.

CHAPTER 24

Courtney and Bryan spent the morning with Vala learning about this new land. They talked about the Queen, the castle, Shifters, and overall life as she knew it. The kids listened intently to the kind woman. Vala was motherly and loving, but they could tell by the men who came in and out of the small headquarters that she was well respected and revered by them. They also figured that she was not a person to cross. Her husband, Griffin, may be the leader of this rebel group, but Vala was the most respected and loved person around.

Courtney and Bryan loved the time they were spending with her learning about the history of Alden. They were shocked that Abby and Mr. Lane were royalty and how quickly Mr. Lane rose to power in a land he was only in for a short time. Learning the history also made them more fearful of what was going to happen to their friends.

"If I was the Queen, I would want revenge. I would want Mr. Lane dead," Courtney said.

"What about Abby?" Bryan asked, "What will happen to her?"

"I'm not quite sure," Vala answered, "I lived in the city and around

Queen Kitane for a long time. She was so distraught when Prince Richard and Princess Abigail went missing, but remember why Prince Richard left. He saw that Kitane was all about Kitane and didn't really care about anything else except the power she had, and how much more she would get when her father died. I believe that she was only upset about them leaving because it embarrassed her, not because she was going to miss them."

Bryan nodded his head in understanding and Vala continued.

"So, to answer your question, no one really knows how Princess Abigail will be received by the Queen. Will she be brought in as the beautiful long lost daughter who has returned to her mother and assumes the role of Princess? Maybe. Yet, it could be very different. She could be the Princess that is now a threat to the Queen. Remember, not many people like her. The Princess could be the heir to the throne that gets the Queen killed, but the Princess could be the heir to the throne that gets the Princess killed." Vala shook her head as she made the statement. "Queen Kitane is very unpredictable. I believe she will want to execute Prince Richard, but I'm not sure about the Princess."

"We can't sit here all day," Courtney said standing up, "we have to do something. We have to find them!"

Footsteps could be heard coming up the hall from outside, "Griffin is here," Vala said knowing her husbands steps.

Bryan perked up hoping for good news or any news for that matter. Courtney sat back down as Griffin entered the room.

"I have some news," he said looking at Vala more than the kids. "There was secret prisoner taken to the dungeon last night. We weren't sure who, but this morning got word that it was Prince Richard."

Courtney gasped, "They got him!"

"What about Abby?" Bryan said.

"I'll get to that. Prince Richard was taken to a trial this morning and was sentenced to death at noon in two days. We had a few men at the trial and all of them told the same story."

"What about Abby?"

Griffin shot him a look that made Bryan shut up quickly. "At the trial, Prince Richard said that the Princess was dead, but also said that he didn't kill her."

"He lied, so they wouldn't look for her," Courtney said.

"That's what I was hoping," Griffin said.

"But," Bryan looked at Griffin to make sure he could speak again, "what if Abby found him when we got separated, and she was killed?" Bryan got through the question, but looked on the verge of tears.

"I thought that, too," Griffin said.

"Griffin, if the Princess was killed here, in our land, you know Queen Kitane would have produced the body to completely condemn Prince Richard," Vala said with confidence.

"I agree," he said, "and that brings us to my next bit of news. The Princess has been seen, just this morning, right around the time of the trial."

"What? Where?" Courtney asked.

"One of our search parties came upon the Princess and the Shifter, it's definitely Lakota," he said looking at Vala, "but they got away."

"They got away?" Bryan questioned throwing his arms in the air. "Some soldiers you have, " he finished frustrated.

"The Shifter told the Princess to run, and then turned into a bear to fight my men," Griffin said staring down Bryan. "Have you ever fought a bear, boy?"

"No," Bryan answered putting his head down in disgust.

"Anyway, she ran. The Shifter changed into an ant to avoid arrows and spears. So, the men chased her through the forest, but could not move as quickly through the underbrush as her, and she got away."

"But, she got away from the Shifter guy too!" Courtney said excited.

"Yes, for now, but they were headed to the castle city and will be there soon."

"She'll be caught!"

"I know," Griffin said, "it is time for you to go to the city. Vala will take you along with a few men. Vala is known in the city and will have no problem getting in and moving around, but you two must change and wear more traditional Alden clothing."

"When do we leave?" Bryan asked.

"A cart is waiting. You must go now to avoid the closing of the gates."

CHAPTER 25

Richard sat in his dark cell thinking over the decisions he had made in his life. He was happy that he had taken Abby when he did, but wondered if he should have left her clues to get to Alden. Would they go find her like they did him? He was afraid they would, but he was really unsure. Richard knew that Kitane was all about power. If Abby was here, then she would be the heir to the throne and put Kitane in jeopardy. This queen might not want that and might just leave Abby alone.

Richard shook his head knowing that his clues may have put Abby in trouble. He also wondered about Mike Pitman. Would his old friend help Abby or even remember the book after all these years? He shook his head again trying to get the thoughts from his mind. If he was going to die tomorrow, he wanted to have a clear head and feel that Abby was safe. He tried to think of other things to keep his mind occupied.

The clicking of the steel lock at the end of the hall always made Richard perk up. He knew it would set off the moans from across the hall, but could give him more clues of the Unknown Prisoner if the guards were talkative. Torchlight streaked across his floor through the trough at the doorway, then the footsteps alerted him of the guard coming down the hall. Suddenly, the stench of the dungeon was broken by the smell of freshly cooked pork. Richard breathed in as long as he could to suck up the beautiful aroma. He knew it wouldn't last long before it was overpowered by the dungeon, so he took another long breath as the footsteps passed him to the cell at the end of the hall.

"Place your hood," came the call from the guard, "and hands on the wall." Richard heard the lock click and the cell door open. Then he could only hear the rustling of movement around the cell. He figured that the guard was cleaning up while the hooded prisoner stood with his hands on the cell wall. After a few minutes, the door creaked closed and the lock clicked again.

"I'm clear," came the call from the guard as he shuffled back down the hall past Richard's cell. There was no pork smell this time, just the flicker of torchlight and more desire to know who was in that cell.

Abby was gone from his thoughts and replace by his desire to know who was in that cell. He had been gone from this land for so long that there were plenty of people he didn't know who could be in that cell. It was the secrecy that was eating at him. If the man was in a cell, there was a reason Kitane was keeping him there and not just killing him off. Richard's conclusion was she somehow needed this man. The only sound explanation to Richard was that he was the maker of the key that opened the door. It made sense because she would want him alive, but not out there making keys for anyone else to leave this world. She kept control over him, but treated him well, except for the being in the dungeon part.

Since he was going to die, he vowed to ask the queen if he got the chance.

CHAPTER 26

Abby and Lakota's pace increased as they anticipated the closeness

of the castle. Yet, their conversation had slowed to a crawl. Abby had

no idea of what to say to a guy that just told her that he liked her. Sure,

she had heard that boys liked her before, but not an older guy and

definitely not directly to her. Usually, it was a friend of hers who came

running over with some gossip about some boy. That was easy to deal

with because Abby could decide if she wanted to talk to him or not.

Then again, most boys stayed away from her because they thought she

was with Bryan.

'Wow!' she thought. Bryan hadn't even been a thought since she

spent the last day and night with Lakota. Her relationship with Bryan

was always special to her. When she was a little girl, she played that

they were married, but as they got older she got teased for hanging out

with him. Then, when it was cool to talk to boys again, he was the one

boy that talking to was natural. She loved Bryan and always would, but

her feeling for Lakota were different.

Lakota was exotic, independent, and so handsome. Abby kept

glancing at him hoping he would say something about liking her again, but he didn't. They just kept walking until Lakota started to slow down. Abruptly, he stopped and put his arm out to stop Abby. As his hand brushed against her arm, she felt tingles run up through her shoulders. She looked at him, but he was intently listening and looking down the path.

"Stay here," Lakota said never looking at Abby, but immediately changing into a wolf. He dashed away into the bushes to their right. Abby was left standing there, almost frozen, missing him already. She wanted to follow him, but trusted that he knew what he was doing, so she waited. Finally, she heard a rustling in the bushes. It startled her, but she was ready, not to fight, but to scream for Lakota. She stared at the spot as Lakota emerged from the bushes.

"Oh, Thank God," she said.

"We made it," he answered, "the castle is just ahead of us. We are going to head through the forest to the main road. It's not far, but a little dense, so you need to stay close to me. A person can get lost quickly in these woods." He reached out his hand for Abby to take.

There was Lakota's hand extended in front of her to hold. She could again feel her face flush, and her palm immediately started to sweat, but she took his hand. He led her through the trees and bushes holding back branches. She tried to follow Lakota's footsteps and place hers in the same spots so she could keep the same pace as him. After a few minutes, she got the feeling that Lakota would rather be a wolf than a man when going through dense forest.

Finally, he stopped, looked at Abby and pushed away a branch in front of him. There in the distance was the castle pushing up into the bright sky beyond a high stone wall. Abby and Lakota were at the edge of the forest only about a hundred yards from the large thick wooden doors that led into the fortified city. Abby stood in awe of the structure before her. It resembled the medieval castles she had learned about in school with a castle in the middle surrounded by a city of houses and stores. All of it was protected by a large wall. According to Lakota, the city gates were opened during the day, but closed for the night. If you did not enter the city before dark, you were locked out for the night.

Abby could see the main road leading to the gates was scattered with people and horse drawn carts moving into an out of the city. These were merchants and farmers from surrounding villages, making their way to the city to sell products, then return home before nightfall. Some were city people who had small fields they tended to during the day and then returned to the protection of the city walls for the night. She also noticed it was easier to leave the city than to enter as a small line was forming in front of the guards.

"You can't just go in and out as you please?" she asked.

"No, those entering the city must state their business to the guards. Most people are let in without a problem, because they live there or are seen every day. If you are not known, then they may ask you questions and decide if you are worthy to enter."

"What about me? Am I worthy?"

"One look at your eyes, and you will be taken directly to the Queen," he said.

Abby looked shocked. "How can I save my Dad, if I can't even get in the city to find him?"

"That's why you're not going into the city."

"What? I have..."

"I know," Lakota said taking both of Abby's hands in his and turning to face her. She immediately stopped talking. "I am going to go into the city and find out if your Dad is even here. They may not have gotten here yet, which would be great because we could then search the road for him. If he is here, then I'll come back and figure out how to get you in the city."

"I have to stay here. Alone?"

"It won't be for long. I promise. Just stay out of sight, and I'll be back." He pulled her to him and gave her a hug. He then pulled back slightly and kissed her on her forehead. Lakota then turned and scurried down the slight incline that led to the main road.

Abby stood stunned. She finally got her kiss, but it was the same kiss her Dad always gave her, and definitely not what she was looking for from Lakota. She sat out of sight at the tree line and watched as Lakota made his way along the road with the rest of the people. It took a few minutes for him to get to the line for the gate. She noticed some people looked at him and sort of shied away from him. It started to bother Abby, and concerned her that Lakota wouldn't get into the city.

Finally, he got to the front of the line. Abby could feel her palms sweating again, nervous that he would be turned away. Lakota approached the guards and walked right through the gate. She was too far away to see if anything was said, but was confused that the guy everyone was noticeably moving away from wasn't even questioned. Abby blinked and shook her head to make sure she just saw what she thought she saw. The guards looked at him and he walked right by them.

Now the waiting began. Abby still confused, but relieved sat watching the rest of the crowd as they entered and exited the city. She was watching the exits more now looking for Lakota to emerge and come back to her. She did keep an eye on the entrance to see if anyone was turned away. She saw one cart get pulled to the side and searched, it was let through. A few minutes later a man was turned away. He threw his arms into the air and seemed to be yelling something and pointing at a guard. Finally, after a few minutes, he walked away.

As Abby watched, she wondered how long Lakota would take to find out about her Dad. Was he just going to ask someone, or turn into an animal and search around? She never asked him to be certain. What she was certain of was that it was starting to get dark. The sun was fading into the horizon and it wouldn't be long before the gates would close. She was also certain that she didn't want to do another night in the woods, especially alone.

There were fewer people on the road now. Abby noticed those emerging into her line of sight were hurrying toward the gate now. Then, one of the guards went and closed the door to the left where people had been exiting. "Oh my God, can he still get out?" she said out loud to no one. There was no movement to close the entrance side yet, but Abby knew it couldn't be long now.

Finally, a figure emerged from the entrance side that was exiting the city walls. It had to be Lakota, but in the twilight, she couldn't tell. She waited and watched intently as the figure moved along the road rather quickly. He was wearing a long cloak with a hood, but Abby felt it could still be Lakota; it had to be. The figure moved closer to her sight line and reached up to remove the hood. He flipped it off his bald head and continued on down the road. Abby almost cried.

Panic set in, and she rushed through the trees and down the incline toward the road. The guards have moved inside the wall except for one who is grabbing onto the large heavy door. He looks around for any stragglers, but cannot see her in the gloom of the night, she's not going to make it, but she runs. Abby runs toward that door, like she is being chased by a lion. The door is half closed and she is screaming, "Wait! Wait!", but she is either not heard or ignored. She continues running and screaming, but the door is about to click shut when she changes her tactic and begins yelling, "Fire! Fire!" She remembered a program in school about child abduction that taught them to yell "Fire", because it would get people's attention.

The door which was all the way shut began to slowly open. The guard's head popped out searching the area as Abby came running at him screaming, "Fire! Fire!"

Abby arrives at the gate out of breath and knowing she can let them get a good look at her eyes. "Thank God," she says out of breath.

"Where?" the guard replied.

"Where, what?" Abby asked hunched over trying to catch her breath.

"Where's the fire?" he asked annoyed.

"Oh, I thought I saw something over there," she chuckled thinking that the fire thing worked. "Can I come in?" she asked.

"State your business!" said the annoyed guard, who never really looked at Abby because he was still searching for a fire.

"My father never came out, I need to find him," she said.

"You look familiar," he said.

Abby dropped her head again and placed her hands on her knees trying to catch her breath, but really trying to keep her eyes and clothes hidden. "My family comes here a lot," she said.

"Come on, Gorn," came another voice from inside, "close the gate. It's just a girl, let her go and let's end this shift!"

"Thank you," Abby said not waiting for an answer from Gorn as she raced in the gate and up the main road bowing to the guards as she ran by them. She stayed at a jog to make sure they didn't ask her anything else. She also knew she had to make it look like she knew where she was going.

Abby could see the castle looming in the distance behind a large wall. All along the road were open air shops that were closing for the night. Abby moved from the middle of the road to the right side of the street along the stores and into the shadows. She didn't dare stop moving in fear that the guards were still watching her. Having no idea where she was going or where to find Lakota, she continued up the street toward the castle. She felt like she was in one of the medieval times movies her dad used to watch about castles and kings. This city was just like the movie sets, but these people weren't actors, they were living here for real. Abby stayed out of the way and kept moving hoping no one would talk to her or even notice the girl in the funny clothes with the Queen's eyes.

Up ahead on her side of the street, she heard music coming from a building. She slowed her pace and looked both ways before running across the street to the shadows on the other side. She felt this would give her a better view of where the music was coming from up ahead. Moving forward, she was happy she crossed the street as she could see the numerous torches and no shadows outside of the music filled Inn. There was also a lot of people in the area in front of the inn, which was obviously the place to go when the day ended in the city. She remembered that a long time ago, inns were not just hotels, but also bar/restaurants.

Abby got as close as she could and slid into an alcove across the street from the Inn. She didn't know what to do next. If she stayed here long, she would probably be seen by someone, but she didn't know where to go next. She couldn't just walk into the inn and yell out, "Does anyone know Richard Lane?" Yet, if she was going to find him, she needed to talk to someone and find out where he might be.

She waited and watched the inn hoping for an idea of what to do. She watched many people go into the inn, but it didn't seem like many were leaving. Then, she saw a few people walking up the street toward the inn. Abby wondered if she should try to talk to them since the trio looked like an older woman with two teenage kids. She couldn't really see them due to the darkness and the hooded cloaks they were wearing to tell if they were her age or not, but she let them pass without a word. She kept an eye on them and saw that they passed the inn and went into a building down the street. "Well, that chance is gone," she thought.

There were a few other people that came outside with drinks, but they were just talking to friends before heading back inside. There were some that came out, looked around and made their way to the shadows and alcoves of the surrounding buildings, which confused Abby until one guy made his way directly toward the place where she was hiding. Abby was ready to run from the alcove, when the man got distracted and moved to another spot only a few feet from her. Unfortunately, it didn't take long for Abby to realize what the man was doing when she heard the sound of water hitting the ground. "Eww," she thought, but also got an idea; she could talk to a drunk.

Abby knew from experience from parties with her dad that drunk people liked to talk and would tell you everything. That could get her the info about her dad that she needed. She also knew that drunks didn't remember things, so any drunk she talked to probably wouldn't remember it. Yet, the best part would be that if a drunk recognized her and told someone that they talked to her, people probably wouldn't believe them. Now, she just had to find the right drunk.

Abby waited in the darkness and watched each person coming out of the inn. A few were stumbling, but they either went away from Abby or were with other people. Finally, an older man came out by himself and stumbled down the opposite side of the road from Abby's position. She made the decision to follow him even though he was headed back toward the gate. Abby quickly snuck across the road getting into the shadows behind the man. She walked quickly and was a few yards behind him. She took a deep breath and spoke.

"Excuse me, sir,"

"Huh," the drunk replied trying to steady himself and not fall when he turned toward the voice. "Whaddaya want?"

"Have you heard anything about Prince Richard?" she asked.

"Where ya been all night? Talk is that he's back and..." the old drunk froze when he finally caught sight of Abby's eyes. He pointed at her, "You...you're..."

Suddenly, an arm came from behind and wrapped around Abby across the top of her chest pulling her away from the drunk. She was startled when she heard the voice behind her say, "Come on, girl, leave that man alone."

It was Lakota.

The old drunk looked as if he had just seen a ghost as Abby was led away by Lakota with his arm still around her. The man shook his head a few times and even rubbed his eyes before turning to continue his walk home. "Nah, couldn't be," he mumbled to himself as he stumbled away into the night.

"What are you doing?" Lakota asked trying to be quiet, but wanting to yell at Abby.

"What do you mean?"

"I mean you can't be here! You'll be seen and captured by the guards!"

"But the gates were closing, and you didn't come back!" she said pushing his arm off of her shoulder.

"I know. It was too dangerous. I was coming to get you now, and I see you chasing down some drunk. Are you crazy?"

"You were going to leave me out there all this time? I thought you were coming right back to get me!"

"Lower your voice. We have to get out of here," he said looking all around the area. "Follow me," he said grabbing her by the hand again. It didn't have the same effect on Abby as the last time he took her hand, but she held on and followed him down the street.

Lakota led him through the streets of Alden. Once they moved off of the main road, it was quite dark and Abby stayed close to him clutching his hand a little firmer. They moved quickly and quietly turning off of one block and onto another through the serpentine of streets with small houses and buildings that Abby couldn't really see to tell what they looked like. Finally, Lakota stopped, and Abby almost ran into him not anticipating it. They were at the corner of a small intersection of streets that looked no different from any other place they just passed.

Lakota turned to Abby and placed two fingers on her lips silently telling her to be quiet. She nodded her head to show that she understood, and he immediately let go of her hand and changed into a wolf.

The wolf just sat in the same place Lakota had been, but sniffed the air all around searching for unseen people in the darkness. It only took a few seconds before Lakota was again standing with her. He took her hand again and led her to the door of the small house on the opposite corner of where they were standing. He reached above the door and took down a key to open the door. He gently pulled the door open and led Abby inside.

Walking through the door put Abby into more darkness as Lakota quickly closed the door behind her. He then let go of her hand and moved about the room. Abby stood frozen not being able to see. Suddenly, there was the flare of a match and a candle was lit, then two more candles followed. The room started to take shape for Abby. She was standing in a hallway with a set of stairs in front of her to the left. A small table next to the stairs held the first candle that was lit. Off to her right was a doorway that led to a living room with a few chairs and a table, while ahead of her down the hall she could see what looked like a kitchen and eating area. Abby looked around wondering whose house this was when Lakota came back into the hall.

"Stay here. I'll be back. I have some ideas about your Dad, but have to check a couple things. I'll be back in a few hours."

"What if the owner comes back?" she asked.

"He won't," he said while walking out the door.

"How do you know?"

"I'm the owner."

CHAPTER 27

Courtney and Bryan had walked for what seemed like hours with Vala along the road that led to the castle. They were given traveling cloaks so as not to draw any unwanted attention. Courtney felt like they were extra long hoodies that went down to around their knees, but were very heavy material like a burlap sack. Both were instructed to put their hoods up and keep them there no matter how hot they get under them.

There were numerous people going to and fro along the road. Bryan noticed that the ones traveling toward the castle were hurrying much more than the people going away from the castle. Those heading to the castle were trying to get to the city before the gates closed, while those heading from the castle were going home to their farms after a long day. Yet, Vala didn't seem to be in that much of a hurry. They kept a steady pace, but Bryan noticed many people on the road were passing them and it was getting darker by the minute. The doors would surely close before they got there, but Vala seemed to know what she was doing, so Bryan kept his thoughts to himself.

Finally, the road thinned out and there were no longer any travelers coming toward them away from the city. The air cooled a little and wearing the hood was now bearable. Courtney started to notice some small fires sprouting up in the forest just off the road.

"What's with the fires?" she asked.

"Those are people who didn't make it to the city before the gates closed. They are camping here for the night."

"Oh my God! We didn't make it? Now what are we going to do?" Courtney said.

"We are fine. We were waiting for the gates to close, so no one sees you two go into the city."

"If the gates are closed..."

"Again, we are fine," Vala said stopping to look Courtney in the eye and reassure her.

"Ok," Courtney said hoping Vala was right.

They continued their walk in the dark, but as the road turned, they saw the shadow of the castle rising in the distance along with the large wall surrounding the city. The road had cleared of other travelers who were now gone or camped for the night in the surrounding woods.

As they silently approached the closed gates, Vala quickly searched the area with her eyes to make sure there were no other travelers in the area. It seemed to be quiet all around them, so they walked right up to the locked gate. Courtney stopped and looked at Vala. She didn't say anything, but Bryan knew she was thinking, 'Now what?' He had the same thought.

They watched as Vala walked up to the two large doors. She went to the bottom corner of the right entrance door and kicked the door making a dull thud sound. She then walked over to the far corner of the left door and kicked there as well. She then moved across to the center of the door and with the sides of both fists pounded twice where the doors come together. They heard the lock unlatch. Vala looked around one more time before grabbing Bryan to help her pull open the right hand door and waving for Courtney to follow. Courtney's mouth hung open and Bryan just smiled feeling there was a lot more to this woman than either of them knew.

As they went through the gate, Courtney was curious as to who opened it, but there was no one in the small guard house that was supposed to be guarding the door. Vala and Bryan quickly pulled the door shut and flipped the iron latch behind them. Vala waved for the kids to follow her into the shadows on the left side of the door. They moved quickly across the road and along the shadows toward the castle.

After moving a few hundred feet down the road, Vala moved them out of the shadows in into the middle of the road, so they wouldn't look suspicious. She now spoke to them in whispers under the cover of the hoods.

"We should look like any other people journeying into the city. Up ahead of us is an inn that will be very crowded with people. We will walk up like we are going to the inn, but we'll go into the building next to it." As she finished the noise from the inn could be heard ahead along with the glow from torches welcoming people to the area. As they approached, Courtney and Bryan saw people mulling about the area, some waiting for friends to arrive and some who already drank too much. Bryan wanted to look around, but kept his head straight and focused on the building they were headed toward.

"I feel like we're being watched," he whispered.

"All the more reason to get inside the safe house," Vala whispered back.

They quickly headed into the building next to the inn. Where Vala removed her hood, as they closed the door behind them.

"Clear," she called and candlelight erupted from the opposite end of the room. Oswyn and two soldiers.

"Ahh," Courtney said as she jumped a little startled by the sudden appearance of the men.

"Sorry to scare you," Oswyn said, "but we have some news."

"About Abby?" Bryan asked.

"Yes," Oswyn answered, "but it's not that good. We have found or, I should say, we have seen Lakota, but Abby was not with him."

"Not with him?" Courtney questioned.

"Yes, he has been in the city and has been asking questions about a prisoner. We're assuming that he is looking for Prince Richard. The problem is that we don't know what he's done with Princess Abigail."

"Oh my God, do you think he killed her or something?"

"That is unlikely, but there are two theories. First, he hid her or left her in the forest when he found out that Richard is here. He might believe that Richard is a bigger prize to give to the Queen. The second theory is that he is trying to help the Princess to find her father. If that is true, then he might help us to save the Princess from her mother."

"What do you think?" Bryan asked.

"I'm not sure," Oswyn answered, "mainly because I don't know how loyal Lakota is to the Queen. He is young and might not care that much about the Queen, or he is young and stupid and will do anything to impress her."

"I have another theory," Vala said and everyone turned to look at her. It was obvious that she was well respected by all of these men and they would listen to whatever she had to say. "I believe that he is helping the Princess."

"Why do you believe that?" Courtney asked.

"It's simple. I think he originally took her because she was a girl, and he wanted to talk to her. Then, he found out who she was and knew he needed to take her to the Queen. It was easy, because the Princess wanted to go to the castle anyway. Yet, along the way, he started to like her. I mean, I don't know anything about this girl, but her friends are loyal to her, and if she looks like her mother, then she is beautiful."

"You might be right," Oswyn said.

"Think about it. Lakota is a teenage boy who is a Shapeshifter. Everyone stays away from Shifters because they're different, but the

Princess stays with him. You think he's not going to fall in love with her? She's the only girl who's probably ever talked to him, and she's a Princess! Any boy would be in love. Plus, when our men came upon them, he told her to run and he protected her. If he didn't care, then he would have just got away and let her go."

"So, now what?" Courtney asked.

Vala looked at Oswyn, and he just smiled. "I know exactly what you want me to do," he said.

"Yeah, she wants you to talk to this Lakota dude," Courtney said, "but we have a bigger problem."

"What's that?" Oswyn asked.

"Pitman left and probably went back to our world. That means that he used the key we stashed by the exit door. So, even if we find Abby and her dad, we can't leave. We don't have a key."

Oswyn looked at the soldiers in the room. "Find out about the Queen's key," he said.

"Queen's key?" Bryan asked.

"If the Queen sent men to pick up Prince Richard, then they had to have a key to go through that door. I'm sure they didn't stash it by the door."

"Yeah, that was a bad move," Bryan said.

"Actually, it was very smart, but you didn't know that you had a traitor in your company."

"I swear to God, if I ever see Pitman again, I'll punch him right in his stupid face!" Courtney said getting agitated.

"I'll hold him for you," Oswyn said. "Now get some sleep, you have work to do tomorrow."

CHAPTER 28

"He lives here?" Abby said out loud to no one since Lakota had left.

She walked over to the table where the candle was for some light. The

candle holder was small like a saucer to catch the wax and had a handle

extended from it. It reminded Abby of a tea cup handle as she took hold

to carry the candle with her. The light of the candle made her feel safe in

the unknown house. She noticed the curtains were drawn for privacy and

even in the dark, she could see the place was dusty. "Obviously, Lakota

doesn't spend much time here, if any," she thought.

Abby began searching around the room for clues about Lakota's life,

but there was nothing in the room, just two chairs in the living room and

a coffee table set between them. It had a drawer that Abby just had to

open, but she actually looked around first to make sure she really was

alone before sliding the drawer from the table. There was nothing inside.

"Who has drawers with nothing in them? In my house we can't even

close half the drawers, because they're stuffed with things," she thought.

This place was very different from her home. There were shelves

on the walls, but no pictures, no knickknacks, nothing but dust on them.

She moved back out in the hall by the front door letting the candle lead the way. The small table where the first candle sat also had a drawer, but Abby's expectations were not great. She slid the drawer open to find a box of wooden matches and six unused candles identical to the one in the base she was holding. She closed the drawer and moved down the hall to the kitchen area.

The kitchen was no different. There were cabinets with some pewter cups and dishes, but there was no food to be found. Abby realized how hungry she was and started to look around some more, opening each cabinet hoping to find some kind of food. Finally, in a top cabinet, she found some mason jars with different types of nuts and dried fruits in them. Unscrewing the caps was difficult, but she managed to get the one with peanuts off. She wondered if they were ok to eat, but was now so hungry, she had to try them. Cracking and ripping open the shells, she devoured half the jar before realizing the mess she was making. She looked around the floor at the spent shells and really didn't care. She could clean it up later.

Next she found some pieces of dried apple mixed with apricots. She sucked them down as well, but now she was thirsty. There was no refrigerator to grab a cold drink from and nothing that looked like it would have drinks in it. She flashed the candle around the room, but was resigned that she would not get a drink in here. Then, she saw a wooden bucket sitting by the backdoor. Abby stepped to it and peered in, but there was nothing. She pulled the curtain from the window of the door and saw darkness. There didn't seem to be anyone around, so she unlatched the door and opened it.

Holding the candle out first with her hand cupping the flame to block the wind she saw a small backyard with an old fashioned well pump. It was metal with a large handle and a spout that had a bucket already under it. Abby quickly grabbed the house bucket and ran for the pump. She placed her bucket under the spout as the wind blew out her candle. She felt for the handle as her eyes adjusted to the dark. She grabbed it and pulled up then down sending a stream of water into her bucket. She quickly took it back into the house. Luckily, she had lit the kitchen candles and had some light to see. The water was a little cloudy, but she filled a pewter cup and drank quickly before she had second thoughts about drinking cloudy water.

Refreshed and full, she relit her candle and explored upstairs, where she found three bedrooms, but two were completely empty. The third had a small bed in it and a table. Abby sat on the bed, which wasn't very comfortable, but lay down anyway waiting for Lakota to return.

Abby jumped up and was standing before she even realized that she was awake. The room was bright with daylight coming through the white drawn curtains. Abby shook her head trying to figure out where she was, and how did she get there. It took a couple of seconds, but she remembered being in Lakota's house waiting for him to come back. She realized that she fell asleep and slept through the night.

She looked around realizing that Lakota wasn't there. She searched the other upstairs rooms, but they were still empty. Walking down the stairs, she realized that she never put out the candles the night before. She threw her fingers through her hair and sighed in relief that the candles just burned themselves out and didn't start a fire. 'I'm so stupid,' she thought. Sighing in relief, she continued to search the house but found no sign of Lakota. She looked out back at the water pump which she now noticed was a dull green color.

She couldn't wait for Lakota any more, and she made a desperate decision to go alone. In her mind, she had deduced that if the Queen was her mother, then she would hear her out and let her dad go. She couldn't be positive, but using herself was the only chance she had. The drunk man had said that the big talk of the night was that Prince Richard was back. If he was right, then the Queen must have him.

Abby needed to hurry, but she also needed a disguise. In the daylight, her clothes would give her away, she needed something else to wear. She ran back up the stairs and searched through the bedrooms again. The room she slept in had nothing of use with a bare closet and no dresser. She went back to the other two empty rooms, both had small closets that could hold some sort of clothing. She whipped open the closet in the first room to find and blanket and what looked like some sort of leather belt. Pulling the dusty blanket onto the floor, she noticed that it wasn't that big and might just cover her enough on the street for her to get to the castle gate. She whacked the dust off of it and wrapped the blanket around her shoulders. Abby flipped the edge up over her head trying to make it like a hood. She didn't have a mirror, but figured she looked like a kid going trick or treating who forgot to get a costume. It would have to do.

Abby peeked out of the curtain to make sure the street was clear. It must have been very early because the street was still empty and the sun wasn't quite up yet giving the sky a light gray and pink color. She needed to hurry while most people were still asleep. Unlatching the door, Abby decided not to lock it in case she needed to get back in quickly. She figured there was nothing to steal anyway.

She flipped the blanket over her head and stepped out into the light. She tried to remember the streets that Lakota took to get to the house last night, but there was almost no way to figure it out. She did know which way they came from, so she headed across the dirt street. Abby walked as fast as she could without running. The blanket was a little warm, but the cool morning air and the swiftness of her pace kept her from getting too hot. Walking with her head down, she listened for activity that would lead her to a main street. Every once in a while she took a peek up to she if she could see the castle.

Finally, there were some people walking down the street to her right. Slowing her pace, Abby followed, hoping they were headed to the main road. After a few blocks, she found she was right. There were more people on this street, but most were too occupied trying to set up their shops or get where they were going to noticed the strange girl wrapped in a blanket.

Spotting the castle gave Abby a destination, and her experience last night gave her a way along the shadows to get there. Slipping down the street to her previous hiding place across from the Inn, she felt like she knew what she was doing. The Inn was quiet now, everyone from the previous night's revelry was still sleeping and could care less about the girl in the blanket sneaking down the street.

Abby crept from her hiding spot and scanned the street noticing a man coming out of the building next to the Inn. He was also scanning the street looking right over to where Abby had just been standing, but she instinctively moved back into the shadows before he saw her. Her heart was racing. 'What's he looking for?' she thought pulling the blanket a little further over her head to conceal her face even more. She was pretty sure he didn't see her, but she wasn't going to chance moving until he was gone.

He didn't seem to be in a hurry, but was definitely looking for someone or something as he craned his neck down the long street. Finally, he moved out onto the street and headed almost the same path Abby had just followed to get there. Little did she know that he was heading to the house she just left.

Abby moved more deliberately now heading straight for the castle gate without looking left or right. As she approached, one of the two guards called out to her. "Be on your way, you homeless wench!"

Abby was surprised, but kept moving toward the guards determined they would listen to her.

"I said, be one your way!"

"I demand to see the Queen," Abby said.

"Oh, she demands to see the Queen," he mocked laughing to the other guard. "I'm sure the Queen would love to see her."

"Yes, she would," Abby said sternly.

The guards laughed to each other. "And why would she want to see you?"

"Because, I'm her daughter," Abby said removing the blanket from her head and staring confidently into the eyes of the guard.

He froze. Of course there was a resemblance, but the eyes were unmistakable. He turned to the second guard, mouth still agape and said, "Go get Raftis." The guard left immediately running across the bridge that led to the castle. Abby was let through the gates and the first guard told her to put the blanket back over her head. He led Abby to the small guard hut next to the gate. Abby complied and found a seat. They sat in awkward silence waiting for the guard to return with Raftis.

It seemed like an eternity for the runner to return. He was completely out of breath.

"Raf...tis...said...cov...er..."

"Relax, just wait and catch your breath for a minute," the first guard said.

Again, they waited as the runner got himself together and finally spoke.

"Raftis said, cover her up and bring her to him. Do not let anyone see her. He also said," the runner's eyes got wide while he paused.

"What?" the first guard asked.

"He said if anyone besides you, me, and him find out about this, he will kill us both."

"Great," the first guy said turning to Abby, "cover yourself up, while we cross the bridge."

Abby stood and covered her head with the blanket. She also pulled her hair down in front of her face, not wanting to get the guards in trouble if someone did see her.

"I will take her," the first guard said, "you stay here and keep your stinkin' mouth shut."

The runner nodded as Abby and the first guard walked away. They made their way in silence across the bridge, Abby keeping her head down as much as possible. She only paused when they reached the middle of the bridge where the gallows where. The menacing nooses hanging out over the water made Abby shudder.

"Keep moving," the guard said, "or you might see me hanging there."

Abby knew by his tone that he wasn't kidding, so she continued toward the castle. When they finally arrived at the doors, they were closed, but Abby soon found they were not locked. The guard pulled open the right door just enough for them to slip into the castle. Abby, like her father was led to the right into a room where Raftis was waiting in a long flowing green robe. Abby kept her head down with her hair in front of her face but kept her eyes up looking at the man in front of her.

"Thank you, Barda," Raftis said to the guard, "you may go."

Abby looked through her hair at the guard, who now had a name. She hoped he would not have any problems because of her. She kept an eye on him as he exited, then continuing to keep her head down turned to Raftis.

"We do not take kindly to imposters," he said.

Abby was shocked. He hadn't even seen her yet and was calling her an imposter. Immediately, she started to wonder if everything Lakota told her about being a princess was true. She really couldn't know for sure, but she didn't really care, her main goal was to help and free her dad. She closed her eyes, sighed, and took the blanket off of her head. She dropped her head and flipped her hair over her head revealing her face and eyes to Raftis.

He stood sternly, his lips pushed tightly together, but Abby could tell by the widening of his eyes that he knew she was the Queen's daughter.

"Who are you?" he said.

"I am Abigail Lane," she answered, "and I am here to beg for my father's freedom."

"And who is this father that you speak of?"

"Richard Lane, the Prince of this land."

"Richard Lane is a prisoner, who admitted kidnapping and killing his daughter the Princess. He is due to be executed tomorrow at noon. So, this Prince you speak of is no more."

"Admitted to killing me? He would never."

"It doesn't really matter, my child, he will be executed tomorrow, and you should leave here now and never ever come back."

Abby looked perplexed. If she was really a princess, wouldn't the Queen want to see her daughter? Why was this guy trying to get rid of her? He obviously knew who she was. "That's why I'm here. To save him."

"Be smart and save yourself," Raftis said, "come with me, and I will insure you get back to your land." He walked past Abby to the doorway where she entered the room to lead her out.

Suddenly, Raftis froze. Abby heard footsteps coming from around the corner, then a voice.

"Raftis, explain to me why..." The Queen froze mid sentence locking her eyes with Abby's. The resemblance was amazing, both Abby and the Queen staring like they were looking at a different aged version of themselves, which they really were. The Queen finally broke the silence, "Raftis...explain."

CHAPTER 29

At about the same time that Abby was entering the castle, Oswyn

was making his way through the streets to the area where Lakota lived.

No one was really sure of which house was his, but Oswyn's spies had

narrowed it down to a specific intersection in the city. Lakota had been

seen in the area often, and they believed one of the houses around this

intersection of streets was his. Oswyn figured he could wait in the area

and hope to catch a glimpse of Lakota and maybe find Princess Abigail.

He arrived at the intersection without a solid plan of what really to

do. He walked up and down the streets a few times, but saw nothing out

of the ordinary. He was able to eliminate a few houses based on the

people who came out of them and went on their way. Finally, Oswyn

tired from his monotonous walk through the area. He stopped on a

corner and just waited. Unbeknownst to him, he was directly in front of

the house where Abby had spent the night.

As much as Oswyn watched, he never noticed that he was also

being watched, by a small mouse hidden in the shadows across the street.

The longer he stayed on the corner, the more agitated the mouse became

until the mouse couldn't take it any longer and morphed into a fly. The fly zipped across the street and landed smack on Oswyn's face. Startled, he took a swipe at it, but the fly was too quick buzzing around his head and attacking Oswyn's left ear. He shook his head and stepped into the street. The fly continued his assault landing on the back of Oswyn's neck, right ear and forehead all in quick succession. Oswyn flailed his arms and shook his head violently, desperately trying to evade the fly. So caught up in the onslaught, Oswyn never noticed the fly land at the base of the door where Oswyn had been standing, change to an ant and scramble under the door and into the house.

Oswyn was still swatting the air for another few seconds before realizing that the menace was gone. He stood in the middle of the intersection, relieved and confused over what just happened. Then, his soldier training took over and he realized the fly could be the Shifter he had been looking for all along. Oswyn replayed the events in his head and realized the fly could be trying to move him away from where he was standing. He quickly took note of the house in his head and moved down the street, away from the area. He situated himself down the street from the house, but at a straight angle that he could not be seen from the door or windows. Then, he waited.

It wasn't long before his hunch was confirmed. The door to the house crept open, and Lakota stepped out searching up and down the street. Oswyn leaned into the shadows unseen. Lakota began walking down the street at a quick pace, right toward Oswyn, who moved deeper into the shadows to a spot where he could no longer see Lakota.

Oswyn's plan was to wait for Lakota to pass and then follow, but that never happened. The wolf was upon so quickly, Oswyn was shocked as he tumbled to the ground.

"Lakota! Please!" was all he could get out before the wolf's jaws closed around his throat.

CHAPTER 30

"My Queen...," Raftis started as Queen Kitane glared at Abby almost certain who she was. Abby's eyes filled up with tears staring at the same eyes she had seen in the mirror countless times. Emotions flowed through her confusion.

The Queen broke the staring competition and yelled at Raftis, "I said explain!"

"We were given word of someone claiming to be the Princess Abigail just a few minutes ago, my Queen. I had her brought here to check if she was an impostor, when you walked in, my Queen. Clearly, she is not the Princess, and I will have her removed immediately."

Abby half heard what he said and turned quickly to glare at Raftis. "Are you serious?" she said. "I have been waiting my whole life to meet my mother, and you're going to deny me."

"Yes," Raftis replied, "Richard admitted himself that the Princess was dead, so you, my dear, are an impostor."

"Thank you, Raftis," the Queen said never looking at Abby. She turned to leave the room.

Abby screamed, "Now I know why my father took me away from you! I know you have him here! Let him go home with me"!

"Raftis, leave us," the Queen commanded as tears streamed down Abby's face. Raftis was gone quickly, and the Queen's whole demeanor changed. "My child," she said, "my long lost child has come home."

Abby was crying but utterly confused, "What?"

"Honey, it was a test. And you passed. You are the Princess, who has come home to her Mommy," she said pulling Abby into her arms and squeezing her as tears welled in her own eyes.

"What?" Abby said still stunned.

The Queen lifted her embrace and Abby could see the tears in her eyes. "There have been a few girls over the years who have come here claiming to be you, " she explained in a loving mother voice. "All of them were seeking power, and when challenged, they all yelled, screamed and carried on about their birthright and heir to the throne. One child even threatened to kill me and take over the kingdom. Yet none of them had your reaction. You are not concerned with the power you have, only with me as your mother and with your father."

"So, you do believe me?" Abby asked.

"Most certainly. I knew who you were when I walked through that door, but I had to be sure. I hope you won't hold it against me."

Abby was really confused now. Two seconds ago, she hated this mean, cold-hearted woman with all her heart, but now, she was so loving and kind that Abby felt bad for yelling at her. She finally managed to say, "I came here for my father...I came to ask you to release him."

"But, my child, he has committed crimes and he must be punished. A Queen cannot just let people commit crimes."

"I understand, but he was just trying to help me," Abby replied.

"Help you?" the Queen said amused, "my child, he kept you from your destiny. You are a Princess and some day, you will be a Queen. What would you be in your world?"

Abby didn't know what to say. She had been told that she could be whatever she wanted from a young age. Her father, her teachers, her friends, just about everyone told her that. She believed them all, until now. In her world, she could never be a queen. She looked at her mother and gave a small smile. The Queen returned the smile and took Abby by the hand.

"Come with me, and I'll show you our kingdom." Abby followed obediently. Any thought of her father had vanished.

CHAPTER 31

Before Oswyn realized it, the wolf was gone and Lakota was standing over him. Oswyn took a second to catch his breath, rubbing his throat in the process and checking his hand for blood; there was none. He tried to find his voice through his tensed up throat, but Lakota spoke first.

"Why are you following me?"

"I...am...Oswyn..."

"I know who you are, I asked why you are following me."

"I was looking for the princess," Oswyn said.

Lakota's eyes narrowed and his fists clenched. "What do you know about her?"

"I know that she was with you. Please tell me that you didn't turn her over to the Queen."

As he said this, Lakota's face changed, and Oswyn saw it, but his words were different than the look Oswyn saw. "I serve the Queen and will do what she wishes."

"Come on, Lakota. I know you don't believe that or think that. Look around, there is no one here except you and I. I was once one of the Queen's men, but now I work for the Fighter's For Alden. We are trying to save the princess and her father. He has already been captured and is sentenced to death. We are trying to save Princess Abigail from the same fate."

Lakota continued to stare at him, and Oswyn felt that he was getting to him. He especially thought he hit a nerve by saying that Abby could be in danger.

"We sent men," he continued, "but you protected her and scared them away. They were dressed as Queen's soldiers, so if you truly worked for her, you could have turned her over then."

That really struck a nerve and Lakota responded, "If you are against the Queen, then I should take you to her now."

"Maybe, but if you wanted to do that, you would have done it by now. We are here for the same reason; to save the princess. I believe we could work together and get that job done."

Oswyn paused waiting for a response, but none came. Lakota just stared at him with the wheels of his mind turning.

"If you take me to her, then we can work together to save her father. I have men on the inside that can help us."

"I can't do that," Lakota replied.

"Lakota, we can do this, but you have to trust me. I know that you like this girl. You chased my men away and were willing to give yourself up for her. She only wants to save her father and go home. We can do this for her."

"I can't."

"Lakota..." but Oswyn was cut off.

"I can't because I don't know where she is," he said rubbing his hands over his face.

"Don't know where she is?"

"No. I left her here last night, but she is gone." Lakota went on to explain how they got into the city, and how he took Abby to his house. Oswyn could tell that he was very attached to this girl. He could also tell that Lakota trusted him enough to tell him all of this.

"You're sure that no one saw you come here with her," Oswyn asked.

"I'm sure. When I left here last night, I stuck around for a while to make sure she was safe. I am positive that no one saw me."

Oswyn could tell that he was sure, but he was more worried about where see could be. "Do you think she went to the castle?"

"She might have. I tried to tell her who she was, but she is all about finding her dad."

"I believe that we have the power to save them both, but I need you to help me. I just need you to get some information."

Lakota just waited to hear the plan.

CHAPTER 32

Courtney paced the halls of the safe house starting to go a little stir crazy. Bryan sat watching her feeling the same way, but trying to save his energy in case it was needed.

"I can't take this any more," Courtney groaned. "We're sitting here doing nothing! I feel like we need to get out there and try to help!"

No one answered her. Bryan just stared at her and Vala went about her business of cooking and cleaning like nothing special was happening. She was by far the calmest person that either of them had ever met. She was so in control at all times with soldiers and messengers coming in and out of the house. Some were there to eat, some to change, and some to deliver messages, but you could never tell from Vala if it was good news or bad. Courtney's ranting meant nothing to Vala, it was like she wasn't even there.

When Courtney realized that her words were getting no response, she stomped over to a chair and heavily plopped down. Bryan almost laughed, but thought better of it.

The outside door whipped open and Oswyn emerged from the light.

Courtney jumped up and ran to him spewing questions so fast, he couldn't keep up.

"Did you find him? What about Abby? Did he hurt her? I swear to God, I'll kill him! Where is she? Did you bring her back?"

"Slow down, child."

"Courtney, let him get a minute's peace, and I'm sure he will tell us everything," Vala said.

"Thank you," Oswyn said as he moved further into the room and sat at the large wooden table. Vala immediately placed a cup in front of him and he took a long draught of the water. This only made Courtney more anxious as she bounced around the room waiting for him to speak. Bryan, on the other hand, never moved. He waited patiently for Oswyn, although, on the inside, he was just as antsy as Courtney.

Finally, Oswyn finished his drink and began to speak. "I was able to find Lakota, by staking out the area where I was told his house was. I had a conversation with him about the Princess Abigail and our search for her. He was just as distraught as us."

"What?" Courtney yelled.

"Yes, I said distraught. He does not know where she is either."

"But he..."

"Oh my God, Court! Will you just shut up and let him talk!" Bryan said breaking his silence and giving Courtney a look she had never seen from him before.

"Lakota told me, that he brought the Princess to his house last night and left her there. He then went off to find out information, presumably about her father. When he returned this morning, she was gone."

"Oh, that's just great!"

"I also think that I convinced him to help us out," he said completely ignoring Courtney now. "Vala, you were right, I think he has a thing for the girl and will try to do what we want," he said smiling.

"But, there is more," Vala said knowingly.

"Yes, when I left Lakota, I went to some contacts and found out that the Princess arrived at the castle this morning and asked to see the Queen. Some people tried to avert her from the Queen, but it was too late. Apparently, they spoke and now the Princess is with her in her chambers."

"Abby will never listen to her! She will do whatever it takes to get her Dad out and get out of there!" Courtney said.

"You do not know the Queen," Vala said, "she is cunning, intelligent and a master of weaving words."

"Abby is smarter than that!"

"Really?" Vala asked, "Is she smarter than her father?"

"No, but Mr. Lane is the smartest person ever!"

"Not smart enough to *not* marry the Queen. He listened to her, fell under her spell and married her all within a month."

"So, Abby has no chance," Bryan said putting his head down and shaking it. "What do we do now?"

"I have some people on the inside who are working for us and will keep an eye on the Princess, but we really need Lakota to come through for us."

"He will," Vala said reassuringly.

CHAPTER 33

Abby was caught in a whirlwind. The Queen led her down the long stone hallways of the castle where decorative tapestries caught the sunlight streaming through high windows. They walked from room to room, each with it's own decor and purpose. There were dining halls and sitting rooms, elaborate meeting rooms and a library full of old dusty books. All of which were created with elaborate stone work that developed an echo throughout as she silently listened to her mother, the Queen, describe each room in detail. The elegance and luxury were beyond her imagination. Yet, it was all so different. She felt as if she had been taken back to Medieval times, where torches hung from wall sconces, crude fireplaces heated rooms, and flowing robes were the clothing of choice. The castle was huge and overwhelming, but nothing could prepare Abby for the throne room.

The Queen stopped their tour in front of large ornate wooden doors guarded by serious stone faced guards and spoke. "And now, my dear, the main room of any castle. The one where you will rule the people some day." She motioned and the guards in unison reached for the large handles and pulled open the huge doors. The room was enormous with large purple banners hanging from the walls and ceiling which arched to a tented roof high above them.

Abby stood motionless, absorbing the power and majesty of the room. She took a deep breath and stepped into the Throne Room. Yet, she could barely see the throne, which was a good hundred yards from the entrance. There was no mistake where she was, though. She strolled down the red carpet with her head constantly moving and seeing something else new in the room. There were six unlit fireplaces on each side of the room with rows of benches near the front of the room reminding Abby of church pews. At the end of the red carpet, there were steps leading up to the gold and purple throne. The high backed chair was adorned with a deep purple seat and backing, which were arrayed with gold and jewels of various colors. A golden scepter lay across the arms of the chair like a golden baseball bat waiting for a batter. Abby paused at the bottom of the steps staring at the massive chair above her.

"Go ahead," the Queen said breaking Abby's trance.

Abby turned and looked at her curiously.

Again the Queen said, "Go ahead," gesturing toward the throne. "Try it out," she continued. "It will be yours some day."

Abby was in awe. She really was a princess and would rule a kingdom some day. She turned and scurried up the polished stone steps fulfilling every little girl's dream in the process. Approaching the chair, she reached out and felt the purple velvet seat with her hand. Satisfied, Abby lifted the golden scepter with her right hand and quickly grabbed it with her left as well. She clearly underestimated the weight of the jeweled object. Steadying herself, she turned and faced the Queen, smiled, and gently sat down on the throne. Surprisingly to her, she found no comfort in the beautiful seat, which reminded her of the huge responsibility that came with sitting there. She remembered the saying, "Heavy is the head that wears the crown," she thought. "And hard is the butt," she added.

Her thoughts were interrupted by the Queen, "You look marvelous on the throne, my child."

Abby looked at her letting the words, "my child" sink in. She was the Queen's child. In a matter of hours, she had gone from a single parent child to the child of a Queen. It was pretty overwhelming, but the thought made her smile and her mother smiled back. Thoughts of her father condemned to death were buried under the thoughts of thrones and crowns.

"Don't get too comfortable though," the Queen said jokingly, "I'm not ready to give it up yet."

"Oh, I don't want it," Abby said hopping up from the throne and skipping back down the steps.

"Then let's go to your chambers," the Queen said with a smile.

"Chambers?"

"Yes, my child, you are a Princess. A Princess has Chambers, and yours have been vacant for a long time."

Abby didn't know what to say. She let the words sink in, 'Princess Chambers'. It was all surreal. She followed the Queen through a door behind the Throne Room and down a long corridor. Again, torched sconces lined the walls with beautiful paintings framed in elaborate gold-leaf. Abby was led through a maze of halls and up a large staircase to the sleeping chambers. The Queen paused to point out large double doors that led to her own chamber, but Abby wasn't taken there. She was led in the opposite direction to another set of double doors draped with a sheer pink cloth. There were soldiers standing guard in pristine brown uniforms, swords at their sides and spears in their hands. Abby noticed how young they looked, not much older than her, but they didn't look very happy either. Their eyes stared straight ahead unblinking, yet wary of the Queen's every move. They were obviously intimidated of her, and she was clearly in charge.

"Gentlemen, Princess Abigail has returned and would like to access her chambers."

Without a word, the soldiers reached and opened the doors in unison revealing the room inside. Abby was speechless, her words lost in the immense beauty of the room. Light billowed through the windows revealing a large sitting area with what looked like beanbags and futons to Abby. They surrounded a large stone fireplace that begged for a fire. On the far side of the room, was a large four post bed draped in pink to match the doors. Abby had slept in king sized beds in hotel rooms, but this made them look like cots. At the foot of the bed was a large tub which was empty, but Abby figured it was for a bath.

She stepped into her room and slowly investigated the area. The place reminded her of a large studio apartment that she had seen in movies. Beyond the bed was a huge, beautifully carved wooden closet. She could have fit all the clothes she owned in that closet with plenty of room to spare. Back, next to the sitting area, there was a table for eating that was large enough for a board meeting and yearning for a feast.

Finally, Abby turned and looked back at the Queen, who remained in the doorway with the guards. She just stared waiting for the Queen to break the silence.

"I will have some of my handmaidens assigned to you this evening. They will attend to your every need," the Queen said.

"But, I don't..."

"Yes you do. You are a Princess and will be treated as such."

Abby knew not to argue with a Queen, especially one that happened to be her mother.

"So, Princess Abigail, I have some business to attend to, and I think you should take some time to rest. The handmaidens will be here shortly with a fine meal. I will check on you later to see how you are how you are fairing."

With that, the Queen exited and left Abby alone in her chambers. She walked over and sat on the bed. It was big, but definitely not comfortable. It seemed to be matted down straw with a bunch of blankets overtop for comfort. At least it was better than sleeping outside on the ground. After a few minutes of gazing around the room, Abby dropped herself back on the bed and stared at the ceiling. So much had happened in the last day that she was happy to have a chance to sort everything out without anyone else around. She had so many questions running through her head. *"Could she really be a Princess? Where was her Dad? Could she save him? Why did he take her away from this life, and her mother who seemed so nice?"* This actually made her angry with her father. *"A girl needs her mother,"* she thought, *"Why would he deny her of that?"* She took a deep breath and remembered her friends. *"Oh my God! I forgot all about them, where are they? Why didn't the Queen mention them? Should I mention them to the Queen? If they were taken by the Queen's soldiers, like Lakota said, then they should be here. Lakota? What happened to Lakota?"* She threw her hands to her head. It was all too much at one time. She felt like her head was going to explode, but she had to do something. She hopped up out of the bed and went quickly to the door. As she was about to open it, there was a knock. She slowly pulled the handle and opened the door. Standing with a pile of clothes and two large basins of water were three beautiful young handmaidens about the same age as Abby.

"Hello, my lady, we were sent by the Queen to wait on your every need. We will begin with a bath."

Abby backed up and let them enter the chambers, but she wasn't sure about taking a bath in front of them. They moved around the room with such ease, filling the tub and motioning Abby toward it. She moved toward the tub, but was unsure about what to do with three strange girls standing there.

"My lady, you may change and enter the bath, and we will wash you," one of the girls said.

"But, I don't even know you, I don't want to get undressed in front of you," Abby replied.

"You may bathe yourself if you like, of course, and we can come back when you are finished."

Abby felt so relieved, "I would rather do that," she said.

"Of course, my lady," the girl said. the others laid out clothes on the bed as the first girl poured something from a bottle into the bath water. Abby could smell the perfume as it hit the warm water. The girls then returned to the door and were let out by the guards.

Abby began to undress placing her clothes and one of the thick cloths close to the tub, so she could reach them quickly if needed. She entered the warm perfumed bath and realized that these people didn't really wash, they just sat in a perfumed tub. She sat in the tub for a few minutes, but the warm water was quickly getting cold. Abby didn't take baths often at home, but when she did, liked to sit and relax for a while before exiting. This was different, she was getting cold and was afraid someone would walk in on her. She hopped out of the tub and dried off quickly. She put her underwear back on before trying on one of the outfits that was left for her. She chose a pale lavender gown which made her feel more like she was going to a wedding than hanging out in her room. She longed for sweatpants and a t-shirt, and would have loved to put her shorts and t-shirt back on, but they were noticeably dirty and would defeat the purpose of taking a bath.

She walked back over and opened the door to find the guards standing at attention with the girls chatting with each other. "You may come back in," Abby said. The girls stared at her for a second in her lavender dress, but proceeded past the guards and into the room where Abby was determined to get to know them.

CHAPTER 34

Sitting in a cell preparing to die was not the nicest way to spend your evening, but Richard didn't really have a choice in the matter. He remembered a movie line from years back, "The anticipation of death is worse than death itself." He hoped it was true. It wasn't dying that bothered him, he felt good about his life and the things he had done. His only reason to try and stay alive was Abby. It always came back to her. What would happen to her if he died? The possibilities were endless because he didn't know where she was. If she was still at home, then his family would surely take care of her and give her a great life, but if she followed his clues and came here, then he was scared. Would Kitane see her as a threat or a daughter? What about the people of Alden? If they despised the Queen as Richard thought, then they may use Abby to gain control and that would put her in mortal danger.

He sat thinking about options, but they evaded him. He could try to beg for his life, but Kitane would take too much pleasure in his death. It would also demonstrate her power to the people. She would prove that she could do the impossible by finding him and executing him, even after all these years. If somehow, Abby had come here and Kitane found her, she would be seen as god-like.

Richard heard the distant lock click and door open as a blast of light filled the hallway and then disappeared. The wall torches gave off a mesmerizing light that flickered throughout the dungeon area. Richard waited for the guard to come with his food, but he passed by him and the now moaning guy across the hall; the Unknown would be first. Waiting patiently for the Unknown to be fed, Richard's thoughts of Abby and dying were dismissed and replaced by the wonder of the Unknown. He hoped for a last dying wish to know who it was and why he was here.

His thoughts were replaced by the sound of the guard returning to Richard with his food. The flickering light showed the plate as it slid through the opening on the bottom of the door. It was basic, a hunk of bread and cheese along with an apple. There would be a jug of water, but that would come later. As the plate slide into Richard's cell, a mouse jumped onto the plate looking for a quick meal. Richard shoed it away with a wave from his hand as the guard finished giving food to the Moaning Neighbor. He was getting used to the food routine and also his furry cellmates that were always looking for some scraps. Usually, the mice went after the plate when Richard was finished eating, which made him leave a few morsels for them. This mouse was stubborn and brave as he jumped back on to the plate and tried to drag the bread away. Richard flicked him off the plate with a swift backhand, but the mouse scurried back to the plate.

"Go away," Richard whispered as the guard exited giving his statement a dual meaning. The mouse jumped away from another backhand and scurried under the door. Richard could see through the flickering light as the mouse, still in the opening at the bottom of the door, looked both directions and hurried back into the cell. Richard smirked thinking that the mouse was checking to see if the guard left before making an all out assault on the plate of food. He followed with his eyes as the mouse ran into a darkened corner of the cell. Richard plopped on the floor with his plate and stuffed a hunk of bread into his mouth. The voice from the mouse's corner almost made him choke.

"Hello, Richard, do not be afraid," it said as a figure emerged from the corner. He was young and shirtless with black hair and knee length pants.

Richard jumped up spitting out the bread and mumbling, "What the..."

"I was sent here with a message for you," he said moving more into the light

"But...how?"

"I am the mouse. My name is Lakota, and I'm a Shapeshifter."

"You're the mouse? What do you mean, you're the mouse?" Then Richard remembered the Shapeshifters. They worked for the King when he was here before, so now they must work for the Queen. *"She sent you,"* he thought.

"I'm also a friend of Abby," Lakota said, which made Richard lose all of the color left in his face and forget that this guy was probably working for the Queen.

"What?" was all he could manage to say.

"I am a friend of your daughter, Abby. I met her on the road while she was looking for you," Lakota said.

"Abby is here?" Richard could feel the tears welling up in his eyes. "Who was she with?"

"She was with me, but..."

"No, when you found her. Who was she with? Did she come here alone?"

"No, she was with a few other people, but they were being

captured, and I rescued her. I didn't know she was the Princess at the time, but..."

"She knows...Oh my God, she knows." Richard dropped to his knees and buried his head in his hands crying.

Lakota didn't know what to do or say, so he just stood and waited for Richard to control himself. His crying made the wailer in the other cell cry out even more than usual.

"She knows, what?" Lakota finally asked.

Richard unburied his head and looked up with tears in his eyes. "She knows that she's a princess. She knows who her mother is. She knows what I did to keep her safe. She knows...everything."

Lakota didn't know what to say again. He just stood as Richard rose from the floor and wiped his tears.

"Abby is not the only one who knows something. I know something too!" his voice was rising now. "I know that the Shifters work for the Queen, that you work for the Queen!" He lunged at Lakota to tackle him, but found nothing but air. Richard stumbled off balance whipping his head around looking for the young man who just stood before him, but he had vanished in the blink of an eye. The movement and Richard's voice made the Wailer howl even louder than before. Richard screamed from his cell, "Shut Up! Shut Up over there!" It must have startled the Wailer because he did just that and went silent.

Richard searched the ground for the mouse, raising his foot to stomp on the slightest movement.

From outside the cell, Lakota watched as Richard did a crazy one-legged war dance around his cell. He finally broke the silence, "I didn't come here for the Queen."

Richard whipped around stomping down his foot to gain balance and stare through the bars.

"I didn't come here for the Queen," Lakota said again.

"But you work for her!" Richard retorted.

"Sort of."

"Sort of? What's that supposed to mean? 'I was sort of sent here to kill you, but I'll be nice about it'"

"No...I... Can I come back in there without you attacking me? I'll explain."

Richard thought for a second. He really didn't have any chance against a guy who could turn into some huge predator a devour him at any second, so he said agreed.

Lakota vanished again and appeared a few seconds later inside the cell.

Richard stood and stared at him still angry, but not really at this kid in front of him, more at his situation.

"Let's sit," Lakota said.

He began by his story of how he met Abby. "I was on a hunt for food when I heard voices in the forest. I came upon a group of men who were dressed as Queen's soldiers, but were not Queen's soldiers. They had all of the right uniforms and equipment, but I shifted a few times to get close enough to hear their conversations. They are a rebel group, who were searching the forest for you."

"Me?"

"Yes, apparently, they have people who are close to the Queen, who are working for them. They knew that you were here and were trying to find you before the Queen got you to the castle. While I was 'with them' a scout came back telling about a group who were moving toward the castle, but were off of the main road and trying to be secretive.

"Abby?" Richard asked.

"Yes and her friends. They set out to find them, and I followed. When they got close, I moved on my own to follow the group myself. I thought they were going to follow them to see where the group was headed, but they descended upon them. Just before they did, Abby separated and went off on her own. I think she had to go to the bathroom.

Richard shook his head and stifled a smile.

"When she was returning is when her friends were captured. I snuck up and took her, before they could. Yes, I was working for the Queen when I did. My goal was to find out who the group was and what they were doing. I did not know that I found the long lost Princess of Alden."

"Who was she with?"

"Two others the same age as her. A boy and a girl."

"Bryan and Courtney."

"Yes, and a man."

"Mike."

"That doesn't sound familiar," Lakota said.

"Pitman?"

"Yes, that's him."

"So, what happened?"

"I led Abby along a parallel path from her friends. I was trying to decide what to do, when through our conversations, I figured out who she was. I then planned on bringing her to the castle and turning her over to the Queen. I mean, I would be a hero."

"You little..." Richard was ready to charge again.

"But I didn't!" Lakota quickly added putting his hands in front of him in case Richard attacked again. "Something changed on the journey."

"Watch what you say about my daughter!" Richard said through clenched teeth.

Lakota looked confused, but continued, "I'm a Shifter. We live very secluded lives. People fear us and shy away from us. We are loners and get used to that life. I spend a lot of time as a wolf, because it keeps people away from me. Then, Abby came along. I didn't want her to know what I was, but she was attacked by some wild dogs and I saved her as a wolf. I had to tell her what I really was. She wasn't happy, saying I lied to her because I didn't tell her. It upset me. I never really cared about anyone before, but I liked having her around and enjoyed her company. Anyway, I vowed in my heart to help her. I led her to the city and had her wait outside, but she got scared and came in on her own. I found her and took her to my house, but she wouldn't wait for me to find out information about you, and I think she came to the castle herself. I'm pretty sure she is now with the Queen."

Richard wasn't used to teenagers pouring their heart out like that. He was still guarded, but his thoughts about Lakota were changing. Either Lakota was genuine and really cared for Abby, or the greatest actor he had ever seen. "So, I'm supposed to believe that a Shifter, who works for the Queen, is here to help a man that the Queen condemned to death?"

"No," he replied, "You're supposed to believe that a friend of your daughter is here to deliver a message to you." Lakota shrugged and gave a slight smile.

Richard couldn't help but believe him. Besides, what other

choice did he have. If Lakota was really there to kill him, he would probably be dead by now. If Lakota planned on killing him, he was sentenced to death anyway. "So, what is this message? If you're here to kill me after telling me all about Abby, I'd be surprised. I still have no where to go. I can't turn into a mouse and slip through the bars, or I would be long gone by now."

"I know, but my message is simple, there is a plan in place to try and save you."

"Try?" Richard asked with a laugh.

"Nothing is for sure, and I am not privy to the plan," Lakota said. "You still could die."

Richard pondered the thought without even knowing the plan. He had come so far and done so much. His life with Abby was wonderful. She had grown into a beautiful and independent young woman. He knew that he made the right choice so many years ago when he removed her from this life and her mother. Yet, he wasn't finished as a father. There was so much more that he wanted to teach her, so many things that she was curious about that he wanted to be there for when she found out the answers. He wanted to be there for so much more of her life; he needed to be there.

He looked thoughtfully at Lakota. "An hour ago, I was prepared to die. I knew that Abby was well prepared to live her life to the fullest. I had a great life and was ready to go. Then, you showed up. You told me about Abby, and I know that I'm not done. I want so much more from life. There are too many things that I need to do...need to know. What do I have to do?"

"Honestly, I don't know. I was sent here because they knew I could get here to talk to you."

"Who is 'they'?"

"Oh, yeah, the people that took Abby's friends. There is a man named Oswyn."

"Oswyn? I know an Oswyn. He worked for the King."

"Yes. He used to."

"Used to?"

"Yes. When the King died, Oswyn retired. Some say the Queen forced him to leave, but he is still very well respected among the soldiers and the people the Queen employs."

"So, he sent you."

"Yes, well his group did. They are called the FFA, Fighters For Alden. Their leader is a man named Griffin. It's funny actually, the Queen knows about the group, but she doesn't see them as a real threat to her. I have heard her say that they're disorganized and 'just a bunch of fools seeking power."

"So, what do you know?"

"I know nothing, just to tell you that there is a plan for your escape and they are working on it and the are trying to help you. I'm pretty sure that Oswyn has some informants here inside the castle, but I don't know who they are. I believe he sent me just to let you know that there is some hope and you have people working for you."

"What about you?"

"What do mean?'

"Why aren't you part of the plan, I mean, you were able to get in here, maybe, you could get me out."

"I wondered why they didn't ask for my help, but figure that they don't totally trust me because I do work for the Queen. If they told me the plan and I went to her, it would be over and you would be dead. Pretty smart actually." Lakota shrugged.

"So?" Richard asked.

"So, what?"

"So, are you going to the Queen?"

"Do you think I am?"

"No, I don't think you care about me, but the way you spoke about Abby, tells me that you respect her and will not tell that there's a plan."

"I won't tell."

Richard liked this kid. Many teenagers would be offended that they were being used without knowing the plan, but Lakota seemed to understand and respect the reservations that this FFA group has about him. "Thank you," Richard replied.

A smile came to Richard's face and Lakota looked at him a little confused.

"What?" Lakota asked

"Can you use your unique talents to do something for me?"

"I am not here to try and save you," Lakota replied.

"I know; this is something else."

Lakota looked at Richard strangely. The man in front of him was condemned to die and he was not asking for help to be saved. It confused Lakota and showed on his face.

"What could you possibly want?" he finally asked.

"I want you to find out who the prisoner is in the cell at the end of the hall." Richard smiled. If he was going to die, he would at least know the Queen's secret.

"That's it? That's what you want?" Lakota asked confused.

"Yes." Richard explained the process the guards go through and how secretive everything about the cell was. In the back of his mind, he hoped that knowing who was in there might help him in his own situation or at least hurt the Queen.

"Ok, I'll be right back." Before Lakota changed the door for the guards was unlatched and someone was coming into the dungeon. Lakota looked at Richard wide eyed and vanished. Richard caught the faint glimpse of a mouse scurrying under the door. The guards made their toward the cells. The moaner began again, while Richard sat back in the corner of his cell listening.

"When ya come down 'ere, ya always gots ta be ready for da smell. One never gets used ta da smell." the lead guard said.

Richard figured that they were training a new guard. He listened as they walked by his cell and the Unknown Prisoner was explained. They started back toward the entrance door.

"Well, dat's it. Ya won't have ta worry about da last cell fer a while. We won't let ya go in der fer a couple weeks and dis one ere'll be dead tamarra," he said pointing toward Richard's cell.

"Ahh!" the second man yelled jumping. "What was that?"

"Jusa mouse," the lead guard said laughing. "Der all ova the place. Ya gotta get usta em," he finished as they opened the door out of the dungeon.

The mouse scurried under Richard's door and exploded into Lakota. He was white as a ghost and his chest was heaving.

"I didn't think changing took that much out of you," Richard said.

"Not...the change...," Lakota said gasping, "the prisoner."

"Who is it?" Richard asked anxiously.

"The...prisoner...is the King!"

CHAPTER 35

"I can't stay cooped up here any longer. I have to get out of here."

"I understand," Oswyn said without looking in Courtney's direction.

"No, you don't! I have to get out of here! I have to go do something!" Courtney said getting louder. "I can't sit here any more!"

"She's right," Vala said startling Oswyn who's head jerked up.

"What?" he said.

"She's right. They should get out of here and take a walk."

"Yea...." Courtney was cut off by the hand of Bryan grabbing her arm to make her shut up. She looked at him, but he just shook his head telling her to shut up and let Vala talk for them.

"Take a walk? Are you crazy?" Oswyn said.

"Courtney, Bryan, please go to another room for a minute," Vala commanded.

Bryan grabbed her arm and couldn't leave fast enough. When they got into the other room, Courtney ripped her arm away.

"Would you please stop grabbing my arm!"

"Sorry, but I was afraid you were going to say something else."

"I don't have to say anything now, Vala's going to win this battle."

Courtney was right. Not two minutes passed and the door open to let the kids back into the room. Vala had a small smile on her face as she pointed toward Oswyn. The kids moved toward him noticing that he was drawing a map for them on some parchment. It was a very crude drawing which showed streets and only a few buildings. After a few minutes, Oswyn looked up.

"I'm not sure about this, but Vala trusts that you will be ok. I'm sending you to see if you can find Lakota."

"Lakota?" Bryan asked shocked.

"Yes, I believe, well, Vala believes that Abby must have talked to him about her friends, and that he won't hurt you."

"I also believe that if Oswyn didn't convince him to help us find out some information, then you two might," Vala said.

Bryan was still shocked. He knew that Lakota helped Abby, but he also knew that the guy was a Shifter who could change into a wolf or a bear and devour them both without even a fight. Suddenly, 'taking a walk' seemed like a bad idea. Courtney on the other hand was eager to go. She listened intently as Oswyn explained the route to Lakota's house. She couldn't wait to get out of there.

"Finally, and this is the most important thing," Oswyn said, "we have many people working for the FFA all over the city and even in the castle. They will not stand out to you, nor will you know who to look for. If you need help or if someone is an FFA member they will recognize this greeting, 'Best of the day to you'. Most people say 'Good Morning' or 'Good Day' and FFA people do too, but if we need to speak to each other privately or need some help, we say 'Best of the day to you'. An FFA member will recognize it and help you. So, if someone speaks to you and you are fine, then say 'Good Day', but if you need help or someone needs you, it's 'Best of the day to you'."

"Ok," they both said in unison.

"By the way," Vala said, "you must stay together at all times. Don't be afraid to turn around and come back. I think it will do you good to get out and see the city a little. It's much better than being cooped up in here all the time. Also, if you see that Pitman guy, feel free to punch him in the face," she said with a laugh.

"You can count on it!" Courtney said with a smile.

They gathered the map and prepared themselves to go to Lakota's house. As they stepped out into the late morning, Oswyn whispered to Vala, "I hope you're right."

Bryan and Courtney set out into the sunlight to find Lakota. The map was pretty easy to follow, but the city was way more challenging than they expected. Courtney and Bryan both grew up in a city, so they were used to crowds of people trying to hustle and bustle from one place to another. They understood how to navigate the movement of crowds and the way city streets worked and how a person had to make it look like they belonged or they would get run over. The streets of Philadelphia had trained them for this adventure. They had Mr. Lane to thank for their many excursions into downtown Philadelphia to museums and historical sites, which prepared them for living in a city. Yet, they were not prepared for the ancient and almost primitive ways of the people of Alden. There were no cars, but the horse drawn carts filled in for them carrying goods to markets and shops. People moved fluidly through the streets, each on their own private mission to get somewhere and get there fast. The problem was that Courtney and Bryan could not stop looking at everyone and their strange outfits and mannerisms. It didn't take long for them to be off course from the map and stuck in the flow of people.

"We need to turn right up here at the next street," Courtney said to a nodding Bryan who was thinking the same thing. They used the turn to regroup and move to the side of the road next to a building that was not an open air store front.

"This place is crazy," Bryan said, "There's so many people. I didn't think the city was that big."

"It's not, look," Courtney said pointing down the street where they turned. Bryan immediately noticed the lack of people. He then turned to look at the street they were just on and realized it was the main street that everyone used. The other streets were almost deserted compared to the one they just left.

"Whew, Thank God for that. I felt like we were in a parade! We should use the map, but stick to side streets to get around."

"Absolutely!" Courtney agreed.

They quickly referred to the map and noticed that they were only a few streets off from where they wanted to be, but they also noticed people looking at them kind of strangely.

"This city isn't big enough to need a map," Bryan whispered.

"Yeah, let's keep moving," Courtney replied.

They did find out that the people here were pretty friendly saying "Good Morning" to most of the people in passing. They listened intently to the greetings to pick up on the FFA code, but didn't hear it from anyone. Finally, after a few minutes, they made it to the intersection where Lakota's house was located. There were people moving freely around the streets, but no one coming or going to the house that was their target.

"Well, we might as well knock," Courtney said as they moved toward the door.

She knocked hard on the door.

"Oh my God Court, you knock like you're trying to bust down the door."

"Sorry, it's the way I knock! I want to be heard!"

There was no answer. She knocked again, making Bryan cringe.

After a minute or so, there was still no answer. Courtney was about to knock a third time when a man appeared behind them almost out of thin air.

"Can I help you?" he asked. Courtney and Bryan were both startled. They didn't know what Lakota looked like, but were pretty sure this man was too old to be him. He was very large and dressed in large worn out boots and gray pants. His shirt was baggy with a short rope tie at the neck which was untied. It reminded Bryan of a large hockey jersey, but didn't hide the man's muscular frame. His shoulder length gray and black hair and beard made him resemble a hairy dog.

"We're looking for a friend," Courtney finally replied.

"What's your friend's name?" the man asked in an extremely deep voice.

"La..."

"Lawrence!" Bryan blurted out cutting Courtney off.

"Yes, our friend Lawrence lives here," she agreed.

"I think you have the wrong house," the man said, "No Lawrence lives here."

Thinking they were in trouble, Courtney responded with the code, "Well, best of the day to you, then," she said looking at the man for a reaction. There was none. He just stared at her.

As the man opened his mouth to say something, a passer by grabbed Courtney by the arm, saying, "Best of the day to you, old friend. I've been looking for you, hurry or we'll be late for the meeting."

Bryan and Courtney were quick to react and go with the new stranger and leave the first man standing by the door alone and bewildered.

They walked quickly with the man putting full trust in the "Best of the day" code. They also continued to glance behind them to keep an eye on the man they just left.

"Forget him. Let's go!" the man commanded. they followed him toward the main street they were trying to avoid. Bryan stole one more quick glance back at Lakota's house, but the first man was gone. There was no sign of him anywhere.

"Where did that guy go?"

"I said forget him! We need to move, now!"

Something in his voice made them go faster, but they still didn't know quite where they were going. After a few blocks, the main street was just in front of them when Courtney abruptly stopped.

"Ok, dude, I don't know who you are, but I'm not going into that mob of people with some guy who I don't know," she said.

"Yeah, thanks, but we only said the code to..." Bryan was cut off.

"Shut up! I know why!"

For the first time, Courtney got a good look at him. He was probably in his early twenties with short brown hair and a bit of scruff on his face. His hazel eyes were kind, but demanding and he was dressed like everyone else in the city. Probably to fit in, she figured. "Ok, so who are you?" she finally asked.

He looked around briefly, then answered. "My name is Chase, and I was sent by a friend to follow you in case you got in trouble, which you did."

"Chase? Seriously? A guy named Chase was sent to chase us?" Courtney said with a laugh.

"Yes, and you couldn't say my real name anyway."

"Real name?" Bryan asked.

"Yes, it's Chastanootcin."

"Ok, Chase," Courtney said, "Where are we going?"

"I'm taking you back to Vala. There is news, and you have to get back quickly."

"About Abby?" Courtney jumped.

"Will you please stop talking? That Shifter is probably listening," Chase whispered.

"Shifter?" Bryan asked, "That's who we were looking for!"

"Not that one! That was Kuruk. He's known as the bear, and he's not to be messed with. He may also be a fly buzzing around right now listening to us, so let's go, and stay close to me."

There was no more time for discussion, since Chase was moving again. They noticed that everyone on the main street was moving in the same direction to the left. They joined the crowd and moved with them steadily. Bryan felt like one of those plastic ducks that little kids pick in the carnival game, just moving along with the flow of those around him.

After a few blocks they began to recognize their surroundings. Chase led them to the right side of the street so they could be plucked out of the duck pond by Vala who was waiting by the safe house.

"What's going on?" Courtney asked as they were quickly wisped inside.

"Give me a minute and we'll explain," Vala calmly answered.

They got inside and Vala led them to the small meeting room where they had first met with Griffin. As they sat, Courtney started, "Ok, so what's...," but she was quickly cut off by Vala.

"He's first," she said pointing to Chase, who had followed them into the room.

"I'm not sure if we were followed or not, I tried to cover, but it was Kuruk. He didn't seem that interested in us. Probably thought they were some lost kids, whose friend played a prank on them and gave them the wrong address. If he wanted to follow, we would have no real chance to get away from a Shifter."

Vala nodded her head in agreement hoping Chase was right, and Kuruk didn't give them a second thought. "Thank you, Chase. I think Oswyn wanted you for another job."

"Ok," he said turning to Courtney and Bryan as he stood to leave. "It was nice to meet you. If you see me around, do not attempt to speak to me unless I speak to you first. I am always around and will keep an eye on you. Good day."

"Is that dude serious?" Courtney said, which made Bryan laugh.

"That... dude, just saved your life from a very dangerous Shifter named Kuruk. He is dead serious, and you would be too without him," Vala said making Bryan laugh again at the way she said "dude". A quick look from her made him stop abruptly.

Courtney seized the moment, "Can you tell us now?"

"Yes. As you saw the city is bustling with people going to the castle. Soon after you left, a Crier came through the street saying that the Queen is supposed to make some sort of announcement when the bridge is full."

"What's that mean?"

"The castle is surrounded by a moat that is more like a lake. The bridge is long and fairly wide, which means most of the city has to be there to fill it. She will probably come out on a boat to speak to the people on the bridge.

"What's the message?" Bryan asked.

"That's the problem," Vala said, "We don't know. There is some speculation, but nothing is for sure. We are pretty sure that she didn't move up tomorrow's execution of Richard."

"Thank God for that, but we have only another day," Courtney said.

"Or it could be worse. Maybe Lakota got caught helping us or Abby, or he told on us, or something will be said about Abby, or Abby said something about you two and she is warning people to look for you."

"Oh no," Courtney said, her face dropping.

"Honestly, I don't think it's that, but you cold be in danger, so we're giving you a choice."

"Choice?" Bryan asked.

"Yes, you can stay here and be protected for a while or you can come with me to hear what the Queen has to say. Just know that if it's about you, we might have a huge problem."

Courtney looked at Bryan and immediately knew the answer.

"We want to come."

CHAPTER 36

"The King? What do you mean, the King?"

"I mean, The King!" Lakota said a little too loudly. "The prisoner in that cell is King Tammany!"

"But, he's..."

"Yeah, he's dead. But I just saw him sitting in a nice chair reading a book. I promise you, he is very much a live!"

"But that's..."

"Impossible? Yeah I thought so too. I swear to you that King Tammany is alive, and the Queen has him jailed and hidden here in the dungeon."

"It does make sense of why no one can see the prisoner. Could you go back and talk to him?"

Before he could answer, the guard door flung open with a thud. Lakota looked at Richard and vanished into a mouse scurrying under the door.

"We hafta hurry!" the guard said jogging down the hall right past the unseen mouse zipping out the door to freedom. "She wants 'em by da dock as fast as possible."

They made it to Richard's cell and yelled, "Put yer 'ands on da wall!"

Richard complied without a question and the guards quickly entered the cell. One shackled his feet while the other ripped his hands down from the wall and chained them in front of him.

"Now, we're leavin', so no funny stuff before the execution!"

"That's tomorrow," Richard said jolting his head toward the lead guard.

"Ya never know now do ya," was the reply.

Richard didn't answer, but hoped the plan Lakota talked about was in place to work today, just in case. All these thoughts crossed his mind as he was led from the dungeon and through the castle. They finally emerged at a small dock situated at the back of the castle. Richard was loaded into a small boat with the two guards and a large man seated in the rowing position. As soon as Richard sat down, the rope was lifted and they pushed away from the dock. The large man rowed in silence with strong strokes that moved them quickly across the calm waters of the lake surrounding the castle. Richard was happy to be outside, but after being in the dungeon for so many days, he couldn't see much. Richard spent most of his time in the boat shielding his eyes from the unyielding sun hoping that his eyes would adjust. He felt the gentle movement of the small boat as they glided easily through the calm still waters of the lake. Richard began to see the bottom of the boat more clearly as his eyes remembered how to see in the bright light. He slowly raised his head to the large stone bridge looming in front of him. He could see the people from the city jammed on the bridge, but Richard could only see the backs of their heads. They were all facing the other side of the bridge.

"She doesn't want me to be seen," he thought. Realizing that the Queen had some sort of surprise for the people. He was hoping that the surprise wasn't his execution. They rowed without detection from the throngs of people on the bridge who were mesmerized and laughing loudly at a show going on in front of them. Richard's boat moved under one of the large stone arches supporting the bridge. One of the guards took the rope he had been holding and looped it around a hook protruding from the side of the arch. *"She wants me to see this, but not been seen?"* Richard hoped. He realized his execution could be the main

part of this little show that was going on in front of him.

On the other side of the bridge, there was a large rectangular wooden dock which was the main attraction at the moment. There were many things going on all at once. Two men were juggling balls and shiny metal rings, while acrobats were tumbling across the long dock. They took turns going back and forth flipping and twirling through the air, while the main attraction was a group of dwarves who were mimicking the other performers and completely messing up to the delight of the crowd. Even the one guard started to laugh before he was stifled by the rower with a look of contempt.

Suddenly, a hush came over the crowd and the performers began to notice. They stopped their performance and stared with the others as a large boat came into view from around the castle in front of them. The boat was much bigger than Richard's with five oars protruding from each side. Richard thought it looked like an old Viking boat, but there was no mast for a sail just the man power of the rowers. He could see the Queen come into view as the boat came closer. She was perched at a rail in the front center of the boat looking like Captain Hook coming for the slaughter. The gallows loomed from the bridge making Richard cringe at the thought of being tossed in the lake to drown.

The Queen's boat approached the dock and the rowers pulled the oars inside the boat. The performers grabbed ropes thrown from the boat and tied the boat down, they then disappeared onto the back of the Queen's boat. The Queen descended onto the dock with all of the pageantry that Richard expected from her and her large ego. Soldiers surrounded the dock with the Queen alone in the middle of the dock. She began to address the crowd.

"Citizens of Alden, for many years, I have had a heavy heart," she began loudly. The crowd was so deadly silent that she was easily heard. "My former husband, Richard, who I have found and is now condemned to death had kidnapped my daughter, your Princess Abigail. He will pay for that crime tomorrow at the bottom of this lake! I had set a goal to avenge her disappearance and your Queen always accomplishes her goals. In capturing Richard, I hoped to find out about Princess Abigail. Richard told us that she was dead, but we all know that Richard cannot be trusted."

Richard lowered his head in the boat knowing that the Queen was making sure the people were totally against him before the execution. She wanted no sympathy for him. He also knew that everything he did and said about Abby was for her own good. He would not apologize for anything.

"Through his fickle words I have found out about Princess Abigail. I, your Queen, has found that Princess Abigail is alive."

For the first time, a sound besides the Queen was heard. The gasp from the crowd was so loud that Richard felt the air being sucked away. Then, the murmurs started and grew into a crescendo so loud that a soldier had to bang his spear on the dock many times to get their attention again.

"Yes," she continued, "I felt the same way when I found out. I sent men far and wide searching for her, but then, when I felt all hope was lost, Princess Abigail returned home!"

Another gasp from the crowd and Richard felt his stomach drop. *"This can't be happening,"* he thought. There was more spear banging from the soldiers and the crowd was attentive again.

"Ladies and Gentlemen of Alden, I present to you, my long lost daughter, your Princess Abigail!" The Queen extended her arm toward her boat and a hush fell over the crowd.

Richard gazed intently at the Queen's boat. He knew it wasn't a bluff and hoped Abby had not fallen under her spell. Yet, he knew how compelling the Queen was, *"For God's sake, I married her!"* he thought shaking his head.

The tears welled up in his eyes when he saw her. Abby emerged from below deck on the boat. She wore a pale lavender dress that was stunning. To Richard, it looked like a prom gown, which he thought was a few years away for her. Richard wanted to scream her name to let her know he was there, but the Queen had placed him in such a way that it would be very difficult for her to see him. Also, the roar of the crowd on the bridge was too much for him to overcome. Plus, Richard feared that yelling might make the soldiers throw him out of the boat. The shackles would be too much to overcome, and he would surely drown. He had to settle for watching Abby walk onto the dock with a cheering crowd as she took her place next to her mother, the Queen. Richard wanted to vomit.

From high above on the bridge, the crowd cheered their princess, while Bryan and Courtney stood in stunned silence with Vala. It was one thing to hear their friend Abby being called a princess, but a whole other feeling to see her actually as a princess. Although they were standing toward the end of the bridge closest to the city, Bryan stood awestruck at the sight of Abby in her beautiful dress.

Courtney had other ideas and began yelling, "ABBY!"

She was quickly stifled by Vala who grabbed her by the arm and yanked her away from the crowd. "Are you crazy?" she said sternly right in Courtney's face. Courtney was so stunned that she couldn't even answer. Vala continued speaking low enough so only Courtney could hear, but brash enough for her to understand, "These people see a long lost princess that they haven't seen since she was a baby. They see an evil father that kidnapped her and took her from them. If they think you know her, then you are an accomplice and will die with Richard! Do you understand?"

Courtney just stared at her trying to process the loss of her friend.

"Do you understand?" Vala said again.

Courtney could only nod, apparently afraid to say anything.

Bryan finally got their attention back to the proceedings at hand. "Look," he said pointing to Abby, "I think she's going to speak."

Abby looked around at the crowd, waving randomly like a special guest in a parade. Finally, the Queen raised her hands and the soldiers banged their spears for silence. It was silent within seconds, when someone yelled, "Long live Princess Abigail!" and the whole crowd started yelling again.

After a few minutes of this the Queen finally got her chance to speak. "Citizens of Alden, your Princess has returned. Although she would like to speak with each and every one of you, she has endured a perilous journey and needs her rest. Over the coming days and weeks, she will be sure to get to know all of you."

With that Abby was gone. Whisked away by the Queen to the protection of her boat. The crowd began to disperse with a lot of chatter about the Princess's return. Courtney, Bryan, and Vala were a few of the first to get out of there and back to the safe house.

When the crowd was gone and the bridge was empty, a small boat undocked from under the bridge and silently made its way around the far side of the castle; unspotted by all.

CHAPTER 37

Courtney and Bryan return to the safe house with Vala. Immediately after they closed the door, Vala turned to Courtney, but she didn't have to say anything to her.

"I'm sorry," Courtney said lowering her head, "I understand and knew I should have kept quiet, but when I saw her, I felt like I had to call out to her. It was like she was under a spell or something that needed to be broken."

"You're right," Vala replied, "the Queen does have her under her 'spell' as you call it. The Queen is very manipulative and the Princess is a young girl, who has never met her mother. I'm sure she's quite impressionable."

"What do you mean?" Bryan asked.

"Do you have a mother?" Vala asked.

"Yes?" Bryan said questioningly.

"Well, imagine if you didn't and never did. Suddenly, one day you meet a woman and find out that she's your mother who you were taken away from. You would be so excited and happy to finally have met her wouldn't you?"

"Yeah."

"Now, take that person who is your new mother and make her a Queen, who can give you everything you ever wanted and make you a real life princess. Suddenly, you'll forget all about your old life and be sucked into royalty."

"I know that I would," Courtney said dejectedly. "We have to do something about this."

A stern knock on the door made them all jump. Courtney and Bryan looked at Vala, who put her finger up to her lip to tell them to be quiet. She called away from the door so as to sound further away, "Give me a minute!" She quickly pointed to a room on the side and ushered the kids in, closing the door behind them.

Another knock followed, but Vala quickly opened the door revealing the source of the knock to be a young man.

"My name is Lakota," he said, "is Oswyn here?"

Courtney heard the name through the door and cracked it open enough to see the guy they had been looking for. She took a good look and quietly closed the door again.

"He's hot!" she whispered to Bryan, who simply scrunched up his face and rolled his eyes. "And he wants Oswyn," she continued.

Before Vala could answer Lakota, Oswyn was walking up the steps to enter the safe house.

"Hello, Lakota," Oswyn said. "How did you find us?"

"I am the sneakiest person you know", he said smiling.

Oswyn smiled back, "Come in." He led Lakota toward the room in the back where Courtney, Bryan, and Pitman were taken when the first arrived, but before they got there Lakota stopped.

"Can I meet Abby's friends?" Lakota asked.

Oswyn looked at Vala, who gave a simple, "Yes."

Courtney was out the door before she finished the word. "Hi, I'm Courtney," she said rushing toward Lakota with her hand outstretched.

Lakota actually took a step back before taking her hand and shaking it. Courtney was in heaven for that split second. She smiled and said, "I'm so happy to meet you. Oh, and this is Bryan." He was trailing behind her, but caught up to shake Lakota's hand.

"Hi," Bryan said.

"Abby told me a lot about you two. I saw you come in here and wanted to meet you."

"What can we do for you?" Oswyn asked.

"I did what you asked. I talked to Richard."

"You talked to Mr. Lane?" Courtney jumped back into the conversation.

"Courtney!" Vala said staring her down again about controlling her mouth.

"Sorry," she replied putting her head down.

"If Mr. Lane is Richard, then yes, I spoke to him," Lakota said making her feel a little better.

"How's he doing?" Bryan asked.

"Let's take this into the back room," Oswyn said leading them out of the front hall.

When they got to the meeting room, Griffin was already there seated. He didn't seem surprised when they entered, probably having already been informed of Lakota's arrival.

"Please, everyone, have a seat," he said.

They all took seats around the table with Courtney quickly and strategically sitting next to Lakota with a sly smile. When they were all seated, everyone looked at Lakota to speak.

"I went to the dungeon and spoke to Richard. He is in better spirits than I thought he would be, but is still worried."

"Understandable," Griffin said.

"He is happy that there is a plan, but seemed more worried about Abby's safety than his own. I admire that. Therefore, I want to help. I believe that my skills can be very useful to try and save him and Abby."

"You want to help?" Griffin asked.

"Yes and no offense to your plan, but I think you need me."

Oswyn smiled. "But, you work for the Queen. Why would you help us?"

"Actually, the Shifters work for the Queen and the King before that. I was born a Shifter. No one ever asked me if I wanted to work for the Crown. It was assumed. Now, I know enough to make my own decisions." Lakota stood up from his chair and began pacing around the others. Thoughts racing through his head. "I don't know what I believe anymore. Maybe, I believe the Queen is not the rightful heir to the throne. Maybe after what I saw today and my talk with Richard, I believe the Queen will execute Richard and then Abby. Maybe, I just like a girl and want to help her. Maybe, I believe all of these things and want the Queen overthrown. I don't know, but I do know that she will not share her power with anyone. This makes me scared for Abby." He sat back down waiting for some sort of response, but happy that he was able to express how he felt.

They all stared at him. Vala breaking the silence, "I love a young man that can make his own decisions."

"Welcome to helping us," Griffin smiled.

"Now, I want to hear your plan," Oswyn said, "I'm sure it's better than ours."

CHAPTER 38

For the first time, Richard could not wait to get back into his cell and be alone. The guards led him there and unshackled his feet and hands. Richard sat in the corner of his cell and sobbed. The sight of Abby was too much for him. Hearing that she was there and with the Queen was one thing, but actually seeing her as a princess was an entirely different feeling.

The Queen had done it again. She had someone under her spell. Many years ago, it was Richard himself that was the one mesmerized by the Queen. Today, it was his daughter, Abby. He longed to switch places with her and take the brunt of the Queen's wrath. He couldn't get the image of Abby in her lavender dress out of his head. She looked so beautiful as a Princess. Richard also knew that being a princess was every girl's dream and that Queen Kitane would use that to her advantage.

The Moaner must have heard Richard's sobs, and he began his antics, breaking Richard of his thoughts. Richard couldn't take it any longer, he jumped up, slammed his fists against the door of his cell and screamed, "SHUT UP! I swear to God, if I get my hands on you I'll rip your moaning throat out!"

The moaning stopped immediately, but Richard didn't know if it was because of him or the dungeon door latch beginning to open. *"Great,"* he thought, *"I should have kept my big mouth shut."* He heard the door opening and the footsteps on the stone floor. There were more steps than usual, and Richard prepared himself for the Queen. He had to keep his composure or he would be dead in a few minutes. He was sure an attack on the Queen would mean immediate death. Richard took a few deep breathes to calm him down before the arrival. The steps got closer and Richard closed his eyes to breathe deeply. He didn't care what she did to him, but now that she had her claws into Abby, he was furious. Another breath and the footsteps stopped outside his cell. He opened his eyes to see shadows under his door. Richard prepared himself with another breath.

Suddenly the footsteps started again, but they moved back toward the dungeon entrance. Richard looked confused, but noticed there was still a shadow under his door.

"Oh my God, is she going to meet me alone?" he thought. *"There's no way. I really might hurt her."* thoughts raced through his head as the dungeon door closed and the footsteps were gone. Richard

waited. Finally, after a good minute, the lock on his door turned and the door pushed open. Standing in front of him in the flickering torchlight was Raftis, the Queen's right hand man. He was alone in a long flowing green robe.

"Hello Richard."

"Raftis? I thought..."

"You thought the Queen was here to see you. No, it's me," Raftis interrupted. "I have come to ask you what you want for your last meal."

"For my last meal?" Richard asked.

"Yes, it is customary for those about to be executed to have a final meal of their choosing."

"You couldn't give me the meal I want," Richard said.

"We could try."

"Ok, I want a Philly Cheese Steak with some fries and a Dr. Pepper," Richard laughed at the look on Raftis' face. "I know you can't do that, so I'll take whatever you want to give me."

Raftis looked at Richard with curiosity. How could a man who was about to die be making jokes?

Richard wasn't making jokes. His anger for the Queen had made him sarcastic. He finally broke the silence and became very serious, "Why did you send the guards away?"

Raftis again looked curiously at Richard, but then smiled. "I have some questions for you."

"Raftis, we were friends. I can never repay you for the help you gave me."

"Keep your voice down," Raftis answered looking concerned.

"I can't thank you enough for the life you have given Abby and me, but I have to ask for your help again," Richard said.

Raftis lowered and shook his head. "That's my question, "he said looking Richard in the eye, "Why is Princess Abigail here? Those soldiers only returned with you. How did she get here?"

Now Richard was the one to lower his head. "Many years ago," he began, "I was afraid for my life. After I left here, with your help of course, I took Abby and began our lives as a father and daughter. I was always afraid that someone would come to find me, but was sure I had the only key to 'my world'. I gave the field journal and key which led me here to a good friend of mine that I rarely see. I told him to bury it somewhere and not give it to anyone unless Abby or I went missing."

"You gave it to Pitman," Raftis said knowingly.

Richard looked confused. "How would you know that..."

"He was here..."

"What?"

"He was here. He used the book and the key to come here. He was treated like a celebrity by the people, the Queen found out and captured him. He was allowed to travel back to your world when the Queen replicated the key and replaced it in your book. She used your key to have Pitman lead the soldiers to you."

"What the ...?" Richard stifled himself before ending his question. He continuously shook his head repeating, "Oh my God!" over and over.

"If it makes you feel better, I don't think he knew what he was getting himself into by coming here," Raftis said. "He just seemed curious, then was in fear of his life, that's why he gave you up."

"I can't believe he used the book," Richard said.

"There's still my question of the Princess."

"So, I was in fear that someone would find me. I set up clues around my house to contact Pitman. When I was taken, I purposely knocked over a bedroom lamp that had 'Call Mike Pitman' written on the bottom. I wanted Pitman to know I was gone and the book was needed. Little did I know that he was the reason I was captured. Abby must have gotten my clue and called him. He must have shown Abby the door to get here."

"You call this Pitman guy a friend?"

"He used to be at least."

"Richard, I must be going. I'm sorry I couldn't keep them away from you. I will make sure your meal is well prepared," Raftis said stepping out of the cell.

"Raftis, wait. I need your help again," Richard pleaded.

"Richard, I..."

"Not for me. I need you to save Abby. She will kill her or jail her as soon as I'm dead. I know it," he pleaded even more. Tears welling up in his eyes. "The cell down the hall..."

"What?" Raftis asked.

"The cell down the hall that no one can go into or know who's in there," he said quickly and almost frantically.

"What about it?"

"I believe the unknown prisoner is King Tammany." He said it. Looking for a reaction from Raftis, but needing to get it off his chest. Raftis looked confused making Richard feel that he didn't know.

"You've been in here too long. You're losing your mind. The King has been dead for years," Raftis said beginning to leave.

"Ok, but I need two things from you. Please help Abby escape. She doesn't deserve any of this. I don't care about me; I just want her to be safe."

"Most people in your position beg for their life, but you beg for your daughter. You're a true father," Raftis shook his head and smiled. "I promise you that I will try," Raftis said closing the cell door.

"And," Richard continued through the door as Raftis left, "Check out that prisoner. I bet you never saw the King's body after he died."

Richard couldn't see Raftis' face, but could tell by the pause in his walk that he was right about not seeing the body. He heard the dungeon door close and dropped his head with a sigh. Richard turned to go sit back in the corner of his cell. It had been an exhausting day, and he was actually looking forward to relaxing a little. That would not be the case.

"Hello, Richard," came the voice making Richard jump backwards into the cell door.

Lakota emerged from the shadows in the back of the cell with a smile of satisfaction on his face for scaring Richard.

"My God! Stop doing that! You're going to give me a heart attack before they kill me!"

Lakota laughed. "Thank you," he said.

"For what?" Richard said doubled over trying to catch his breathe and relax his quickly beating heart.

"For caring about people. I decided to help you before I heard you ask for Abby's safety, because I thought you were a good person. I heard what you said and you proved it. Also, you didn't say how you found out about the prisoner, which protects me. So, Thank you."

"How much did you hear?"

"I came in when Raftis did." Lakota tried to stop himself there, but he couldn't stop himself from asking questions after what he just heard. "Raftis helped you escape all those years ago? I thought he was loyal to the Queen? Do you think he'll help Abby?"

"Slow down," Richard said with a chuckle. "The answer to all three questions is 'Yes'."

"How could he help, but be loyal to the Queen?" Lakota asked, "That doesn't make sense."

"There are a few things you don't know about Raftis. First, he has been around the Queen for a long time. He secretly loves her."

"What?"

"We became friends when he realized that I wanted out of my relationship with her. He helped me to get me away from her, so he could be with her."

"But they're not together," Lakota said confused.

"Honestly, I don't know what their relationship is. Also, I don't really care. Another thing you don't know is that Raftis wants power. He lives for it. He loves his role as the Queen's advisor, but wants more. He wants to be King."

"But..."

"He knows it's a long shot, so he loves his position. Yet, he is always looking for ways to advance his role. That's why he will help Abby, she is a direct threat to his power."

"And why he'll investigate the King being the prisoner."

"Exactly," Richard said with a small smile.

"Wow," Lakota said shaking his head, "when I decided to help Abby, I didn't know I would be in the middle of a love triangle/power struggle thing. I was just being nice."

"Welcome to life," Richard said. "Now, what's the plan?"

CHAPTER 39

Abby woke with a start. She quickly sat up in bed looking around the still unfamiliar chambers taking a second to remember where she was. Then, realizing that this wasn't a bad dream that she wanted to wake up from, she sighed.

The last few days had been the craziest days of her life. She sat in bed thinking about all that she had gone through, "*I traveled to a different world with my friends, lost my friends*," she paused. "*Oh my God, Bryan and Courtney, what could have happened to them. I hoped the Queen would say something about them, but she didn't. If I say something, then I might give them away. What about the servant girls? Would they know about her friends? Should she ask them?*" Abby's mind was racing from one subject to another. "*What about Lakota? Where's he? And my Dad? Oh my God, he's being executed today!*" She jumped out of bed not knowing what she was going to do or how she was going to do it.

The door opened quickly and the servant girls rushed into the chambers. The lead girl, whose name was Nessie spoke first, "Are you ok, my lady?"

"Ah...yes...I just jumped out of bed," Abby replied looking around as the guards scanned the area behind the servant girls.

"Good day, then. It's about time to get ready," Nessie said, "the Queen has sent over your old clothes for you to wear to the execution."

"My old clothes?" Abby questioned with a scrunched up face.

"Yes, my lady, you need to be reminded of the old wretched life you led at the hands of the criminal. Your new life as a Princess fully begins after the execution," Nessie explained.

Abby still looked confused, but she knew the Queen certainly had her way of doing things. She took her t-shirt and shorts from Nessie and noticed they were still a bit dirty. There was a quick awkward silence before Nessie realized that Abby was waiting for everyone to leave before she dressed. Nessie ushered everyone from the room and closed the door with a smile for Abby.

Abby quickly dressed and felt so comfortable in her old clothes. It was almost refreshing after being paraded around the day before as a Princess. Then, again, she remembered the feeling of everyone staring at her and cheering for the princess. It was the most amazing feeling of her life, and she couldn't wait to tell Bryan and Courtney about it.

The door opened again slowly and Nessie poked her head inside.

"Are you ready?" she asked, "It's time to go."

"Time to go?" Abby thought, *"She's acting like we're going to the movies or something! My father is about to die!"*

Abby didn't move and Nessie looked at her quizzically. Nessie then turned to the guards who entered the room. Abby still didn't move. She wanted to see if they would force her. They moved toward her and she exclaimed, "I want to speak to my mother!" That backed the soldiers up a few steps.

"Then you shall," Nessie said and pointed to the door. Abby could do nothing but head toward it. The guards fell in behind her almost as if they expected her to flee.

Abby was surprised, she had felt that the guards were there to protect her, but now it seemed they were there to watch her. *"Which was it?"* she thought as they led her through the halls of the castle toward the Queen's chambers. Abby could hear the guards behind her in step and surely keeping a close eye on her. Nessie led the way, but the other servant girls stayed behind. Abby being marched to the Queen felt more like a prisoner than a princess.

Arriving at the Queen's chambers, Nessie turned to everyone and spoke, "Remain here, until I clear your presence with the Queen. Without another word, she disappeared into the Queen's chambers.

Abby was left staring at the door waiting. The soldiers behind her stood at attention waiting for the Queen and not wanting to appear relaxed if she came through the door. Abby turned and looked at them and almost laughed. They were stone faced and so serious. She thought of Courtney and how she would be making some snide remark about them; it made Abby smile. She also noticed how young they were, not much older than her and just following orders. She shook her head thinking, *"These poor guys really have no life."*

The door opening made her turn back around as Nessie emerged from the chambers. "You have two minutes," she said and held the door for Abby.

Abby entered the Queen's chambers rather reluctantly not really knowing what to expect from this meeting. The room was magnificent with large tapestries covering the stone walls and a beautiful four post bed that was covered with a sheer linen. Abby scanned the room for her mother, but she was not there. She moved further into the room, her eyes catching movement in another room off to her left. Abby stopped and waited for her mother to come out. She figured that she was already disrupting, she might as well wait.

It didn't take long for the Queen to call for her, "Princess Abigail? Are you there?"

"Yes," Abby answered a little apprehensively.

"Well, come in here child, I don't have time to waste."

Abby took notice that she was apparently wasting the Queen's time and began reluctantly walking toward the room where the Queen's voice came from. She barely got to the room when the Queen, dressed in a flowing red gown came walking toward her with a huge smile on her face.

"Well, my child, you look fabulous in your old clothes," she said speaking quickly. "I'm sure you're here to ask for Richard's life. You probably want to execute him yourself, since he took so much away from from you, but I need to do this. I will do this for me, for you, for us!"

Abby was so confused that she didn't know what to say. She just stared dumbfounded as the Queen continued.

"It is a glorious day in Alden. Soon, very soon, you will be out of those hideous clothes and dress as a proper princess to rule with me. Now, today will be difficult, so Raftis will accompany you to the execution, and you will stay with him throughout the proceedings. You will ceremonially come and stand with me when it is over. The people will then see your old clothes and note the symbolism of the change."

Abby never said a word, but she never had the opportunity to speak. As the Queen finished, she saw an opportunity, "I wanted to..."

The Queen cut her off, "you don't have to thank me, my dear.

Just you being here is thanks enough for me. Now, it is almost time, so," the Queen moved toward the door, "Nessie!" she hollered. "Nessie will take you to Raftis, now run along."

Nessie shot into the room hearing the last part about Raftis and ushered Abby out of the room. The guards closed the door before Abby could even glance back. She was quickly ushered through the halls which were completely empty.

Finally, Abby arrived at the entrance to the castle. Raftis stood by the open castle door in his flowing green robes. As Abby approached, he took total control.

"Thank you Nessie, I'll take the Princess from here," Raftis commanded.

The guards stopped along with Nessie as Abby approached Raftis. She felt awkward, but continued toward him. The guards and Nessie stood and waited.

Raftis quickly became agitated and shooed them away, "I said, I'll take the Princess from here, now, be gone!"

The soldiers quickly turned in unison and marched down the hallway, but Nessie was more reluctant, "But, I am the Princess's handmaiden," she said.

"I will not tell you again," Raftis said calmly. Nessie turned and walked away, but not without an evil glance back at Raftis.

Raftis didn't even blink, but did not look at Abby or say a word until they were alone. Then, he looked deep into Abby's eyes.

"Those eyes," he said, "so much like your mother's. Yet, everything behind them is different."

Abby was becoming uncomfortable. She was used to comments about her eyes, but this was different, Raftis was staring at her soul. There was something that made her stare back and not look away though. Without breaking their eye contact, Raftis reached for her hand and placed a small cloth in it. He then closed her hand around the cloth. Abby could feel something inside the cloth, but didn't look down at it, keeping her eyes on Raftis as he spoke.

"Do not open this until you need it. Put it somewhere safe and do not let anyone know you have it until the time is right. It is a gift from your father, Raftis said without breaking eye contact.

"But...how will I know when the time is right?" Abby asked.

"You'll know," he said breaking the eye contact and taking

Abby's other hand to lead her toward the bridge where her father was

soon to die.

CHAPTER 40

Courtney couldn't take it any longer. She had been up since the first sign of light and had sat patiently for what seemed like hours for others to wake. She waited for any type of noise outside her room to barge out and begin the day, but there were none. Finally, she had had enough. Looking over at Bryan sleeping comfortably on the bed across from her, she shook her head and jumped on top of him to wake him up.

"Get up!" she whispered

"What the heck!" Bryan said groggily, "What's wrong with you?"

"You gotta get up! I can't sit here any longer waiting! He's going to die today! We have to do something!"

"They are doing something," Bryan said rubbing his eyes, but not really pushing Courtney off of him.

She hopped off of him, but stayed on the bed, "Yes, THEY'RE doing something, but WE have to do something."

"Listen, Court, we have to trust them. I really think we would be in the way. I don't think Vala would..."

"In the way? What do you mean, 'in the way'? I want to help!"

"But..."

"No, Abby is not going to go with them. She doesn't know them. If she sees us, she'll come with us. They even said that the Queen probably has her brainwashed or something. We need to be there! Please, Bry."

Bryan shook his head, "You're crazy," he said, but inside he knew she had a point. Abby probably wouldn't go with them. She didn't know them at all. "But, you're right," he added. "We'll have to wait until they all leave and then sneak out."

"Yes!" she exclaimed jumping back on top of him and kissing him on the cheek, "You're the best!"

Bryan was at a loss for words. The last girl he ever expected to kiss him would be Courtney. He was shocked, but it made him smile.

The next few hours were like a whirlwind in the house. There was a flurry of activity with men and women slipping in to see Vala for a few seconds and then slipping away. Bryan and Courtney sat in the eating area and just watched. They saw Vala's interactions with everyone and thought that Griffin and Oswyn are in charge, but realized that Vala was really running this show. Especially, since Griffin and Oswyn were nowhere to be found. Vala explained that they had some setting up to do and left before sunrise. Finally, Vala gathered her things and explained why it was important for Bryan and Courtney to stay behind.

Courtney wasn't really listening; her mind was already made up. All she heard coming from Vala was, "Best for Abby...can't chance getting caught...we'll do all we can...hope you understand..." Courtney just continued to nod her head in agreement and hope Vala would leave so they could get going.

Bryan sparked Courtney's attention by asking a question. "Where will you be on the bridge?"

Courtney tried not to give him a look, but her eyes were digging a hole through him. "*Oh my God! Shut up,*" she thought.

"What do you mean?" Vala asked wondering why he asked that.

"Well," Bryan said noticing Courtney's anger and choosing his words wisely, "I just thought that when we were there before, we were nowhere near Abby or anyone in charge. We could have never saved her."

"You're right. This time I will be on the castle side of the bridge and that is why we cannot take you two," Vala replied.

"Oh," was all Bryan could say without the wrath of Courtney coming at him again.

"Now, I must be going. The bridge will be crowded. If things go awry, someone will be sent to escort you from the city. I will make every effort to be that person."

With that, Vala turned and left the room heading toward the door. Neither of the kids spoke until she was gone and the house was empty.

"I thought you were going to mess the whole thing up," Courtney said.

"I know, but I figured if we knew where she was going to be, we could stay away from her."

"That's exactly what we're *not* going to do. I want to be near her so we can get near Abby. She's not going to go with Vala."

Bryan sighed, "Maybe you're right."

"I am. Now, let's go."

Vala made her way across the bridge in a timely manner. The crowd was starting to gather, but it was still going to be an hour or so before the execution. Vala moved quickly and inconspicuously through the people. She got about halfway across the bridge to where the gallows were and the hangings took place and stopped. She made her way to the side of the bridge where Abby was introduced the day before. There was speculation on why the Queen didn't just bring her to the town square for the introduction. Griffin felt the Queen didn't want anyone to get too close to Abby. The same would be true for Richard. The Queen would drown him because if he was brought to the bridge for hanging, too many people would be too close to him and there would be a chance for escape.

Vala pondered these things as she peered over the side of the bridge to the platform/dock below. Large men in boats with taunt ropes attached to the dock were rowing hard to move it away from the bridge so everyone could see the spectacle that was soon to take place. Vala smiled, "*She may be evil, but she sure is smart,*" she thought.

Vala then turned and moved across the bridge to the other side. She became more isolated on this side since the crowd had gathered to watch the men pulling the dock into place. She quickly looked over the side seeing that this side of the bridge was abandoned with everyone's focus being the dock. She smiled again knowing the people's attention to the execution would be the key to saving Abby.

Vala proceeded to move toward the castle blending in with the people as she went. She did not notice the two cloaked figures with hoods up, who were also using the crowd to move across the bridge.

Suddenly, Vala moved to her left and as quick as a cat turned and doubled back toward the center of the bridge again. Courtney and Bryan who were once twenty yards behind her and trying to keep her in sight were now in front of her with Vala moving toward them. Bryan, who was leading stopped on a dime, turned toward Courtney to shield both of their faces from Vala and did the only thing he could think of to hide. He grabbed Courtney in an embrace and planted a huge kiss on her joining their hoods and concealing their faces from the approaching Vala. Vala, just feet away, turned again and headed back toward the castle.

After a good thirty seconds, the make out session was over and

Bryan unlocked his lips from Courtney. Nervously looking around and waiting to see Vala next to them. She was gone.

"Where'd she go?" he whispered.

"What the hell was that?"

"It was the only thing I could think of that would hide our faces."

"Seriously?"

"Sorry. Now, where is she?" Bryan asked.

"I don't know, my eyes were closed," Courtney smiled.

"Well, she'll definitely have to go toward the castle, so let's go that way," he said matter of factly.

"Ok," was all Courtney could say. She followed Bryan again confused. *"I just had my first real kiss from a boy, and it was only to hide his face. My life sucks,"* she thought shaking her head.

They made their way through the people toward the castle. As they got closer, Bryan started to slow down the pace.

Finally, he turned to Courtney and whispered, "How far do we go, we're almost at the castle door?"

"There's Vala," she whispered nodding toward the dock side of the bridge.

Bryan and Courtney made their way through the crowd to the area behind Vala. They stayed out of her line of sight and left a good group of people between them. They only wanted to keep an eye on her and be close when the time was right.

As they waited, the crowd was building. Bryan hoped that the bridge could hold all of these people. The dock side of the bridge looked like a bunch of concert goers trying to rush the stage. The hoard stretched all the way across the bridge and engulfed almost the whole width except for a thin line of daylight which ran along the opposite rail.

Courtney looked at Bryan concerned about being able to get out of there quickly if they needed to, but Bryan had other thoughts. The jostling of the people was pushing them closer to Vala and there was really nothing they could do about it. Now, only about five rows of people separated them, but Courtney couldn't imagine them getting any closer to her since they were now pretty much packed in together.

A hush came over the crowd as a loud horn signaled the arrival of the Queen. Most people turn toward the castle doors. Bryan and Courtney realized that those people were now looking toward them.

Courtney thought she was getting another kiss when Bryan grabbed her by the waist and spun her toward the castle. It never came though as he was only shielding her from everyone's view. While shielding Courtney, he kept an eye on Vala to make sure she didn't spot them. Bryan found it interesting that she was one of the few people who didn't turn toward the castle. It didn't take long for people to realize that the castle doors were not opening. The horn blowing continued, but there was still no sign of the Queen.

Finally, some yelled, "There!" and pointed off in the distance. Bryan saw the Queen's boat that Abby rode on turning the corner of the lake by the far side of the castle. The boat approached slowly, but as it came into focus the Queen could be seen standing proudly on the bow. Her dark purple robes blowing in the wind and a huge smile on her face. Bryan scanned the other passengers for Abby, but she could not be seen. As the boat drew closer, he split his attention between the boat and scanning for Abby and Vala. He watched her to see if there was any sign of movement from her. He leaned over and whispered to Courtney, who was still huddled close to him.

"Keep an eye on Vala, and I'll watch the boat for Abby."

"Ok, but she doesn't look surprised at the Queen's entrance," she whispered back.

"I know. I think she knows where Abby is, so keep watching."

The Queens boat arrived and ropes were thrown overboard to tie it to the side of the dock. The Queen made a grand entrance down the gangplank and stood in the middle of the dock. She raised her hands and everyone went silent.

"Today is a day of reckoning. A day that we have longed for for many years. It is a day when a debt is repaid. Many years ago while swimming, the prisoner expressed his fear of drowning. So today, his fear will be realized."

A rumble when through the crowd. A man grabbed Courtney's arm and shook her, "I wanna see him hang!" he shouted at her.

She pushed him away with out taking her eyes off Vala. Bryan shot the man a look of anger, and he moved away murmuring about hanging.

The Queen raised her hands again. "I understand that you want to watch him suffer, but knowing his fear will be satisfaction enough. Today, we will be rid of the ghosts of the past."

She turned to one of the soldiers next to her and nodded. He in turn nodded toward the boat. Two huge men came walking down the gangplank struggling to carry what can only be described as a boulder. They brought a hush to the crowd and then a gasp as two more men followed with another boulder. They walked to the far side of the dock and placed them at the very edge. The second pair almost knocked theirs into the lake, which brought a sigh and laughter from the crowd. Bryan noticed there were large iron chains with shackles protruding from the boulders

Someone in the crowd yelled again, "There!" and everyone began pointing off in the distance again. There was a small rowboat approaching. A large man, his back to the crowd, rowed while three men sat silently. Bryan recognized Mr. Lane in the middle, although he needed a shave and apparently a good shower. The guards on each side of him sat stone faced as they approached the dock.

When they arrived, Courtney elbowed Bryan and flicked her head toward Vala. She was now beginning to look around a little more, turning toward the castle and leaning over the side of the bridge. She was obviously looking for something or someone. Courtney figured it was Abby. Then, there was motion to their right at the castle door. The door opened ever so slightly and a man with dark hair and a perfect goatee slid out of the door. He was wearing long green robes and scanned the area before turning back to the door. He reached his hand out of view and when he pulled it back out, he was leading Abby from the castle.

Courtney almost screamed. Bryan hugged her tightly so she wouldn't, "Shhhhhh," he whispered. Courtney was so stunned, not only to see Abby so close to them, but because she looked like Abby. She was dressed in shorts and a t-shirt, which were quite dirty from her travels. Bryan thought she looked much more comfortable than she did dressed as a princess. It made him smile, but the procession of guards that emerged through the door behind her wiped that away quickly.

They cleared a path toward the bridge railing giving the man in green and Abby a clear view of the dock and the soon to be execution.

Seeing that Abby was well guarded, Bryan turned back to the dock and noticed that Richard was already chained to the boulders by his ankles. His back was the the water so he could face the people with his hands tied in front of him. Courtney continued to follow Abby's movement forgetting about Vala until she noticed Vala sliding herself closer to where Abby was standing. The guards, who had cleared people away with ease, paid no attention to Vala as she slid to within a few feet of Abby and the green robed man.

The Queen raised her arms again hushing the crowd. "I present to you the prisoner for execution. Guards!" she hollered, "move into position."

The four huge boulder guards moved into position to push the teetering rocks into the lake, looking to Bryan like football linemen ready to attack.

"Normally," the Queen continued, " we would ask the prisoner for any final words. But we don't care what you have to say!" she finished by spitting in Richard's face.

The crowd was stunned. Many turned to their friends to discuss what they just saw. Bryan turned to Courtney, who didn't see the gesture because she was still watching Abby. He noticed more movement at the castle door. A huge man emerged, the same man they saw at Lakota's house. He tried to remember his name, *"Kuruk?"* he thought, but scared is what he felt. Kuruk looked right at Bryan and smiled.

"Oh, crap!" Bryan said grabbing Courtney, "We gotta go!"

"What?" she questioned.

"We gotta go! Now!"

Courtney followed Bryan's gaze to the huge Kuruk who was now moving toward them.

"I can't leave Abby!"

"We have to!"

They turned to run and saw Richard being pushed off of the dock to his death.

CHAPTER 41

Abby gasped. She watched the bubbles explode on the surface where her dad had just been. The Queen smiled and turned toward the crowd with her arms outstretched in triumph. Abby threw her hands over her face, but the tears were flowing.

Raftis quickly turned her away from the scene. "Guards, lead us away!" he commanded. The guards turned and headed toward the castle, but Raftis did not follow. He leaned over to Abby and spoke to her quickly.

"Many years ago, I helped your father escape this place with you. His dying wish was for me to help you escape again. You must get out of here or you will be the next one in the bottom of the lake. She is only using you to gain the people. She made you wear your old clothes to present you as ungrateful for what she is trying to give you. You must go, or you will die. As we walk away, a woman will stop you and take you away. Trust her she is good."

Abby was trying to listen through her tears and grief, but not much was registering. She only knew that she needed to run and someone was going to help.

Raftis began moving behind the soldiers leading Abby by the hand. They walked a few steps when Abby felt someone take her other hand and in an instant Raftis let go. Raftis moved to the right toward the castle doors while Abby was led to the left away from the doors and the backs of the soldiers.

Abby turned and peered through teary eyes at the woman leading her away. She looked kind, but determined as she glanced at Abby and smiled. "I'm Vala. I'm friends with Courtney and Bryan," she said. Abby was confused. How could this woman be friends with her friends?

Vala led Abby into the crowd, who were mostly interested in a commotion going on not far away, but involved a large bearded man pushing his way through the people. Abby felt a presence come up on her left and suddenly everything went dark.

Abby twisted and turned throwing her elbows so her wasn't captured, but the darkness was disorienting her.

"Easy, honey, it's just a cloak to hide you," Vala said calmingly.

The words helped calm Abby and she stopped fighting long enough for daylight to appear. She now had a long, gray hooded cloak over her, which concealed her old clothes except for her sneakers. She felt like she was wearing an over sized hoodie, but Abby realized that besides her eyes, her old clothes were going to make her stand out in the crowd.

They moved along through the crowd who were still giving their attention to the side of the bridge where Richard just plunged to his death. Most of the people didn't really know what they were looking for to happen, but they were used to hangings that sometimes took a few minutes. Then, there was the viewing of the dead man hanging for all to see. Today, there were questions over how to handle a drowning. Would someone be sent down to bring up the body? Would the Queen declare him dead without seeing the body? No one knew what to do.

This helped Vala and Abby to make their way across the bridge virtually unnoticed. When the arrived at the bridge gate, the guards were missing. Vala actually looked confused. She already had a plan in place to deal with them, but it wasn't necessary. In the distance, they could see the guards and the large bearded man chasing after two cloaked figures. Vala was able to lead Abby off of the bridge and behind the first building on the right. There was a horse drawn cart waiting for them with a man at the reigns and a pile of hay in the back.

"Hello Chase," Vala said.

"Hello, Vala and Princess Abigail," he said nodding to them both.

Vala shot him an evil look.

"Oh, sorry. I forgot. Vala and," he paused, "Abby," Chase finished nodding to them.

Vala nodded back and ushered Abby into the back of the cart.

"It's going to be hot, but you must stay under cover until we get out of here," Vala said.

Abby, who still was crying and trying to figure out what was going on, just nodded. Abby hopped in the cart face down, and Vala pushed a large amount of hay over her. Little did Abby know that she was leaving the city in the same manner that her father arrived. The cart started to move, and Abby felt the gentle back and forth movement of the wheels to be relaxing, but relaxing made her think.

She couldn't believe that her father was gone. He was her world. What was she going to do now? She wanted to go home, but had no reason to go. Her life was always so great and now, her dad was dead, her mom killed him, her friends were gone, and she was in a hay cart with two people she didn't know. *"Now what?"* she thought. She heard the muffled voices of Vala and Chase above her, but couldn't make out what they were saying.

"Be calm going through the city gate. I have a friend who will check the cart and let us go, but the other guard could get suspicious if we don't act natural," Vala said.

"Ok. Ah...do...you know who the people running away were?" Chase asked reluctantly.

"Please tell me those kids stayed in the house," she said shaking her head.

"Ahhh...they didn't."

"Was that Kuruk chasing them?"

"Unfortunately, yes."

"I had them followed. I hope someone is getting Oswyn."

"Me too."

"Let's hope," Vala said, "Now, here is the city gate. We are farmers returning home with our hay that we didn't sell."

"Ok."

The cart approached the gate quickly. The city was pretty much deserted due to the execution. The two guards at the gate were the only people around.

"Seems kinda fishy when people leave in da middle of an execution," the first guard said turning to his partner.

"Yer right, no one else is leavin'," the second guard said.

"The execution's over," Vala replied, "drowned 'em in the lake." No one buying anything today, so we're goin' home."

"Shouldn't a even tried to sell on the day of an execution," Chase said jumping into the conversation.

"Yer right," the second guy said.

"We'll remember that for next time," Chase added.

"All right, well, hurry home before the rush," the first guard said.

"Yeah, get outta here," the second guy chimed in with a quick wink to Vala.

"Thank you sirs, and have a nice day," she said.

They headed through the gate and out onto the open road without a hitch. As they journeyed down the road, Chase pulled to the side and let Abby out of the hay. She had to stay sitting in it in case they met up with anyone, but at least it wasn't as hot. Abby didn't have much to say, she was still sobbing throughout the ride, but tried not to think of what just happened. Vala and Chase didn't talk much, so the ride was rather boring until they met up with a man on the side of the road.

Abby started to pull hay onto herself, but Vala told her it was ok. They rode up to the man, exchanged pleasantries, and he walked away for a few minutes. When he returned, he had a horse with him. The man and Chase unhooked the horse that had been puling them and switched it with the new horse. Abby was shocked at how elaborate this plan to save her was.

"Why the change?" Abby asked when they started moving again.

"Honey, the goal is to get you to the door and home. That journey can take days, but if we can switch off the horses, then we can cut the time down to about a day if we keep moving. You need to return as soon as possible."

"But, I have friends here," Abby said pushing hay off of herself, " I can't leave without them!"

"I know," Vala said, "we're working on it."

CHAPTER 42

"Don't stop!" Courtney yelled to Bryan as the approached the Bridge guards and ran right past them.

"Hey!" one of the guards yelled. He and his partner started chasing the two cloaked figures as they ran down the main street of Alden. The guards were in full chase mode when they were pushed to each side of the street from behind by the largest man they had ever seen.

The first guard yelled again, "Hey, what the...?"

He shut up quickly when he realized that Kuruk, the Shifter, was the one who pushed them. Both guards regained their balance and continued to follow the chase until the cloaked figures turned down a side street. Kuruk immediately turned into a wolf and began gaining on the figures. The guards both stopped remembering their vacant post, and knowing the Shifter would take care of this problem, they stopped the chase and headed back to their post. They were too late to see Vala and Abby exit the gate and head through the town.

Courtney and Bryan ran through the streets, trying not to look back. Then, they heard the snarl of what they thought was a dog.

Courtney glanced behind her to see the wolf gaining on them quickly.

"We can't get away!" she yelled ahead to Bryan.

Turning left at the next street, Bryan was trying to head back to the safe house, but the wolf was now too close for comfort. Courtney was right, they weren't going to get away. Another quick left and they were over taken.

The wolf cut the corner and zipped in front of them. He turned to face Bryan and Courtney and changed back into Kuruk in an instant. Bryan stopped abruptly, and Courtney almost ran him into Kuruk.

"I knew you two were up to something," Kuruk snarled.

Bryan and Courtney were too out of breath to respond. They just stood in terror of the large menacing man looming if front of them, both of their chests heaving and sucking in air.

"I should have known you were friends of the princess. I should have taken you to the Queen the first time I saw you sneaking around Lakota's house."

Bryan was trying to act confused, like he didn't know what this man was talking about, but it wasn't very convincing.

"Now, it's time to see what the Queen thinks about you two sneaking around."

Suddenly, Bryan was thrown back into Courtney knocking her to the ground and landing on top of her. He rolled off of her as quickly as possible hoping she was not hurt and he was not about to be killed. He tried to get up, but Courtney pulled him back to the ground.

"Look," she said pointing toward Kuruk.

Bryan turned and looked up to see two wolves attacking each other. They snarled and snapped growling and twisting around each other. He and Courtney slid back away from the fight, helping each other to their feet.

Suddenly, one of the wolves turned into a huge bear that pinned down the wolf. Then the wolf turned to a bear, but was still pinned down, struggling to get away. Bryan and Courtney were now to their feet trying to back away from this fight without taking their eyes off of the combatants.

The pined bear was still struggling when the most amazing thing they had ever seen happened with both combatants changing rapidly into the same animals at the same time. Bears to wolves to rats to spiders to mice to raccoons to badgers to bears and finally to men. In every change, one of the animals was still holding down the other. When they became men, Kuruk was on the ground being held down by the smaller figure of Lakota. He turned to the kids.

"I won't be able to hold him for long," the Lakota said through a straining voice, "get out of here!"

They didn't need to be told twice. Bryan and Courtney ran as fast as they could to get back to the safe house, both glancing behind them once to see the same shifting dance still going on behind them.

When they arrived at the main street, there were still only a few people leaving the bridge. They continued their race to the house hoping they could beat Vala back without her knowing they ever left.

They ran to the door, looked quickly behind them and quietly entered the house. Stepping lightly in the foyer, they walked toward the first room and Griffin was standing there with his arms folded looking menacingly at them.

"You missed your escape ride," he said sternly. "We plan a full escape for everyone and you two screw up the whole plan. Your ride, with Abby on board, has left, and now you may be stuck in Alden forever."

"Oh my God!" Courtney said. "We just wanted to help. There was this guy, that Shifter guy, Kuruk. He chased us and..."

"I know," Griffin interrupted. "We figured you were captured or dead. How did you escape Kuruk? Oh, I know, you didn't, and he just came in here with you as a bug or something and you gave away our house!" Griffin was getting angrier as he stood there.

From behind him, he whipped out two short swords and swung them expertly around calling out Kuruk. "Show yourself, Kuruk!" He glanced around the room quickly stopping only when Bryan spoke.

"He's not here," Bryan said.

"You don't know what he is capable of!" Griffin groaned.

"I know, but really, he's not here. Lakota helped us."

"What? That's impossible, Lakota was..."

"It was Lakota," Courtney said, "He kept changing into the same animals as Kuruk, then quickly changed into Lakota and told us to run."

Griffin looked confused. "Are you sure?" Griffin asked shaking his head.

"Yes, we're sure. Why don't you think that Lakota would help us?" Bryan asked.

"He was supposed to be helping Richard. He shouldn't have been there to help you." The thought of this made Griffin lower his swords.

"We're sorry," Bryan said, "We really were just trying to help. We thought Abby would see us and go with us, but then Mr. Lane was pushed to his death and..."

"You were told that we had a plan. Apparently, you don't trust us that much. We told you that we were going to try and save them. You're lucky to be alive."

They had nothing to say. They both just lowered their heads, Courtney's eyes welling up in tears both for Mr. Lane and for herself.

"Get yourselves together, we have no time to waste and an angry Shifter who will still be looking for you," Griffin said.

He led them through the house to a back door that they had not previously seen. There was a horse drawn cart waiting for them. It was filled with baskets of vegetables. Courtney sat up with Griffin as he drove the cart out onto the road. Bryan sat quietly in the back amongst the corn and carrots. Griffin told them they would proceed slowly until they got past the guards and out of the city. Then, they would try to make up for lost time. They were to keep quiet and let him do any talking.

The streets were still fairly deserted as they made their way toward the city gate. Bryan scanning the area behind them for Kuruk or anyone else for that matter. They approached the gate and the same guards that Vala and Chase passed not long before. They were standing looking bored and waiting for someone to head into or out of the city.

"Well, whata we have ere?" the first guard asked laughing. "I don't remember ya comin' in this mornin' and I know I woulda remembered you," he added pointing at Courtney.

"Yeah, but there were a buncha people comin in this mornin," the second guard said recognizing Griffin and trying to talk to him with his eyes.

"Awww, but yer a cutie, honey," the first guard said. Courtney bowed her head and bit her bottom lip. She wanted so bad to tell this guy off, but knew it would be a problem.

"I guess ya didn't sell much today?" the second guard said trying to change the subject.

"No, just trying to get my family home before the crowd."
Griffin replied tapping his hand on Courtney's leg to reassure her not to
say anything.

"Family? She must look like er mother," the first guard said
cracking himself up. "Hahahahaha."

"She does," Griffin said, "Have a good day." He began moving
the cart through the gate.

"Good day," the second guard called out as they moved away.

Bryan, sitting and facing the rear of the cart stared down the first
guard as they left. He wanted so bad to yell something at him, but like
Courtney, bit his lip and used his eyes to curse the man out.

They were a good half mile away from the gate when Griffin
picked up the pace and finally spoke.

"You were great back there. I'm glad you didn't say anything. I
know you wanted to," he said to Courtney laughing.

"You have no idea!"

They continued down the road moving as quickly as possible to catch up with Vala and Abby.

CHAPTER 43

The Queen was so satisfied with herself that she stood for the longest time just staring at the spot where Richard went under. The crowd watched her and didn't really know what to do. Questions started to flow through the people. Is she ok? What is she doing? Are we supposed to stay here? Are they going to pull his body up? Finally, after enough time for Vala and Abby to be out of the city, the Queen turned to the crowd. The murmurs stopped and everyone waited for her to speak.

"I officially declare the prisoner, former Prince Richard dead. No one can survive under water for that long. Originally, I was going to bring his body up and hang it for all to see, but I am disgusted by the sight of him. I want the fish and other creatures of the lake to eat away at his disgusting body. After one week, we will pull the remaining mess from the lake to show what happens to those who go against the Queen."

When she paused, the crowd gave a small cheer, not in approval, but because they didn't know what else to do. The Queen then looked toward the castle door searching for Princess Abigail, but she could not find her in the crowd. She raised her hands again for silence.

"Princess Abigail came today to watch the end of her past life. She wore her old 'Traveler' clothes as a sign of her previous life. Today, she will change those clothes and her life. She has already been taken into the castle to change and will be presented to you shortly. Today, is a splendid day and in honor of this occasion, all of you are welcome at sundown for a feast in the Great Hall."

The crowd erupted! There had not been a feast in the Great Hall for years. Many of the younger people of Alden had never attended one. A rumble went through the crowd as everyone began talking at once. The young people were asking the old people what to expect. The old people telling about wonderful feasts under King Tammany and how different things were back then. Everyone hoped this was a sign of change under the Queen. A change they have been waiting for since the King's death.

The Queen raised her hands again to get everyone's attention. "The Great Hall will open at sundown. Now, you should all go and prepare yourself for the feast. Wash yourselves and dress in your best clothes for this will be a night to remember!"

The crowd erupted again and the Queen turned and went back to her boat. The crowd began to hurry off of the bridge. Most of them were trying to hurry home in order to get ready and return as fast as possible. The thought being that the first people back would be the first to enter the Great Hall. As the Queen's boat sailed away and rounded the far side of the castle, the bridge was almost cleared. The town was a bevy of activity. People were hurrying everywhere to get home and get ready. The farmers that lived far from town were going to friend's houses to get ready, while some still tried to hurry back to their farms. The guards at the gate that had time to talk with Vala and then Griffin were almost run over by the horses and carts spewing out of the city. They finally just moved aside and let everyone go. They also decided that when people returned, they were going to just let them enter.

The Queen entered the back of the castle and marched toward the Throne Room with a look of disgust on her face. The castle was alive with activity as servants were hustling here and there trying to get things together for the feast. Guards were also running around quickly looking like they lost something, but the Queen was too focused to notice. The Queen's face gave her a sort of people repellant. There was hustle and bustle everywhere, but no one came near her. Everyone from guards to servants avoided her like death.

Finally, she reached the Throne Room where guards whipped open the doors and she stepped into the emptiness.

"I want Raftis, the Princess, and all of my guards in here now!" she commanded to the guards that were following her. The scurried quickly to find Raftis and round up the guards.

The Queen ordered the Throne Room door to be shut and only opened again when they were assembled.

She strolled up to the throne and sat. The nasty frown on her face slowly changed to a satisfied smile. "I did it," she said out loud, "Richard is gone." She sat alone relishing the thought of him suffocating under the lake and the fish devouring his body.

Three loud knocks on the door ended her daydream and the scowl came back to her face. The doors opened slowly and Raftis entered in his green flowing robes. The guards marched in formation behind him. Raftis approached the Queen confidently and stopped at the bottom of the steps leading up to the throne. Raising his right hand to stop the troops. They did so in unison with highly trained precision. The Queen was impressed, but did not show it at all.

"You summoned us, My Queen," Raftis said.

"Yes, Raftis, but where is the Princess?"

"The Princess is indisposed at the moment, My Queen."

"What does that mean? I want her here," she replied.

"I understand that, My Queen, but she was very upset at the proceedings of today. I felt it best for her to be alone for a while. She needs to gather herself for the feast, so that she can be properly introduced to the people."

"Upset? This should be the happiest day of her life."

"I agree, My Queen, but sometimes things get jumbled up in the mind of a child."

"Raftis, I am counting on you to have her here and ready for tonight. I will accept no excuses. The girl must be happier than she's ever been. Do you understand?"

"Yes, My Queen," Raftis said turning and giving a look to Zareth, who was standing in front of the soldiers.

Raftis moved toward him and whispered as he walked by, "Find her."

"Now, for my guards. Zareth," the Queen said looking toward him.

Zareth marched toward her with precision. He stopped and stomped each foot together when he was directly in front of the throne. "My Queen," he said.

"Zareth, you are one of my finest men. I trusted you to bring Richard back to me, and you did. Tonight will be a challenge for you and your men. There will be a host of people here and after drinking, some of them may get a bit rowdy. I trust that your men will not take kindly to anything they deed unnecessary."

"Yes, My Queen. We will be ready," Zareth nodded.

"Good. Your job will be to stay with me and the Princess as our personal protectors."

"Yes, My Queen. I will be ready," he nodded again.

"Good. Now everyone should prepare themselves for the evening. Dismissed."

Zareth turned toward the guards and commanded, "About face!" The whole group turned as one. "March!"

They filed out with Raftis walking next to Zareth. When they exited, Raftis turned to Zareth. "We need to find her before the feast, but we have to be discreet about it. She cannot know we have lost her."

"We? I didn't lose her!" Zareth said. "You were in charge of her!"

"Correction," Raftis said, "We were in charge of her, your guards and I. I led her with your guards back to the castle, when I turned to see if the Queen needed me, and now she is gone. What type of training do you give your men that they don't pay attention to what's going on around them?"

"You will not pin this on me! I was with the Queen the whole time. I didn't lose her!" Zareth was now a little in Raftis's face.

Raftis did not back away, but stated calmly. "The bottom line is that we both need her found."

"It won't be pretty if she's not," Zareth agreed. He turned and directed guards to quietly find the Princess.

Raftis quickly left the area. He had a lot of work to do to prepare for the feast and the Queen's questions about Abby's disappearance. He was sure there would be questions.

CHAPTER 44

Abby had never been to Sono, but she liked the small village in the middle of the woods. They rode down the road and into the clearing with small wooden houses all around. Abby was quick to notice that there didn't seem to be anyone around and that sparked her interest.

"Is there anyone here?" she whispered to Vala.

"There may be a few older people here, but most people went to the city. Their curiosity would make them go. It helps us, because no one will know that you're here, not that any of these people would tell anyway," Vala said without whispering.

"They wouldn't?"

"No. Most of these people do not like your mother. They miss your grandfather, and they would absolutely love you."

"Love me?" Abby asked confused. "Why would they love me?"

"Honey, you are the heir to the throne. You are The Princess of Alden. You are hope for these people. If the Queen was gone, you would lead them."

"Oh my God! I'm not a leader! I'm just a kid!"

"Exactly. That's why they would love you," Vala said with a smile.

"They would love me because I'm a kid?"

"No, they would love you because you're humble. You don't think you're better than them. You don't think you're entitled to anything. Unfortunately, your mother does. She thinks she's superior to all of these people, and no one likes that. They hate that."

"How was my Grandfather?" Abby asked.

"Like you. The people loved him and he loved them. He listened to their needs, their wants, and their fears. They loved him and trusted him because he was fair."

"I wish I could have met him."

"Me too," Vala said as she stopped their cart in front of a large wooden house. "Welcome to Sono."

Vala and Abby exited the cart and entered the house. Abby was led to a room with a table and chairs that looked like a meeting room. There was a basket of bread and fruit on the table along with a pitcher and some wooden cups.

"Eat," Vala said in the same manner that she did to Abby's friends just a few days ago. "I'm going to feed and water the horse, so we can continue our journey shortly," Vala said. With that she exited the room.

Abby was left by herself for the first time in a while. It didn't take long for her to start crying again. She thought of her life and how symbolic it was for her to be sitting here alone. Her father was gone, her mother was an evil Queen, and she was left alone. Abby reached under her cloak and into the pocket of her shorts. Inside was the wrapped cloth that Raftis gave her. She felt it with her hand, but was not sure if now was the time to take it out. "A gift from your father" Raftis had said. She felt so alone. She needed her Dad and needed him now. She grasped the cloth and puled it from her pocket placing it on the table in front of her.

Abby closed her eyes, took a deep breath and began to unwrap the cloth. As she unfolded the cloth, she saw the key. The same key that was in the journal Pitman had given her. She sighed and began to laugh and cry at the same time.

"Even in death, you tried to take care of me," she thought looking up to the ceiling toward heaven. *"I already have a key to get*

home hidden by the door, but I will use yours to be sure." Abby sighed again thinking about how much her father loved her that he would somehow make a deal with Raftis to save her. She rewrapped the key and placed it back in her pocket. Then, she realized that she was hungry and grabbed an apple from the basket.

A few minutes later, she heard the door open and Vala walked into the room.

"I have a present for you," she said.

Before she could say anything else, Vala was knocked out of the doorway by an overexcited Courtney who rushed toward her. Bryan quickly followed behind. It was the greatest group hug ever with smiles and tears at the same time. They held each other and cried for a long time. Finally, Bryan broke the silence.

"I'm so sorry about your Dad," he said, which only made the tears flow more.

Through sniffles and sobs, Abby asked, "But...how did you guys...get here?"

"Griffin brought us," Bryan said.

"Griffin?"

"Yeah," Courtney said breaking her hug and pointing the Griffin standing in the doorway. "We were supposed to come with you, but we were stupid." She put here head down, then looked to Vala, "We're so sorry, Vala. We should have listened to you."

"It all worked out. I just don't know how you two are not dead. Not many people have ever escaped from a Shifter."

"A Shifter?" Abby said looking at Courtney.

"It wasn't Lakota," Griffin said. "It was another one named Kuruk, but Lakota..."

"Lakota?" Abby interrupted.

"Yes," Griffin said confused, "he saved them."

Abby smiled, thinking of Lakota and how he had saved her for the wild dogs.

"We met Lakota before that," Courtney chimed in, "He's hot!"

"I know," Abby said wiping away a tear and blushing at the same time.

"Oh God," Bryan said shaking his head.

"Jealous much?" Courtney said with a smile.

"So, Lakota saved them from Kuruk?" Vala asked Griffin.

"It appears so. I don't know how else they would have gotten away."

Bryan proceeded to tell the story of how they got away, and how Lakota was holding Kuruk down while they were changing into different animals.

"Wow," Vala said.

"It was so cool," Bryan added.

Vala turned to Griffin, "But...if...?"

"Yes, I know," Griffin interrupted her.

"Know what?" Abby asked.

"If Kuruk tells the Queen, then Lakota is in a lot of trouble," Griffin answered quickly before throwing a glance at Vala. "I think Lakota exposed himself only to let Abby know he was ok."

"That makes sense," Vala said. Now," she said turning to the kids, "you should all eat and get some rest. We will be leaving for the door soon."

"I can't leave," Abby said.

"What?" Bryan said.

"I can't leave. I have to go back and get my Dad's body."

"You can't go back there!" Courtney blurted out.

"I can't leave his body there. I just can't!"

Abby's tears came flowing again. Courtney and Bryan were quick to comfort her, and soon, all three of them were crying together. Vala and Griffin just stood to the side of the room, with Griffin stealing glances out the window.

"I have an idea," Abby said pulling away from them. "Vala, can you go back and get Lakota. Lakota can get his body and bring him to me. No one will suspect him."

"Abby..." Vala started to say, but was cut off.

"Please!"

"But..."

"Please! I can't go home without him. I can't leave him here!"

Vala moved in and took over hugging Abby. "It's ok. I understand. Now listen to me. You have been through a lot today. I want you to try to rest..."

"But..."

"Just for a couple of hours. We will be leaving very early in the morning. I will talk to Griffin and come up with a plan, but right now, you need to rest."

Vala led Abby from the room still embraced in a hug. Abby's face was nestled against Vala's chest and shoulder as Vala led her to the back of the house. The others followed them to a large bedroom with two straw beds in it. The room was rather bland with white walls and shuttered windows which were blocking out most of the light to the room. Vala sat Abby on the far bed closest to the window.

"Rest here, and we will talk in a little while. We still have a long journey ahead of us. It will not be easy to hide a Princess, so you will need to be alert. Now, it's time to rest before people return."

Vala stood up as Abby slid down onto the bed. She didn't think she would be able to sleep, but knew she needed the rest. Vala took Courtney by the arm and led her from the room. She closed the door behind them and led the others down the hall to the meeting room.

"Do you think she'll try to escape like these two?" Griffin asked gesturing to the kids.

"No. She won't leave them again, and those shutters are nailed shut. She's not getting out of that room," Vala replied with a smile.

Griffin laughed. "Ok, then."

"Now, we need to prepare," Vala said.

"You're really going to let her go back?" Bryan asked.

"No chance," Vala said abruptly. "She can't go back there now. You may only have one chance to get out of here, and we have to take it."

"Yes, we may seem safe, but that is only because the Queen does not know that Abby is gone yet. When she does, word will spread quickly, and the door will be blocked. There may already be guards there that we will have to fight. That is why you need to eat and get some rest. You're going to need it," Griffin said again walking over to a window and peeking out.

"What are you looking for?" Bryan asked reaching for a huge

hunk of bread.

"Huh?" Griffin asked moving away from the window.

"Yeah," Courtney said, "you keep looking out all of the windows. Do you think there coming to get us?"

"Not yet. I'm waiting for a Oswyn. He's supposed to meet us here. I thought he would be here before us."

"I'm not getting worried that it didn't work," Vala said.

"We can wait until morning," Griffin said.

"What didn't work?" Courtney asked.

"Part of our plan," Vala said and then went silent.

Courtney couldn't take the silence for long. "Well, are you going to tell us?"

"Not yet," Griffin said.

"If Oswyn is not here when it's time to leave, then, I'll tell you," Vala said with a look that told Courtney the conversation was over.

They sat in silence and ate. Griffin continued to check the window, while Vala quietly walked down and peeked in on Abby, who was sleeping. Although her mind was racing, she was so exhausted from the day that she fell asleep quickly. Vala smiled knowing the sleep would do her well. Vala ventured back into the meeting room and talked Courtney and Bryan into going to bed. They went to the rooms where they had been previously in Sono.

Vala and Griffin sat and discussed what could have happened to Oswyn, but there were too many possibilities to be certain. They were at a loss.

Finally, Griffin stood up and left to get some sleep. Vala sighed and followed, yet she knew she wasn't getting much sleep worrying about Oswyn.

CHAPTER 45

In preparing for the feast at the castle, most of the people of Alden just stayed in the city and found a place to wash themselves. The journey home and back to the city would be too much for many of them to accomplish in just a few hours, so the city remained a throng of people. They hustled and bustled from here to there, many staked out a piece of land around the lake and bathed themselves there. Looking like a crowded beach on a holiday weekend, the lake became a large bathhouse.

Inside the castle was the same flurry of activity with workers preparing food and running errands to get ready. The biggest issue for the castle staff was that the Queen did not alert them to her plan of having a feast. They were ill prepared. Instead of bringing fresh meat to the castle, animals and butchers were brought in to kill and cut up the meat just minutes before it was thrown over a fire to be cooked. The smell of cooking meat was everywhere throughout the castle.

The other thing that was extremely present in the castle was the huge numbers of guards who were actively searching the castle for the missing Princess. Raftis was also active in leading groups from here to there in search efforts. He knew that a good act would help to keep his name out of speculation for her disappearance. He also had everyone believing that she was last seen with a group of guards after he handed her over to them.

As the time approached for the feast to begin, it was apparent to the guards that they were not going to find the Princess. Now the talk was about who was going to tell the Queen, and what was her reaction going to be. The guards began arguing over who was going to work the door. That job was usually the one that no one wanted to do, but tonight everyone wanted to be as far away from the Queen as they could get.

As the crowds gathered on the far side of the bridge, the guards took their places and prepared for the rush of people into the castle. The gates were opened and the people began to trickle through. The first few began running across the bridge to try for the best spots at the tables in the front of the Great Hall. As more and more people were let in the pace slowed to a normal walk across the bridge. Most of the people content to just be there walked at a leisurely pace.

Inside the Great Hall, there was a beautiful display of food along the side wall. The people filled bowls with various meats, fruits, vegetables, and bread. Servants stood by the tables making sure the food was replenished and everyone had enough to eat.

As the party goers milled around eating and swapping stories of long lost parties in the great hall, horns began to sound announcing the arrival of the Queen. Conversations stopped in midsentence and all eyes turned toward the doors behind the head table. Guards on each side of the double doors reached for the handles and began to slowly open the doors. The Queen stood in the doorway for a moment before making her way into the room. She was stunning in a gold and silver sequined gown. The crown on her head was beautiful with glistening diamond chips, which seemed to sparkle even more with the background of her dark hair. The gown and crown brought out the beauty of her ridiculous eyes and their radiant color. She took a few steps into the Great Hall and held out her arms for all to see her.

The crowds cheered and clapped even though most of the people didn't really like her, they cheered out of respect and fear. No one wanted to be the one not clapping.

After turning a few times like a model on the runway, the Queen stopped, put her hands up and lowered them for the people to be silent.

"I welcome you to the first feast the Great Hall has seen in a long time, " she began. "Some of you remember when this was a common occurrence. I would like to make it such, but feel that we should use these feasts as celebrations in order to make them special. Today, marks a new beginning for our kingdom. We have buried the past and resurrected the future." At those words, the Queen began looking around the room for the Princess, but she was not present.

"Where is the Princess?" she whispered to Raftis, who had made his way to the front of the crowd.

"She must not be ready, My Queen. We think she is hiding in the castle somewhere. I have sent guards to find her and bring her here immediately," Raftis said.

"Continue the feast and the Princes will be presented to you shortly," the Queen said to the people. They began their conversations again and went back to their food.

"This is unacceptable, Raftis! I want her here now!" she said gritting her teeth.

"I'm working on it, My Queen," he replied.

"I don't want you working on it! I want her here now!"

The Queen was so loud that everyone and everything stopped. All eyes turned to her as she stared down Raftis, who seemed oblivious to all of the eyes watching him. He just stared back at her as if to say, *"What do you want me to do?"*

Everyone watched the stare down with heightened interest. If anyone could challenge the Queen and get away with it, it was Raftis. This time was different. There was a full audience of almost everyone in Alden. If the Queen wanted respect, she had to respond.

Suddenly the far doors of the Great Hall banged open and a small group of soldiers ran inside. The crowd parted and the ran right up to the Queen. The crowd was completely silent waiting on every words the lead guard spoke.

"My Queen," he started, "we have been investigating and searching. We have god information that the Princess was last seen on the bridge with Raftis. Then, he turned her over to a woman and she hasn't been seen since."

The Queen actually took a step backwards. "She hasn't been seen since the bridge? But I was told that she..." She stopped in mid sentence letting it all sink in. She knew that she had been betrayed. Betrayed by her most faithful servant, Raftis.

"Guards," she commanded. "Seize him!" she yelled pointing at

Raftis. The guards were on him in a second. Raftis never moved, never spoke, and never even looked at the Queen. She continued, "Ladies and gentlemen, we have celebrated the cleansing of the past. It will continue tomorrow at dawn when we will execute Raftis by hanging him from the bridge! Take him away!"

The crowd was stunned. Raftis was her most trusted advisor and the closest friend she had. Now, she was going to kill him. Raftis never flinched. The guards took him away like he expected it to happen. When Raftis was gone the Queen continued.

"Feast tonight and we shall finish off my past tomorrow!" With that, she turned and left the Great Hall. The people continued to feast and party through the night.

The Queen went through the doors from which she entered. When they closed behind her, she turned quickly to yell commands, but the person who always took them was gone, condemned to death. She looked around and spotted Zareth. She commanded him to send men to guard the door. She felt the Princess must be headed there. She had to stop her and finish this once and for all. Zareth quickly grabbed a couple of men and told them to prepare horses for the journey.

"Wait!" the Queen stopped him.

Zareth looked confused. "My Queen, the journey to the door takes time, we must be gone to catch up to them. They have quite a head start."

"I understand, but first, I want the key. You will bring it to me before you leave. I do not want you to take it with you. That key can be no where near that door," she said.

"But...I do not have the key, My Queen," Zareth said looking scared and realizing the problem he was going to have explaining the whereabouts of the key.

"Where is it!" she replied with gritted teeth seemingly already knowing the answer.

"Wh--, wh--, when we re--, re--, returned, Zareth stuttered.

"Oh, spit it out Zareth," she commanded.

"I gave the key to Raftis. So he could give it to you," he said as quickly as he could.

"Then you better get to that door and bring the Princess back, or you will be joining Raftis," she commanded again.

Zareth was gone. Barking out orders while gathering his men.

The Queen returned to her chambers as angry as she had ever been. Even her chamber maids knew to leave her alone. The Queen ripped off her dress and placed the crown on her bed stand. Dressing for bed, she sat on the bed and slammed her hands down to her sides. She actually wanted to cry, but it would only be out of frustration. Kitane couldn't remember the last time she cried from being sad or upset. She took a deep breath and went over the events of the past few days in her mind.

"Richard was dead," she thought. *"Was he dead? He has to be. I watched him go under. I was there and he didn't come up. No one came to help him. He's dead,"* she convinced herself. *"And Princess Abigail, did she want to leave? Or did Raftis want her gone? What child would give up being a Princess? I bet Raftis led her away. Did he give her my key? He has betrayed me for the last time. I bet she betrayed me too! She's just like her rotten father. I will reunite them when Zareth finds her! She will not treat me like her father did!"*

Queen Kitane threw herself back on the bed. She was more mentally exhausted than physically, she laid there for a long time before calling out to her chamber maids. They came flying through the door, ready to please and hoping not to get yelled at or worse.

"Wake me in a few hours. I want these party goers to watch Raftis hang at dawn. And tell Zareth to find Gawain!" she said waving them away with her hand and moving into a better sleeping position. The girls did not have to be told again. They were gone as fast as they arrived.

CHAPTER 46

The plan was to take two carts and separate if they were followed or attacked by guards. He was preparing the second cart loading it with a few small water barrels when he heard the clop of hooves moving into Sono. He turned quickly and waited for the horse to come into view, hoping it was Oswyn. Vala heard it too and came rushing out the door telling the kids to stay inside just in case. She moved from the house and knew from the smile on Griffin's face that it was Oswyn.

Vala turned and called to the house, "Come out! It's him!" Without waiting for the kids, Vala hurried to Griffin's side. She turned and saw Oswyn's large black horse trotting down the road toward them. He was still a good hundred yards away, but it was unmistakably Oswyn. He was a mere fifty yards away when Abby, Bryan, and Courtney arrived.

"Oswyn made it," Bryan said.

"Who's with him?" Courtney asked.

Sitting next to Oswyn on the bench was a dark cloaked figure with the oversized hood shadowing the person's face. Bryan felt a chill like the Grim Reaper was coming to take them away. If the person was holding a sickle, Bryan would have been running.

"You'll see," Griffin said.

When they were about twenty yards away, Oswyn stopped the cart. The cloaked figure stood and flipped off the hood.

Vala and Griffin both smiled.

"Oh my God!" Bryan said.

"What the?" Courtney's question was interrupted by Abby.
"Dad?" Abby asked.

Richard was already scrambling off of the cart. Abby began slowly walking toward him.

"Dad?" she said again a little louder.

Richard was down and moving toward her. Abby broke into a run and jumped into his arms, the question turning into a statement.

"Dad!"

The sound of relief in her voice was indescribable.

Courtney cried. Bryan cried and hugged her, while Oswyn walked past the reunion and hugged Vala. Griffin patting him on the back.

Abby pulled away to get another look at her Dad. Tears filled both their eyes and they hugged again.

Abby finally spoke, "But...how? I saw you drown!"

"Let's go inside and we'll explain," Vala said.

Courtney shot her a look. "You knew?" she asked a little angry.

"Yes," Vala said.

"Oh my God, you knew and didn't tell us! You let us cry and have our hearts torn out and... You knew!"

"I knew the plan, but didn't know if it worked. I couldn't get Abby's hopes up, not knowing the result."

"That makes sense," Bryan said.

"Shut up, Bryan! Do you hear her? She knew!" Courtney yelled breaking out of Bryan's hug and storming into the house.

"I'll take care of the horse," Griffin said.

"Thanks," Oswyn said with a smirk. "This should be fun."

They moved into the house, Abby still wrapped around her Dad. She didn't want to ever let go. Courtney was already seated at the table waiting for the explanation of Richard's resurrection. Everyone found a seat around the table, Abby sat close to her Dad and continued to hold his hand and sob in delight.

"So you knew that her father was alive and continued to let her cry and be depressed, Courtney said directed at Vala.

"No, I..."

"Oh yeah, you didn't know for sure, but you knew he might be alive and never said anything! You let us think he was dead!"

"Yes!" Vala said taking the offensive and quieting Courtney. "I knew there was a chance, just a chance that he was alive and I didn't tell! I didn't tell for a lot of reasons!" Vala was standing now and pacing around the small room. Courtney wasn't even thinking of speaking.

"First, I wanted Abby to know how ruthless the Queen was and what she was capable of doing. Second, I wanted her fear and emotion to propel her to run away. If she knew her father could be alive, she would have wanted to go back and find him! Finally, I didn't want her to experience his death again if he wasn't alive! How awful would it be to watch your father die, be told he's still alive, and then find out he's dead? I didn't want Abby to experience that, and I'm *not* sorry about it!"

Vala finished her speech and sat down. Courtney sighed clearly defeated.

"Ok, so you're pretty smart, but how the heck are you still alive?" she said looking at Richard. "I... We watched you plunge to the bottom of the lake with huge rocks chained to you."

Richard stood up still holding Abby's hand. "It's a long story," he said releasing Abby's hand and standing behind her chair with his hands on her shoulders.

"I was visited in my cell by a friend of Abby's," she looked up at him confused for a second. "Lakota came to see me and tell me that there was a plan to save me." Abby smiled and blushed making Courtney lose her angry look and smile at her.

"We sent him to find out some information about where Richard was," Oswyn said, "but we didn't tell Lakota the plan because we didn't know if he was working for the Queen or not."

"He scared the crap out of me," Richard said laughing. "I saw a mouse run under the door which was normal, then Lakota was standing behind me. I thought I was dead. He explained what was happening and we talked for a while."

Richard dug his hands a little into Abby's shoulders showing her that he knew her affection for Lakota. She blushed even more.

"Then, Lakota came back to us with a plan of his own. He wanted to help," Oswyn said. "He has such unique talents that we had to say yes."

"Ok, so Lakota is great, and Abby loves him, and... Can we get to the point?" Courtney was back to her old self again.

Richard laughed, "Certainly," he said, "It was actually very simple. Lakota came back the night before the execution and sat with me until the guard was asleep. He then slipped out as a mouse, turned back into Lakota and slipped the keys from the sleeping guard. He then quietly brought them back to me. I quietly escaped and headed for the dock where they took me to watch you," he said grasping Abby's shoulders again.

"I slipped away in a small boat with Oswyn and hid out for the execution. Lakota locked the cell back up, slipped the keys back and took my place. He also held my hand long enough that he could turn into me."

"Oh my God, Lakota was executed?" Abby said.

"Relax. He's fine," Richard said comforting her again. "He took my place looking like me and was plunged into the lake. Did I mention that Lakota can turn into a few different types of fish?" Richard said with a laugh.

"Oh," Abby said relieved.

"It was brilliant!" Richard said.

"So, Lakota plunged into the lake and turned into a fish which unchained him, and he swam away as a fish," Bryan said.

"Yep," Richard said smiling. Then to Abby he said, "By the way, I like him."

Abby couldn't take it any more. She covered her red face with her hands and hoped the embarrassment would stop. Yet, she had a question.

"Are you sure that Lakota was able to change to a fish and get away?" Abby asked.

"Yes," Oswyn said confidently, "We tested him."

"What?" Bryan asked.

"We tested him. I chained him up and dropped him into the lake at a shallow part where I could get him out if necessary. He shifted and swam away. We did it three times. Now, no one saw him get away, but I'm sure he did," Oswyn said.

"He did," Bryan said, "Remember, he helped us after the execution."

"That's the main reason why I didn't say anything," Vala said. "Griffin and I can't figure out how that happened. There should have been no way Lakota could have made it to help you after helping Richard."

"I don't care how he did it, I'm just glad he did," Courtney said.

Oswyn looked confused, so they told him the story of Kuruk and how Lakota saved them.

Abby continuously smiled. She longed to see Lakota and thank him, but knew that was a long shot. He had to go back to the Queen to make things look normal, but a girl could hope. She also hoped Kuruk would not tell the Queen about him.

"Now, what are we going to do?" Bryan asked.

"We're going to the door and getting out of here!" Courtney said looking at Bryan like he was crazy.

"Did you forget Pitman?" he came right back at her with the crazy look. "I'm sure he didn't stick around here, so our key is gone."

"I found out from Raftis that the key they gave to Pitman to take back before was the key the Queen had made. They let Raftis through the door, so we don't even know if that key works," Richard said.

"But if we go to the door and there's no key..." Bryan started to say when he was cut off by Abby.

"I have a key," she said matter of factly.

Everyone turned to look at her in disbelief.

"What?" Courtney asked.

"I have a key," she said again pulling the cloth from her pocket. She began unwrapping it, while everyone's eyes were glued on her. Slowly, the key was revealed to everyone to the delight of everyone.

"Where did you get a key?" Richard asked kneeling on the hard floor next to Abby placing his hands under hers to cradle the key.

"You gave it to me," she smiled.

Richard looked confused.

"You didn't give it to me directly, but Raftis gave it to me and said it was a final gift from you."

Richard hugged her tightly whispering, "Raftis is a great man."

"Lakota is a great man," she whispered back.

"Yes, he is," Richard said holding onto Abby for a while.

"We have work to do," Griffin said and he, Oswyn and Vala left the room to prepare for the journey to the door. There were horses to gather and supplies to pack. Abby took the time to catch up with Richard about the events that had occurred and how they followed the clues he left. Courtney and Bryan told their side of the story and how they ended up seemingly captured, but really saved by Griffin and the FFA. The conversation changed when they approached the subject of Pitman.

"I really want to talk to him and find out what happened," Richard said.

"No way, Mr. Lane!" Courtney got heated quickly. "He needs to get punched in the face, and if you don't want to do it, I will!"

"I totally agree that he needs something, but you don't know him that well."

"I know that he screwed us all over!"

"Yeah, he did, but I still want to know his story," Richard said laughing.

"It's not funny, we all could have died! Technically, you did die!"

"I know, Court. It's not funny, you're just so passionate about it, it made me laugh.

Courtney sat with her arms folded angrily. Richard and Abby just watching her to see what she would do next. Bryan got up, walked over to Courtney and grabbed her hand. He pulled her to her feet with her looking confused at what he was doing. She didn't even speak from confusion.

Bryan stood her up and wrapped his arms around her hugging her tightly. She didn't refuse, Courtney just stood there with her arms at her sides until slowly she reached up a little and hugged him back. Abby was stunned. Her mouth hung open as she looked at her Dad who was just smiling. After less than a minute, Bryan let go of his hug and went back to his seat and sat.

"What was that?" Courtney finally managed to say.

"We've been through a lot. You needed a hug," Bryan replied.

"Thanks," Courtney said blushing slightly and quickly sitting down.

"Awww," Abby said with a smile.

The door opened and Griffin poked his head in for a second. "Time to go," he said.

The journey to the door was long and tedious, but the countryside was beautiful. The kids didn't notice how beautiful it was on their journey to the castle, they were too busy following Pitman and sneaking along the parallel path. Now, they were on the main road which meandered through wooded areas, over rolling hills, and separated farmer's fields. Due to the feast, the land of Alden was deserted. No one was on the road and the fields and farm houses they saw were empty.

This made things much easier for the travelers. They could sit in the carts without being covered up, which gave them the opportunity to see the beauty of the land around them.

After a few hours of riding, Griffin turned and directed the kids and Richard to get under cover. "We're approaching a small village around the bend ahead. They may have let someone behind to keep watch, so you should be out of sight."

They quickly buried themselves in hay and tarps. Abby holding onto her father's hand for security. It was warm under the cover, but they felt safe with Griffin, Vala, and Oswyn leading them.

Abby could feel the turning of the cart as the went around the bend, after a few hundred yards the cart slowed to a stop. She suddenly heard a voice that she didn't recognize.

"Is the execution finally over?" the man said.

"Yes," Griffin replied, "it was over yesterday."

"Then where is everyone? I've been waiting for them to get back!"

"Oh," Griffin said, "the Queen announced a feast for last night in the Great Hall. They probably all stayed."

"Glad they cared about me!" the man said sarcastically.

"Yeah, it was a last minute thing," Vala said. "We have a long journey and couldn't stay."

"Apparently, my village did!" the man said angrily.

"Hi, I'm Oswyn, since no one is around, could we get some food and water for our horses?"

"My name's Flack. Might as well," the man said, "I got nothing else to do. "

Flack set up food and water for Vala, Griffin, and Oswyn at a small house, while feeding and watering the horses. Richard and the kids stayed quiet until everyone was in the house eating.

"They better not be long," Courtney whispered.

"They better get me some food," Bryan whispered back, which elicited a look from Courtney.

Back inside the house, Vala was sure to sneak some food away from the table for the others when Flack wasn't looking. They sat for a few minutes making small talk and discussing the feast and the execution. Flack seemed to want to talk, not because he really had anything to say, but he was bored with no one around. Finally, Vala ended the conversation by telling Flack that she needed to get home to her sick mother. Flack quickly grabbed the remaining food and wrapped it in a cloth for their journey.

"Well, thank you for your hospitality!" Oswyn almost yelled much too loudly making Flack turn and look at him confused. Oswyn hoped that Richard and the kids took the hint and hid themselves before they got outside. They did, just scrambling into the hay before Griffin showed up at the carts.

"Thanks again," Griffin said jumping up onto the bench and grabbing the reigns.

Oswyn and Vala hopped into the other cart and quickly began moving away. Flack could barely say goodbye before they were headed down the road away from the village.

As the horses ambled through the trees on the outskirts of the village, the travelers came to bend in the road that would put them out of sight of Flack if he was still watching them ride away. After the bend, Oswyn called back to the kids and Richard that they could come out. After removing the hay and Bryan pulling pieces of it from Courtney's hair, Vala reached back and handed them the cloth wrapped food.

"Vala!!!!" Bryan said happily, "You're the best!"

"Best what?" she asked not understanding.

"Just the best...the best everything," he laughed.

Vala smiled realizing it must be a complement of some sort.

They ate and talked the ride they had left to the door. Richard was getting anxious about getting there. Oswyn tried to calm him, letting him know that they had people in place to slow down any pursuit from the Queen's guards. Yet, Vala agreed with Richard.

"We must make good time," she said, "by now, she knows and there are people hunting us. Maybe even Shifters."

This made Abby sit up and pay attention. "Shifters?" she asked.

"Yes, they can move much faster than the guards through the forest and across the land. Especially, Gawain. He is known as the hawk."

"Oh great!" Courtney said, "some crazy Shifter bird will definitely catch us!"

"Yes, he will, so stay alert. Our biggest hope is Gawain, himself. He tends to stay away from the castle. Hopefully, the Queen cannot find him to send him in time to catch us."

"Oh, that's encouraging," Courtney said sarcastically, "Our best hope is that the crazy Queen and the crazy bird will not get together and kill us."

"Actually, yes. That is our best hope," Vala said bluntly.

"Wonderful."

They went a few more miles without anyone speaking, but they were all on high alert scanning the area for a sign of anyone or anything that could be watching them. Bryan held his head up scanning the sky for any birds and praying not to see a hawk. Abby searched the forest and ground areas looking for a wolf. She was more concerned with trying to find Lakota then worried about a hawk.

"Do you think Lakota is coming to find us?" she asked Oswyn.

"I'm not sure. I hope he does, though. We could use his help if Gawain arrives."

"How is he related to Gawain?" Abby asked.

"Related?" Courtney questioned.

"Yeah, all of the Shifters seem to be related somehow, like they all came from the same ancestor with that ability," Abby said.

"That's pretty cool," Courtney said.

"Gawain and Lakota are cousins," Oswyn said with a smile.

"Why are you smiling?" Abby asked.

"You really like this guy."

Abby blushed and put her head down.

"Is he cute?" Courtney said quickly making Abby pop her head back up. "Not Lakota," she said, "Gawain. I mean if their cousins and all," she finished with a laugh, which made Bryan's head shoot down from the sky and give her a very cold stare. The others noticed and turned away smirking. "Oh my God, I'm kidding," she finished.

If nothing else, Courtney found out exactly how Bryan felt about her. *"Maybe that kiss did mean something,"* she thought smiling on the inside, but still wondering if Gawain was cute.

The ride continued and so did the scanning of the forest and the sky. Not many people ride along a road hoping to see a wolf and dreading the appearance of a hawk, but that's just what they were doing. Luckily for them, they saw neither. Their journey continued without incident for many hours when Vala broke the silent ride.

"Up ahead, we will exit the woods into the final village of Dalusia. The door is a few short miles from the village," Vala said.

"I remember that place," Bryan said.

"Yeah, that's the place that Pitman said the people followed us after we walked through," Courtney agreed.

"He made us leave the road," Abby said to her Dad.

"I know, honey. We're almost home," Richard said encouragingly.

"I know," she replied.

"I think you guys should hide as we pass through Dalusia. I don't think anyone is there, but these people are far from the castle and there's a chance they stayed here instead of going to the execution," Griffin said

"I agree", Oswyn said.

"Whatever you say is fine with us," Richard said.

They immediately began covering themselves in hay and the

tarps. Oswyn and Griffin slowed the carts until everyone was well hidden. Even under cover, they could tell by the sound of the cart when they left the forest into the clearing before the village. They listened intently for voices and sounds of life as they entered the village. Oswyn led the way past the first small house that seemed abandoned. Griffin followed in his cart trying to stay close, but leave enough room to take off if Oswyn was attacked.

The air seemed to be still. Griffin noticed Oswyn, the soldier, sitting a little straighter on his bench as they passed the next set of houses on each side of the road. Up ahead was clearly the small marketplace where there should be people milling around buying items and food, but it was empty. Oswyn was not relaxed though. His eyes scanned the houses as Griffin turned and checked behind them. The road was deserted, but when Griffin turned back, he saw Oswyn handing the reigns to Vala as he silently slipped from the cart and hurried between two houses.

Oswyn slipped a knife from his belt as he slid between the houses still listening to make sure he heard the clop of hooves and the creaking of the moving carts. With the stealth of a true warrior, Oswyn snuck behind the houses and moved toward the marketplace. He kept to the shadows as he crept along stopping suddenly and double backing toward the houses he came through to start. He ran full speed through the houses and back to the carts. Vala had rode to the marketplace and was passing by, but Griffin had yet to make it there when Oswyn hopped up onto the bench next to Griffin.

"He's here," he whispered.

"Who?"

"Gawain. When we get to the last open air building on the left, the hawk was perched inside along the back rafters."

"Ok, I'll look."

They continued keeping a close eye on Vala as she passed the building housing the hawk. Nothing happened, but they approached cautiously, both men on high alert. Griffin peered toward the back of the building, but saw nothing. Oswyn looked concerned. "*Could Gawain have seen him?*" he thought. Then he spotted him. The hawk was perched on top of the last building exiting the village.

"Do you see him?" Oswyn said.

"Yep."

"Me too. What should we do?"

"Definitely keep them covered up," Oswyn said in reply.

They continued through the village glancing at the hawk without staring. Griffin sped up slowly to catch up with Vala without being too conspicuous. When they finally exited the village they entered a wooded area again. Griffin sped up quickly to catch Vala calling to her to slow down. Oswyn, still perched next to Griffin glanced back to the village and saw the hawk still perched upon the last building and still watching their every move. Oswyn turned back to see movement coming from the back of Vala's cart. He jumped from their moving cart and raced to the front cart trying to stop them from uncovering themselves.

Just as he arrived at the cart calling to them, "Don't Move! Don't Move!", it was too late. Abby's head popped out from the hay. Oswyn stopped almost frozen, but he turned and watched as the hawk squawked and took flight. Oswyn's shoulders dropped as he turned back to the cart.

"I'm sorry," Abby said, "I couldn't understand what you were saying. I'll cover up again."

"It's too late," Oswyn said, "Gawain is here, and he just saw you."

"Oh my God!" Courtney said popping out next to Abby.

"What do we do?" Abby asked.

"We have to get to that door," Oswyn said sternly.

He turned and hopped up next to Vala taking the reigns and flicking them to get the horse moving again. His goal was to get out of the woods where they were under the cover of the trees and out into the open. There they would have a better view of Gawain if he tried to attack.

Bouncing around in the back of the cart and trying to get back under cover was not most comfortable ride they ever had. It was kind of like trying to get a coat off in the car while driving down the highway. They were bounced around quite a bit before the cart began to slow down and the sounds from under the cover of the hay and tarps changed for them to know they were finally out of the woods. Oswyn turned around to make sure Griffin was still right behind them when he saw Griffin pointing toward the sky. Oswyn was afraid to look, but saw the hawk circling high about them. He sighed.

"You might as well come out," he said, " he knows you're here."

Oswyn pulled the cart over to the side of the dirt road. Griffin pulled up next to him.

"What do you think?" Griffin asked.

"I think he knows we're here and they're with us. So, we go to the door, which is only about a half mile up ahead. While they get through the door, we fight him off. He might stop fighting once they're gone," Oswyn said.

"You really want to fight a Shifter?"

"No, but there may be no other choice."

"Let me talk with Gawain," Vala said, "Maybe I can convince him to let them go."

"Good luck with that," Griffin said turning to the back of the carts. "You guys can come out. We've been spotted and need everyone to be ready to fight to the door."

Richard popped out first followed by Bryan, then the girls.

"Wow, we're almost there," Richard said. "I heard your conversation. Maybe if Gawain sees me, he'll help us because Lakota did. We can tell him the story."

"That's a good idea," Vala said. "It can't hurt!"

Griffin stood up and lifted the bench where he was sitting. Reaching inside, he pulled out a bow and quiver of arrows along with two short swords. Oswyn did the same, draping a bow and quiver over his shoulders. He placed two short swords at his feet and handed Richard a longer sword.

Abby looked shocked. She had never thought of her father as a fighter, but the way he grasped the sword and bounced it up and down feeling the weight made her think that he had done this before.

"What?" Richard asked her noticing her perplexed look.

"You can sword fight?" she asked.

"While I was here before, I was trained in the long sword and short sword, but it's been a very long time," he answered.

Abby shook her head, "It's like you have this whole secret life that I know nothing about."

"Actually, you do know about it now," he laughed, but she still looked serious. "Believe me Ab, I tried to forget about this place and this life. I was almost finished with it, when they came and got me. I need to get back to our real lives, and if it means fighting for it, I will."

"Yeah, Mr. Lane!" Courtney said emphatically.

Abby smiled. It actually felt good to know her Dad wasn't just a nerdy history buff.

The carts started moving again. They could see the bridge crossing the creek at the bottom of the hill they were starting down, but most of them panned the sky looking for Gawain. He was out of sight, which put Oswyn on high alert. They slowed as they approached the first bridge which Abby knew as the Route 13 Bridge at home. As they crossed slowly, they saw the hawk. He was perched on the far railing of the Red Lion Bridge to their left.

"Come on Gawain!" Oswyn yelled, "Show yourself!"

The hawk took off from it's perch and flew over them. Vala had notched an arrow, but did not fire. She was always for a more diplomatic approach.

He flew high above them circling the area, higher and higher he went as they all watched.

Bryan finally broke the stupor. "He's up there, let's go!" he called.

"He's right," Griffin said jumping from the cart and heading left toward the Red Lion Bridge. The others scrambled from the carts to follow. Across the bridge they went making a hard left and sliding down the embankment toward the covered up tunnel leading to the door. Stepping into the gently flowing creek, they were almost there when the cry of the hawk snapped all of there heads to the bridge behind them. He was perched above them, eyes intense, mouth open, with that high pitched screech filling their ears. Wincing from the sound, their faces turned to shock when the hawk turned into a man.

CHAPTER 47

Before dawn, the Queen was awake and moving quickly through the castle yelling at the guards. Demanding they round up any guests who were passed out drunk from the celebration and lead them to the bridge. She, herself, was shooing people out of the castle toward the soon to be execution site. Outside, a horn was sounding to alert the people of Alden that the execution was about to happen and they should gather at the bridge. Most people were too scared to not show up. If the Queen could kill her ex-husband and now her most trusted advisor, then anyone could be killed by her was their thought; they were right. So, the bridge began to fill up with people. The set up was different from Richard's drowning with a full section roped off. From the center of the bridge, where the gallows were, all along the right side railing to the door of the castle there was a path that was about four feet wide roped off. People gathered right up to the rope trying to get the best view.

On the right side of the castle doors, there was a small stage set up with two guards standing at attention. The crowd gathered and the discussions started about the stage and why it could be there. There was also talk about the execution being late. Many people wanted to return to their farms and lives, but they were force to remain for the execution at dawn. It was now past dawn with the sun already in the sky and the people were getting antsy when there was another horn blast and the castle doors opened.   Raftis was marched out with guards on each side and his hands tied behind his back. He looked so different to the people. Raftis was always well dressed and perfectly groomed, but today he was completely disheveled. His hair was a mess and his clothing was even worse. He wore a dirty gray tunic that looked like it had never been washed. It was such a change from the man they all knew, that there was an audible gasp from the crowd. Many people turned to the person next to them to ask if it really was Raftis. They soon agreed that it was. Following Raftis from the gate was the Queen and her entourage of guards with a huge smile on her face. They all walked up the steps of the stage and turned to face the crowd.

Raftis lowered his head and prepared for the Queen to speak. He knew to just listen and not react to anything she had to say. He had been around her for so long, he could almost predict word for word what she would say.

"Ladies and Gentlemen of Alden," she began, " these are monumental days. Yesterday, we witnessed the execution of the past as we move into the future. Last night, we feasted and partied to symbolize a new beginning and welcome it. Today, we finish off the past with the execution of my former advisor, Raftis. For many years, I trusted Raftis with everything I did, but I have found that he has betrayed me on more than one occasion. The final straw was yesterday, when the Princess went missing. It made me think about all the things that have been a mystery here in Alden, and the common denominator in all of those things has been Raftis."

The crowd began murmuring about her claims and looking at Raftis for some sort of rebuttal, but he remained true to himself and never moved or raised his head.

"I have on good authority that Raftis helped Richard escape with the Princess many years ago," she continued over the murmurs which only grew louder with her claim. "He was in charge of the Princess and now she is missing also. It makes me wonder how many other times he betrayed me. That will soon be the past, as Raftis will hang from the bridge in a few minutes. As for the Princess, I have a reward for the person who finds her and brings her to me."

Now the crowd was in full conversation. "Reward? What is it?" they asked out loud. There were quick dreams of gold or silver and what

could be bought. Then, the chant of "Reward...Reward...Reward!"
started. The Queen relished the moment before raising her hands for
silence.

"The reward is Raftis' job. I need a new advisor and all the fame
and fortune that comes with it."

Now the crowd was cheering and beginning to run from the
bridge, when the horn sounded again at the command of the Queen.

"Anyone who leaves before the execution is not eligible for the
reward!" she shouted and the people stopped abruptly. "Now, in order to
have his job, he needs to be gone."

The Queen walked across the stage to Raftis and stood directly
in front of him. Raftis remained still with his head down not daring to
look at her. The crowd was hushed and waiting for what she would do.

"I have been loyal to you, and you treat me with disrespect.
Even now, I am going to give you a chance to speak your final words
knowing what you have done to me."

Raftis raised his head finally and looked her in the eye. He did
not speak yet, but was longing to do so.

Looking Raftis in the eye, she said, "As you give your final words, know that you have betrayed me for the last time!"

She stared him down, hoping the thought of death would make him crack and break down in front of the people. Yet, Raftis smiled. He nodded his head at her and sighed.

Finally, Raftis spoke, "You are wrong," he said and the crowd gasped. "It is now that I betray you for the last time. Guards!" he yelled.

Everyone was stunned. The doors of the castle opened and a regiment of guards walked out. They were followed by a figure in a gray hooded cloak, much like the one Raftis was wearing. The guards parted and the figure walked onto the stage and turned to the people flipping the hood off of his head. The crowd was stunned, the Queen gasped and looked at Raftis, who smiled. Suddenly, the crowd dropped to a knee in the presence of King Tammany.

The Queen was shocked and yelled, "Imposter!" Yet, guards gathered around her so she couldn't go anywhere.

King Tammany just laughed and turned to the people who had no doubt it was really the King. He lifted his arms up for them to rise.

"You know I was never one for all the bowing," Tammany said. "For many years," he began, "you were told that I was dead and in essence, I was. Locked away in the dungeon by my daughter."

The crowd gasped, but he continued. "She was so power hungry that she couldn't even wait for my real death," he laughed, "but being locked away has revived me, the stress of ruling was taken away from me, and I have had much time to reflect, but I have lost many years. Thanks to Raftis and the curiosity of Prince Richard, I am back from the dead, and I am ready to lead you again. Guards, seize her and place her in the dungeon."

The guards surrounding the Queen, grabbed her tightly, leading her away. She resisted and complained mightily, "Let me go! I am your Queen! Your ruler! I command you to let me go!" They didn't listen to her at all.

"Make sure you put her in Richard's old cell, for mine was much too nice!" Tammany called out making the crowd cheer.

The chat started and echoed throughout Alden, "Long Live The King! Long Live The King!"

CHAPTER 48

Vala had an arrow notched and aimed at the hawk when he changed, but she did not fire.

Abby screamed in shock as the hawk turned into Lakota. She rushed across the creek toward the embankment, but Oswyn stopped her.

"It's Lakota!" she yelled as Oswyn held her back, "Let me go!"

"No! It might not be Lakota! It might be Gawain looking like Lakota!"

"He's right," Griffin said.

As the truth hit Abby, she stopped trying to pull away. She knew that Oswyn was right. Gawain was pulling the dirtiest trick ever, and he had sucked her right into it. Now, she was angry.

"You're not Lakota! Show yourself Gawain!" Abby yelled.

"Yeah, Gawain! We're not fooled!" Courtney yelled.

"Keep moving toward the door," Richard whispered without moving his lips.

Courtney backed up a step and Bryan followed, but Abby stood her ground. She was too angry to move. Oswyn stayed by her side and Vala kept the bow at he ready position.

"I am not Gawain. I am Lakota," he said.

"Oh yeah right!" Courtney yelled.

"Prove it!" Griffin yelled back making Richard, Bryan and Courtney look at him.

"Can he?" Bryan asked.

"Yes," Griffin muttered, "the Shifters can take the shape of someone, but they don't have their memories. "Abby ask him a question about your time with Lakota that only he would know."

"Yes, ask me anything," Lakota said.

"Ok," she said to Griffin. Then turning to Lakota, she asked, "What warning about you did the old woman give me?"

Lakota laughed, "She told you to never trust a Shifter."

"Yes, and I don't!" Abby said.

"Everyone says that," Oswyn said, "He could have guessed that."

"Ugh," She grunted, "then what did you turn into to save me from the dogs?"

"A wolf," he replied changing into a wolf and then back to Lakota.

"Again, too easy," Oswyn said.

Abby sighed and was about to ask again when Lakota interrupted her.

"Should I tell them about how we met, and I saved you from being captured, or how I protected you during the night as a wolf, or how mad you were when you found out I was a Shifter and how I apologized. Maybe, how I was falling in love with the way you looked at me, and how hard it was to leave you outside the city gates, but you didn't listen and came in anyway. I could tell them how I took you to my house, the same house that Oswyn came looking for me to help your father, or how a Shifter can turn into a fish and save your father's life. All for you, Abby."

"It's Lakota," Oswyn said with a smile.

Abby sloshed through the water toward the embankment, but Lakota jumped off the bridge, disappeared for a second and landed as

444

Lakota in front of her. They embraced in a huge hug. Abby only pulled away enough to kiss him on the lips to which Lakota kissed back; a first kiss to last a lifetime.

Suddenly, Richard, Courtney, and Bryan were upon them in a group hug. Making everyone laugh.

"How did you get away from Kuruk?" Bryan asked.

"Kuruk?" Lakota asked.

"Yeah, when you were wrestling around with Kuruk to save me and Court."

"I don't know what you're talking about," Lakota said confused.

"But, we saw you," Courtney said, "you told us to run."

"You saw me? I stayed swimming around as a fish for a while. You couldn't have seen me."

"But, you fought with Kuruk and changed into you."

"I would never fight with Kuruk, but..." Lakota smiled, "my dad, Mika, would. He's the only one who could change into me. He must have saved you."

"That makes much more sense," Vala said.

"He has done that before. I stayed a fish, then went back to the castle. When I heard the Queen was sending people here, I turned into a hawk to get here quickly, and then with hawk eyes being so good, I could read your lips about Gawain. I knew that finding a hawk would be easier as a hawk, so I stayed in that state waiting for Gawain to show himself. He is not around, I would sense it, but the Queen's men are only a few miles behind you."

"You must go then," Oswyn said.

"But..." Abby said sadly.

"There is no but. You must go now until things are taken care of around here," Lakota said.

"He is right," Vala said.

"The plan is already in effect," Lakota said.

"What plan?" Griffin asked.

"Oh, I forgot, you all were gone. The Queen planned to execute Raftis this morning because of Abby's disappearance."

"Oh my God," Abby said.

446

"No, Raftis has a plan to expose the Queen and bring King Tammany back into power," Lakota said.

"But King Tammany is dead," Vala said.

"I never told you," Richard said, "In this running away mess, I forgot. The King has been imprisoned for years and is alive."

"That changes everything!' Vala said.

"I will fill them in on the details, but you really should go," Lakota said. "The guards have to be close now, and they don't know about the King."

Abby pulled out the key. Her pure excitement of finding Lakota again was over in just a few minutes as she hugged him and began crying.

"It's ok," he said, "I will see you again."

She looked at him and was ready for another kiss when a cry came from under the bridge along with the splashing of water.

"Wait! Wait!"

They all turned from their goodbye hugs to see a dirty and battered Mike Pitman emerge from under the bridge.

"Wait! Please take me with you," he begged.

Oswyn laughed at the sight. While Griffin turned to Richard and said, "Say the word and he's over."

Richard shook his head no with a sigh.

Pitman pleaded, "Please Richard, I'm so sorry. Mary left me with the kids. I was lonely and bored and looking through that book was something to do. I didn't know what I was getting myself into. Our hidden key doesn't work, please take me with you."

No one moved as Richard sloshed through the water to Pitman. He got right in front of his old friend and punched him so hard in the face that everyone heard his nose break. Pitman hit the shin deep water with a splash and blood gushed from his nose.

"You did know what you were getting these kids into though!" Richard yelled standing over him.

"Yeah Mr. Lane!" Bryan said as Richard turned back toward them.

"I feel better!" Courtney said with a smile.

The good bye hugs continued quickly, as Pitman sat in the water wiping his bloody nose on his dirty shirt.

"You know, if Tammany is back, then you'll all be welcomed here," Griffin said to Richard.

"I know, but lover girl and these two," Richard said pointing to Abby, Courtney, and Bryan, "have to go back to school, but there's always Winter break."

"Did you hear that?" Abby said to Lakota, "I'll be back in a few months."

"And I'll be here waiting," he said with a final kiss.

They moved to the entrance of the tunnel and disappeared one by one toward the door. Richard, who was last, yelled to Pitman, "Well, are you coming or are you going to sit there and bleed to death?"

Pitman didn't need a second invitation. He jumped up and ran to the tunnel stumbling and wiping his nose in the process. As he disappeared into the tunnel, Abby turned the key and opened the door and went through. Richard pushed Pitman ahead of him and pulled the key out as he exited Alden clutching the key in his palm.

Lakota joined Griffin in his cart as they followed Oswyn and Vala away from the bridge before the guards arrived.

On the other side of the door, the group made their way past the graffiti filled bridge and up the embankment. Pitman's car was gone, probably towed after being left for almost a week. He walked behind the others until he decided to make a right toward the hospital to get his nose checked out. Richard and the kids continued toward home, but life would never be the same.

Made in the USA
Middletown, DE
06 July 2018